more . . .

"Surprising and satisfactory . . . Jean Hager is at her best when she writes about the Cherokee people, whom she portrays with insight and compassion."
—*Southbridge Evening News* (MA)

❀

"[Jean Hager] pays admirably Hillerman-like attention to cultural and geographic detail."
—*Roanoke Times*

❀

"Hager's writing style is unusually clear. . . . That makes reading enjoyably fast."
—*Sunday Republican* (CT)

❀

"Bright and witty, crammed with fascinating characters. . . . These books are a treat in both the lively characters and the original settings. Mystery readers will find them charming and informative about the lives of the Cherokees who are still trying to protect their heritage."
—*Ocala Star-Banner*

MYSTERY NOVELS BY JEAN HAGER

Featuring Chief Mitchell Bushyhead

THE FIRE CARRIER
GHOSTLAND
NIGHT WALKER
THE GRANDFATHER MEDICINE

Featuring Molly Bearpaw

SEVEN BLACK STONES
THE REDBIRD'S CRY
RAVENMOCKER

JEAN HAGER

THE XXXXXXX FIRE CARRIER

THE MYSTERIOUS PRESS

Published by Warner Books

A Time Warner Company

MYSTERIOUS PRESS EDITION

Copyright © 1996 by Jean Hager
All rights reserved.

Cover design and illustration by David Tamura

The Mysterious Press name and logo are registered trademarks of Warner Books, Inc.

 Mysterious Press Books are published by
Warner Books, Inc.
1271 Avenue of the Americas
New York, NY 10020

Visit our Web site at
http://pathfinder.com/twep

Ⓦ A Time Warner Company

Printed in the United States of America

Originally published in hardcover by The Mysterious Press.
First Printed in Paperback: May, 1997

10 9 8 7 6 5 4 3 2 1

Author's Note

I'd like to thank my editor, Sara Ann Freed, who somehow seems to know what I'm trying to say, even when I don't, and whose encouragement and insightful editorial suggestions spur me to put forth my best effort.

Also, I must express gratitude to Frankie Sue Gilliam, whose writings provided much of the information on the "Spook Light"; and Dr. Kay Steen, who answered my medical questions and whom I would never have known except for that wonderfully supportive organization, Sisters in Crime.

Jean Hager
Tulsa, Oklahoma

1

Henderson Sixkiller huddled beneath the patchwork quilt he had stolen from a clothesline the other side of the Delaware County line. Double wedding-ring pattern. Now, there was an irony for you.

He knew the pattern because his mother had helped his sister make one before she got married more than twenty years ago. It didn't seem possible to Sixkiller that she had been married so many years, but to Jessie, it must seem like a couple of lifetimes.

The wind rose, sounding like a beast with its paw caught in a trap. It reminded him of the time he'd found a bobcat in a trap when he was a kid. By the time he'd happened on it and released it, the animal had been trapped so long its howling had dwindled down to mere reflexive moans. That's how this wind sounded, anguished but resigned.

Sixkiller shivered and gnawed the last of the meat from the rabbit's bones, then sucked out the marrow. He'd downed the scrawny creature with a blowgun dart, grabbed it, and snapped its neck while it lay stunned—or sick, who knew? He was too hungry to worry about the rabbit's health. He'd spent a good two hours—after he was too tired and hungry to walk any farther today—finding and hollowing out a cane stalk and whittling darts. Then he took out the rabbit on the first try. It was nice to know he hadn't lost his touch.

The wind rose higher, howling now, like a she-wolf. He

tossed away the bone and pulled the quilt closer around him. Brrr, even his bones were freezing. *Unu-la-ta-nee'*, the Cold Moon, was a hell of a time to break out of jail. So far it had been the coldest January in seven years.

The Apportioner hadn't shown her face for the past two days as he trudged down back roads, through woods, and across open fields. By the time he'd shot the rabbit, his feet, in the cheap, thin-soled shoes, and his legs clear to his knees were numb with cold. He'd had to risk building a fire to cook the rabbit and coax the feeling back into his limbs.

As darkness closed in on his campsite deep in the woods, he'd let the fire die. He was still in unfamiliar country and didn't know how close he might be to a house. If somebody saw his fire and reported it, the law might catch up with him before he'd done what he had to do.

He'd been lucky to find this place, a concave rock outcropping with an overhang that provided a little shelter from the wind.

Tomorrow he should reach his old stomping grounds, where he knew every hill and gully and cave within miles. He sat still, thinking about the old days and the friends he'd known since they were students at the tribal boarding school in Buckskin.

They were scattered now, most of them married, some for the second or third time. As far as he knew, he and Jeeb Shell were the only two who had ended up in jail, but Jeeb always had liked living on the edge. Jeeb raised marijuana on forty acres he owned across the county line. Sixkiller had been helping him harvest a crop ahead of a rainstorm when the whole damn Delaware County Sheriff's Department had descended on them.

Pot was the second biggest cash crop in Oklahoma, and it was just Sixkiller's luck that the sheriff had staked out that particular field. He tried to tell the man he was only helping out a friend. He wasn't going to profit from the sale of the weed. He didn't even use the stuff.

The sheriff had said that was a darn shame, tough turds and

all that, but Sixkiller had not really expected sympathy from the law. They gave him five years. He'd been scheduled to be transferred to Big Mac, the state penitentiary in McAlester, today. It would have been next to impossible to break out of Mac. So he'd run while he could.

With his luck, he figured it was only a matter of time until they caught him, but he was glad to be going home, anyway. This must be how a homing pigeon felt as he neared the home coop. The closer Sixkiller got, the easier he felt in his skin. He hoped he could stay free for a while, long enough to get the jailhouse smell—a combination of stale urine, sweat, and disinfectant—out of his nostrils.

Lying down with a corner of the quilt tucked under his head, he closed his eyes and tried not to think about how cold he was. Soon he drifted into that hazy world between waking and sleeping.

He could see his ma and his sister, bending over the quilting frame in the front room, stitching that quilt for Jessie, as clear as if it had happened yesterday. Ma telling the old stories. How the Cherokee warrior killed the *Uk'ten'*. How the first corn grew out of the Corn Mother's grave. How Thunder gave power to the birds. How the spirit deers, *Ahw'usti'* and *Ahw'equ'*, came to the aid of people who showed them proper respect.

Ma, dead four years now, had been a conjuring woman, and she had taught Jessie the love charm that the *Aniqunehiyat,* the Little People, taught her when she was a girl. Ma said it would guarantee that the man Jessie chose would love her so much he would never leave her. In his dream, Ma began to sing the words in Cherokee.

Yu-wu-sti-i nu-do-qu-hno i-ya nu-da-gua . . .

He couldn't get enough of looking at her and listening. Amazing how much a grown man could miss his mother. He reached out to touch her—and jerked awake. All his muscles groaned and Ma was gone.

He sat up and rearranged the quilt and rested his head on his drawn-up knees. There had been a blanket on that clothesline with the quilt. He wished he'd grabbed it too, while he was at it.

To take his mind off his troubles, he started to sing softly to himself.

> I am the Little Person
> From the Sunland.
> I speak wisely.
> No one can do so much so easily.
> My clothing I received from the Lightning
> Which is never lonely.

He wasn't sure he had the words exactly right, but he was close enough.

Poor old Jessie. She used to sing that charm song all the time.

It worked, Ma. That SOB's gonna love our Jessie to death if somebody don't stop him.

Suddenly he lifted his head and sat very still. Off to the north he heard a sound in the woods. He waited a long time, motionless and hardly breathing, but heard nothing more. Must have been an animal. A coyote, maybe, sniffing the scent of roasted rabbit on the wind. He relaxed and thought again of his sister.

The last time Jessie had visited him in jail, she'd been like one of those cornhusk dolls Ma used to make, except with all the husks knocked out of her. Talking in that dull monotone as though it took all the energy she could muster to push the words out. Saying she couldn't stand it no more. Saying she wanted to die.

He had told her to stop wallowing in self-pity and *do* something. Her boys needed her. It was like pissing in the wind. She'd just looked at him with dead eyes and said they'd be better off without her.

It nearly killed him, seeing Jessie like that; and he knew

that if she was to be rescued, he'd have to do it. The law sure hadn't stepped in. He reckoned they were too busy jailing hardworking folks whose only crime was cultivating a cash crop to feed their families.

Any way you sliced it, it was up to him. So here he was, waiting for the daylight, too hungry and sore to sleep. Freezing his butt off in the backwoods of Cherokee County.

The next morning when Sixkiller awoke, surprised to find he had slept at all, *Anisga'ya Tsunadi'*, the Thunder Boys who were the sons of Kana'ti, were wrestling. Keeping an anxious eye on the dark clouds in the west, he ate the last of the crackers he'd brought with him from the jail. He'd stuffed them in his coat pockets and, after several days, the ones that weren't soggy were reduced to crumbs. He ate every last crumb and broke camp.

It started sleeting as he picked up the hollowed-out cane stalk and whittled darts and trudged onward with the double wedding-ring quilt wrapped around his head and shoulders. The first thing he had to do when he reached the outskirts of Buckskin was find some place to dry his clothes and the quilt. The second was to get food. He would be no help to Jessie if he came down with pneumonia or, for lack of nourishment, lost his resolve.

He would approach Buckskin from the east, where houses were scattered through the woods and along the shores of Lake Tenkiller. Some of the newer ones were year-round residences, but many were occupied only during the summer. These ranged from big, three- and four-bedroom jobs to one-room cabins without modern plumbing. He'd like to find one with an indoor toilet, but his main concern was that it be in a secluded location, out of sight of other houses.

By midday he'd left the sleet behind, but the quilt was soaked and the cold penetrated to his bones. The thing that kept him going was the thought that by nightfall, if he could keep up his pace, he should have found shelter from the raw January weather.

The possibility of spending another night unsheltered in the woods wasn't his only anxiety. About the time it got dark, he would enter the area where it was said that *Atsil'-dihye'gi'*, the Fire Carrier, wandered. For as long as he could remember, he'd heard stories about the evil spirit that went about at night with a light. He'd never seen the light himself, he'd only heard the reports of sightings when he was a boy. Ma had seen the Fire Carrier once, when she was a young woman. She was coming home from a friend's house, and it had followed her, but she whipped up her horse and got away.

A couple of years ago, some medicine men got together and made medicine to drive the Fire Carrier away. He hadn't heard of any sightings since, but then he'd been in jail for months. And the thought of going into that territory was worrisome. What if the Fire Carrier's medicine was stronger than the combined medicine of several medicine men? Or what if the Fire Carrier had been driven away two years ago but had decided to come back?

Despite his qualms, he had to go there to find a hidey hole for his base of operations, and then he'd rescue Jessie. As dusk crept over the land, he combed his memory for a song of protection. Only one came to mind, and he chanted:

Listen! His soul shall be without motion.
Under the earth, where the black war clubs move about
Like ball sticks in the game.
There his soul shall be, never to reappear.
Cause it to be so.
Under the earth the black fog
Shall never be lifted from him.
So shall it be.
Your soul shall never be knocked about.
Cause it to be so.

He thought it was a song to protect warriors going to battle, but maybe it would shield him from the Fire Carrier too. His Cherokee was a little rusty, but he'd got most of the words right. In a way he *was* going into battle, but a different kind from the old days. His fight was with one man who had a black heart so full of meanness, it was destroying the people he was supposed to protect.

Sixkiller tried to remember a song more suited to his situation, but he couldn't. So he sang the same one over and over, as darkness embraced him. He only wished he had paid more attention to Ma when she taught him and Jessie how to protect themselves from night walkers and other evil spirits.

When he began to see the lights of dwellings, he stopped singing, just repeated the words over and over in his mind. He was so hungry and exhausted that he was getting punchy. So, when he saw a light that was different from those in house windows, he couldn't be sure he wasn't hallucinating. The light appeared to be about a football field's distance from him. It bobbed up and down, then moved in a horizontal line.

He squeezed his eyes shut, and when he opened them again the light was gone. Relief flooded through him, leaving him even weaker than before. Minutes later, he stumbled upon the vacant cabin.

2

Monday morning at the Buckskin Police Station, Chief of Police Mitch Bushyhead was at his desk, going through the mail and in-house reports that had accumulated over the weekend.

The temperature outside hovered around fifteen degrees, with a below-zero chill factor. Snow and/or sleet, depending on the temperature, was forecast for later in the day. He'd tried to talk his sixteen-year-old daughter, Emily, into letting him drive her to school. Since he'd given her an '85 Mustang for Christmas, she'd been behind the wheel most of the time when she wasn't asleep or in class. His suggestion that he drive her today had met with stubborn resistance. He'd given in after she promised to go straight home from school if there was ice or snow. Now he made up his mind to go to the high school at three-thirty and pick her up if the roads were hazardous. The Mustang could sit in the school parking lot all night.

He picked up the last envelope, uncovering several messages. The handwritten note on top, dated two days ago, was from Virgil Rabbit, Mitch's crony and one of the officers who had worked Saturday.

The sheriff came by this morning to bring us up to speed on those horse ranch burglaries. The Circle D, Ray Desmond's spread south of town, was hit Friday night while all the family and hired hands were at a horse

*show. Desmond's tack room was cleaned out. They lost
ten saddles, plus blankets, halters, bridles, leads, bits,
and other supplies. About $40,000 worth of tack &
equipment. I notified area law-enforcement agencies and
placed descriptions of the items with the others in our
file and made copies for everybody in the department.*

Mitch didn't doubt the forty-thousand-dollar estimate for a
minute. Ray Desmond raised racing quarter horses and show
horses. His stables were nicer than some people's houses, and
Ray cared for his horses as though they were his children—
some said better than his children. At forty thousand dollars,
Desmond's estimate was lower than some of the other reported losses.

That file containing reports on the horse-ranch cases and
descriptions of stolen items was getting pretty thick. Leaning
back in his chair, Mitch did a mental inventory of the equine
tack and equipment burglaries that had occurred in Cherokee
County and surrounding counties the past several months. If
he remembered correctly, the Circle D made nine horse
ranches that had been hit. The Oklahoma Equine Association
was offering a ten-thousand-dollar reward for information
leading to an arrest. The sheriff's and police departments
around the state had been checking sales and auctions in their
jurisdictions for the stolen items, but none had surfaced.

The thieves had to be hauling the loot out of state to dispose
of it. And it wasn't as though they were smuggling diamonds,
either. This stuff took up a lot of space, and it was being transported right under the collective noses of law officers in numerous counties and municipalities. But they couldn't stop
every truck and van they saw. They had neither enough men
nor the legal grounds for such an operation.

Mitch laid the memo aside and picked up the next one,
which was also dated the previous Saturday and signed by
Virgil Rabbit.

The Delaware Co. Sheriff's office reported Henderson Sixkiller broke out of jail this morning (fax attached). I contacted his sister, Jessie Hatch. She claims she hasn't seen him.

Mitch reached for the phone, dialed the Delaware County Sheriff's office, identified himself, and asked the woman who answered if Henderson Sixkiller had been apprehended. He hadn't. Mitch thanked her and hung up. He read the fax, which described what Sixkiller had been wearing when he broke out.

It would be stupid of Sixkiller to head for Buckskin, where he was well known, but you never could tell. More often than not, criminals *were* stupid. Mitch wrote a memo to his officers, including a description of Sixkiller.

Be on the lookout for escaped convict Henderson Sixkiller. Resided in Buckskin until his arrest (for the cultivation of marijuana) about five months ago.

Physical Description

Full-blood Cherokee Indian.
Age: 38

Height: Approx. six feet
Weight: Approx. 175 lbs.
Last seen wearing Delaware Co. prison-issue dark blue twill pants & gray cotton shirt.

He used the Xerox machine in the common room to make copies for his four officers. Virgil and Duckworth would probably recognize Sixkiller on sight, but Mitch wasn't certain that his youngest officer, Charles "Roo" Stephens, would. And he doubted that Shelly Pitcher, who'd been with the department only seven months, had ever seen Sixkiller.

Helen Hendricks, the dispatcher, glanced up from her crossword puzzle. "Things are awful quiet this morning," she said. "Feels like the stillness before the storm. Makes me nervous."

"If that bad weather comes through, it'll liven up around here. You'll be taking fender-bender calls the rest of the day." He walked around the big common room, dropping a memo in each desk's in-file box. "Did Duck and Shelly go on patrol?"

"By way of the doughnut shop," Helen said, snorting. "I give Duck another month till he gains back all the weight he's lost. Again."

Last year, Mitch had instituted weight and fitness requirements for his officers. Twice now, Duck had lost thirty pounds, then turned right around and put the weight back on. Mitch either had to ignore his own regulation or nag Duck into going on another diet. Well, he wasn't Duck's mother. He'd let it go for a while. The past few months hadn't been easy for Duck. When Mitch had hired Shelly Pitcher, the first female officer in the Buckskin Police Department, he'd partnered her with Duck on the day shift and transferred Roo to evenings with Virgil; he'd figured Duck, the departmental chauvinist, could benefit from a little consciousness raising. The first few weeks, he'd thought Duck was going to run her off. But Shelly gave as good as she got and they'd eventually come, at least, to tolerate each other.

"What's a six-letter word for *stale?*" Helen asked.

"Beats me," Mitch said.

"Shoot," Helen muttered, "what good are you, Chief?"

Mitch glanced at Helen. She was bent over her crossword puzzle, her salt-and-pepper hair falling forward against her cheeks. After Helen's third divorce recently, she had quit coloring her hair and let it go natural. Mitch liked it better this way. Helen swore she was off men for good. Mitch had felt called upon to say something, so he'd told her how sorry he was about the divorce. Helen had shrugged and said, "Life's a tragedy, Chief. Don't you know that?" It was a rare self-revelation for Helen, for she'd sounded dead serious.

Unaware of his perusal, she frowned and gnawed the eraser end of her pencil. Shaking his head, he went back to his office.

He switched on the portable radio and shuffled through the remaining messages, none of which required his immediate attention.

The forecast for snow or sleet later in the day was repeated. Then a country singer came on with a tale of woe about a guy whose girl left him with the mother of all hangovers and a heart weighed down by sorrow.

Mitch knew how he felt. He hadn't heard from Lisa Macpherson, his daughter's former English teacher and Mitch's former lover, for six weeks. Lisa had moved to California in early September to teach at a junior college and get her Ph.D.

They had communicated frequently at first, but his last letter and the messages he'd left on her answering machine had not been answered. Maybe his urging her to come to Buckskin for Christmas had been a mistake. Maybe she hadn't known how to say no, so she'd just stopped answering his letters and calls.

Whatever, he figured the next move was hers. Meanwhile, he tried not to imagine her with other men.

He switched off the radio and went out to the common room for a cup of coffee. Helen had put the crossword puzzle aside and was filing her nails. *"Rancid,"* she said.

"Say what?"

"A six-letter word for *stale. Rancid.* "

"Oh." He took the coffee back to his office.

By noon, the temperature had risen to thirty degrees and it started to snow. Mitch, Duck, and Shelly were called to the scene of three non-injury car wrecks. By three-fifteen, two or three inches of snow lay on the ground.

Mitch grabbed his coat from the rack in his office, shrugging it on as he walked into the common room. Shelly and Duck were at their desks, writing up the accident reports. Helen was on the telephone.

"Duck," Mitch said, "tell Helen I'm going to pick up Emily. Be back in half an hour."

"Wait a minute, Chief," Helen called. She placed her hand over the phone's mouthpiece. "It's Millicent Kirkwood. She's got her tail in a knot. Says there's a man on her porch and he won't leave."

"In her dreams," Duck muttered from his desk.

It wasn't the first time Millicent or Polly Kirkwood, elderly spinster sisters, had called the station to report a man had been in their house or was trying to get in. Neither Mitch nor his officers who had responded to the calls had ever found any evidence that the men were other than figments of the Kirkwood sisters' imaginations.

"Cut the old gal some slack, Duck," Helen said. "Even if she is imagining it, she's scared to death."

Duck threw one arm over the back of his chair and leaned back, his close-set, mismatched eyes—one brown, the other hazel—crinkling at the corners as he prepared to deliver one of his antifeminist pronouncements. "What the Kirkwood sisters need is—"

"A good lay," Helen finished for him.

Shelly looked at him over the top of her reading glasses and gave a contemptuous sniff. "Yeah, right. Thus speaks our resident expert. The cure for all female woes, according to Officer Duckworth."

Duck sucked in his gut and threw out his chest. "Thanks for the compliment, Pitcher. 'Resident expert.' I like it."

"Jerk," mumbled Shelly and returned to her report.

"Come with me, Duck," Mitch said. "We'll check out the Kirkwood sisters on the way to the high school."

"Chief Bushyhead and an officer are on the way, Miss Kirkwood," Helen was saying as they left.

After engaging the four-wheel drive in his Toyota Landcruiser, Mitch started the engine and eased into the street, tires crunching the fresh snow. In bad driving weather, he used his Toyota instead of a patrol car. "It's probably another false alarm, but one of these days it might not be, and we're getting paid to find out."

"Okay by me," Duck said. "I'd rather do that than stay at the station with those two dames giving me a hard time."

"You ask for it, Duck, always smarting off."

"Aw, women got no sense of humor."

"Hate to tell you this, buddy, but you're just not a nineties kind of guy."

Duck adjusted the heater vent and flopped back in the seat. "Tough toenails," he mumbled, offended.

Mitch turned on to the Kirkwoods' street. The snow had stopped for now, but dusk had come early because of the heavy cloud cover. Light yellowed several windows along the street. Mitch pulled into the Kirkwoods' driveway.

"Guess what," Duck muttered. "Nobody's around. Big frigging surprise."

"Footprints are leading to the porch, though," Mitch said. They got out of the Landcruiser and followed the prints up the walk. They were big enough to have been made by a man's shoes.

"Probably one of them Jehovah's Witnesses," Duck said. "Carrying his briefcase full of pamphlets, and Millicent and Polly thought it was a bomb." He cackled at his own wit.

Mitch switched off the engine.

"Those JW's get out in all kinds of weather," Duck said. "Dicey down at the café says they have to make a quota, so many calls a week. Like a Fuller brush man. A couple of 'em showed up at Dicey's house on Christmas Day when she had wall-to-wall kinfolks. You believe it?"

Dicey and Duck's wife, Geraldine, were waitresses at the Three Squares Café. "Christmas isn't special to them," Mitch said. "They don't believe in holidays."

"Really? But that would make every day like every other."

"I think that's the point."

"Weird," Duck observed unoriginally, "but I guess it takes all kinds."

The footprints went up the steps to the Kirkwood sisters' porch and toward the front door where they reversed and descended to the yard again. "Somebody was here, all right," Mitch said and rang the bell.

They heard several locks and bolts being released and the door opened a crack. The safety chain was still engaged. Millicent Kirkwood glared at them through her rimless spectacles.

"Afternoon, Miss Millicent," Mitch said.

"Oh, it's you."

"Naw, it's Captain Marvel," Duck said under his breath.

She released the chain and opened the inner door wider, talking to them through the glass storm door. "He came up on the porch, sat down right up against the front door, and wouldn't budge." Her long, sharp nose twitched. "Poor Polly came very near to fainting."

Polly Kirkwood, Millicent's plump, rosy-cheeked sister, peeked at them over Millicent's shoulder with a little gleam in her eyes. "Did not," she chirped and wiggled her fingers at Mitch. Last spring, Polly had discovered a dead body in the woods behind the Kirkwood house, but this was undoubtedly the most exciting thing that had happened to her since.

Millicent ignored her. "When I told him I was calling the police, he cursed me, Chief."

"I felt sorry for him," Polly said. "I wanted to give him a blanket and something to eat."

"Oh, hush up, Polly!" Millicent snapped. "If one of us didn't have a little common sense, we'd have both been carried off by some crazed rapist long ago."

"You wish," Duck mumbled behind Mitch.

"I don't think he would have hurt us," Polly protested. A little giggle escaped her. "His language was shocking, of course—as bad as you hear on TV these days. But he wasn't too steady on his feet. I fear he'd been imbibing, Chief."

" 'First the man takes a drink,' " Millicent quoted portentously. " 'Then the drink takes a drink. Then the drink takes the man!' " Millicent, a retired schoolteacher, had a quotation for every occasion.

"Did you see where he went?" Mitch asked.

"No, but we heard him," Millicent said. "Snorting and carrying on like a bull elephant on a rampage. He's under the porch."

"Now? I mean, still?" Mitch asked.

"I haven't looked, but we haven't heard him leave."

Mitch and Duck tramped back down the steps and went around to the side of the porch, where it was high enough for a man to crawl under. Mitch banged on the porch floor. "You, under there! It's the police. Come on out."

There was a groan, but no one emerged. Mitch muttered an oath and stooped down to peer into the darkness beneath the porch. He could make out a form huddled against the concrete-block foundation. "Hey, podner, you can't stay under there. You'll freeze to death. Come on out now, or we'll come in after you."

The form didn't move. "Old biddies, wouldn't let me in." The words were slurred. "Lemme alone. Ain't comin' out."

"Looks like we'll have to go get him," Mitch said.

"Damn, slobbering drunks," Duck grunted as he got down on his knees beside Mitch and squinted at the man. "It's wet under there. We're gonna get mud all over us."

On all fours, Mitch crawled into the dank-smelling darkness.

"Oh, hell," Duck muttered and followed at Mitch's heels. They each grabbed an arm and pulled the cursing, protesting bundle out from under the porch.

"Old hags," the drunk wheezed as they pulled him to his feet. His rumpled coat and trousers were covered with mud. "Hissing and yowling like two treed cats. I wasn't gonna hurt 'em."

Mitch wasn't too surprised to recognize the mud-streaked face of Amos Flycatcher. Mitch could count on the fingers of one hand the times he'd seen Amos stone sober. "Amos, what in tarnation is wrong with you? Stumbling around in this weather, scaring old ladies, hiding under the porch like some no-account, egg-sucking hound."

Duck was puffing and scowling, trying to shake some of the mud off his trousers. "Crap, Amos. Look at this. Mud up to my butt. I just got these pants out of the cleaners too."

Amos grinned sheepishly, revealing a gap in the top row of big yellow teeth. He tried to shrug off Mitch's grip on his arm, but Mitch held on, not wanting to get into a foot race with Amos.

Amos pulled himself up and said indignantly, "Nobody can be meaner than a woman when she sets her mind to it. Nutty old bats wouldn't let me in."

"I wouldn't let you in, either," Duck said. "You look like a train wreck and smell like a brewery."

"What did you want in the Kirkwoods' house, anyway?" Mitch asked.

"It's cold, man," Amos explained, as though to an idiot child.

"Where's your car?" Mitch asked.

"Somewhere," Amos said vaguely. "Lost it."

Mitch led him toward the Landcruiser. Millicent and Polly were watching them through the storm door. Mitch waved at them. "Everything's under control, ladies."

Millicent couldn't resist a parting shot. She opened the storm door and yelled, " 'Woe unto them that rise up early in the morning, that they may follow strong drink.' "

"Aw, shut up, you old witch!" Amos yelled back.

But Millicent was not finished. "God-fearing people aren't even safe in their own houses. I've a good mind to arm myself!"

"Just what we need," Duck groused. "Guns in the hands of two goosey old maids."

"You phone us if you need us, now," Mitch called.

"Don't encourage 'em," Duck groaned.

"Come on, Amos," Mitch said. "We'll take you home. You

can find your car tomorrow." It was certain nobody was going to steal the ancient rattletrap.

Amos halted and dug his heels into the snow. "No! Anyplace but home."

"Serve him right if we threw him in a cell till he sobers up," Duck growled.

Mitch jerked hard on Amos's arm with one hand, nearly unbalancing him, and opened the back door of the Landcruiser with the other. "You're trying my patience, Amos. Get in." He shoved him into the car, knowing that later he'd have to scrub the back-seat upholstery.

Amos lived out near the lake, a good six or seven miles from town. Mitch climbed into the driver's seat while Duck got in on the other side. Mitch checked his watch. It was after three-thirty. He'd missed Emily in order to haul a stupid drunk out from under a porch.

"I'm a citizen, I got my rights," Amos whined from the back seat. "I demand you take me to jail."

"Well, there's a new one," Duck said.

"Can't go home."

"Why are you so set against going home, Amos?" Duck asked. "Afraid of your old lady?"

"She left," Amos said morosely. "December twenty-four." His voice caught. "Mer-rry Christ-masss."

It sounded as if Mrs. Flycatcher had finally had her fill of Amos's binges. After twenty-some years. The woman was a saint to have put up with Amos this long. "Where'd she go?" Mitch asked.

"Her mama's, I 'spect. Won't take my phone calls. Won't come home. Hey!" His voice rose shrilly with alarm. "Don't turn here. I told you, take me to jail."

"Why should the city feed and house you?" Mitch asked. "You can sober up at home."

Amos burst into tears. "Can't stay there," he blubbered.

"Aw, Amos," Duck groaned, "don't take on like that. I know the place must remind you of your wife but—"

"It ain't that! It's *him*. He's been back more'n a month! I seen him out there the last three nights, in the woods behind my house. You leave me there, he'll come and get me."

Duck rolled his eyes at Mitch, then pulled out a handkerchief and passed it to the back seat. "Here, wipe your face, bozo. A grown man, crying like a baby. It's disgusting."

"I seen him," Amos blubbered. His words had become slower and more slurred. "He'll get me."

"Who'll get you?" Duck asked.

"The Fire Carrier," he mumbled, and the next thing they heard was a loud snore.

"He's passed out," Duck said. "I guess that means we'll have to carry him in his house."

"Probably," Mitch said, wondering if Emily was home yet.

"A perfect windup to a perfect day," Duck grumbled.

"Who did he say would get him?"

"Sounded like he said 'fire carrier.'" Duck shrugged. "What do you think that means?"

"No idea."

"I bet he's been blind drunk ever since his wife left. Probably hallucinating, seeing fire. Like some boozers see bugs or pink elephants."

Every man to his own horrors, Mitch thought as he imagined Emily's Mustang careening out of control. He shook the image from his mind and headed out of town.

3

Before returning to the station, Mitch detoured down Pawnee Street. The Mustang wasn't in his driveway. He was about to pass on by and check the highway on the way to the high school when he saw a light in the living-room bay window. He and his late wife had spent years remodeling the old Victorian house. When its roofs and eaves were snow covered, like now, it had always reminded him of something out of Charles Dickens. At the moment, though, Dickens was the farthest thing from his mind. He made a sharp turn into the driveway, sliding a little.

Duck had scooted down in the passenger seat with his head resting on the seat back. The quick turn threw him against the door. "What in—?"

"I didn't leave a light on," Mitch explained.

Duck peered at the house. "Oh." He resettled himself. "I'll wait here for you. Holler if you need me."

The front door was unlocked. Mitch stamped the snow off his boots on the porch and went in. "Emily?"

"Daddy?" She walked out of the kitchen, and relief made him feel weak. She was wearing jeans, a red-and-blue plaid flannel shirt of Mitch's that fell to her knees, and white crew socks. She raked a strand of long brown hair out of her brown eyes and smiled at him. When she looked at him with her head tilted to one side like that, she was so like her mother that Mitch's throat felt tight. The memory of Ellen took him unawares sometimes, like a shadow passing over the sun. Other times he couldn't remember her face.

Emily stood on tiptoe to kiss his cheek. "Hi," she said. Noticing the mud on his trousers, she jumped back. "Ick. What happened to you?"

"It's a long story. I'll tell you later." He looked her over carefully and was grateful to see no bruises or scrapes. "I was worried about you. I wanted to get to the high school in time to bring you home, but something came up."

She put a hand on her hip. "Don't worry about me, Daddy. I'm practically an adult."

He wished she wouldn't remind him. "Where's the Mustang?"

She made a face. "It wouldn't start. Jimmy Doolittle drove me home."

Mitch tried to place Jimmy Doolittle but couldn't. It must have shown on his face.

"You remember Jimmy. I introduced him to you a couple of weeks ago, when he came to take me to a movie. He's in my class, plays basketball. We're going to the sock hop together on Friday."

"Oh, yeah," Mitch murmured, vaguely remembering a tall blond boy. Last year, Emily's sophomore year, she had gone steady with Kevin Hartsbarger, now a senior, and Mitch had worried constantly that they spent too much time together. He'd been secretly glad when Emily told him she and Kevin had decided to date other people, but now he almost wished she'd get back with Kevin. The past couple of months, he never knew which overgrown boy-man would turn up at his house next, though evidently Jimmy Doolittle now had the inside track. He knew so little about some of these kids. So he worried as much as ever. Obviously, none of them was good enough for Emily, he thought unabashedly. Of course, every father thought that and, no matter how many times Emily told him not to, it was the role of fathers of female offspring to worry.

"I'm making chili and cornbread for supper," Emily said. "What time will you be home?"

Since his wife's death two years ago, Mitch and Emily had alternated making dinner during the week. They ate a lot of quick, one-dish meals; this winter they'd had stew or chili about once a week. On the weekends, when he had more time to spend in the kitchen, Mitch usually fixed at least one big meal, with salad, meat, vegetables, and dessert. Or they went out for Sunday lunch.

"I'll try for five-thirty," he replied to her question and headed for the stairs.

She called after him, "Can you check on my car? I really *need* it."

He washed his hands and changed into clean trousers. Back downstairs, he went into the kitchen where Emily was stirring chili in a pot on the stove. "I better get back to work now. I'll call the Texaco station, see if somebody can take a look at the Mustang."

"Good. Maybe they can get it running and bring it by here tonight," she said hopefully. "Temple and I were planning to go shopping tomorrow after school. The cheerleaders are getting new shoes. Temple and I are supposed to make recommendations, and Temple's car is in the shop getting a new transmission. So I *have* to drive, Daddy." Temple Roberts, a wide-eyed redhead, was Emily's best friend. They had been pom-pom girls last year, but this year both had been elected to the cheerleading squad. Mitch wasn't exactly sure what the difference was, only that being a cheerleader seemed to be a more coveted position.

He nodded, while deciding to tell the mechanic to keep the Mustang a day or two, until driving conditions were back to normal. The cheerleaders could wait a couple of days for their shoes. "Gotta go, sweetheart. And you left the front door unlocked again. Lock it behind me."

"I forgot," she said. She followed him to the door and he hesitated on the porch until he heard the bolt click into place.

Duck had been napping. He yawned and straightened up when Mitch got in the Landcruiser. "Everything all right?"

"Yeah, her car wouldn't start. Some kid named Jimmy Doright or Doolittle—something like that—brought her home."

Duck looked over at him and grinned. "You're doing the daddy thing again, Chief. What's wrong with Jimmy Doolittle? The way you said that makes it sound like he's some kind of juvenile delinquent."

"For all I know, he's a cat burglar. I only met him once. I don't know anything about him. Do you?"

Duck shrugged. "I know his folks. They're good people, so Jimmy's probably okay."

"When Lisa was at the high school, I could always ask her when I wanted the inside dope on a student."

"Speaking of Lisa—"

"Skip it," Mitch said flatly.

"If you ask me—"

"Nobody did."

Dr. Rhea Vann entered the examining room and closed the door behind her. She'd returned to Cherokee County less than a year ago to take charge of the Cherokee Nation's family clinic in Buckskin. By now, she knew most of the patients who came to the clinic, having treated them previously.

She'd seen the woman huddled on the edge of the examining table three times before today. Her name was Jessie Hatch, she was forty years old and the mother of two teenaged boys. The first time Rhea saw her, she'd set a broken arm, the last time she'd taken a couple of stitches in a cut above Jessie's left eyebrow. Today, Jessie had a black eye and her face was swollen and bruised.

Rhea clasped the cool disc of the stethoscope that hung around her neck, warming it with her body heat. The woman met her gaze briefly, then looked away, embarrassed. Rhea stepped up to the examining table and parted the back of the cotton gown. "What happened this time, Jessie?"

"I fell." The words were barely audible.

Rhea placed the stethoscope's disc on Jessie's back. "Take a deep breath and let it out slowly."

Jessie's breath turned into a gasp of pain. "I can't breathe deep. It hurts too bad. I—I think I may have broke some ribs."

Jessie grunted whenever Rhea touched the right side of her rib cage. "We better get X rays," she said finally. She went down the hall to the staff lounge. Her medical assistant, a combination practical nurse and technician, Marilee Steiner, was taking her first break in a busy day.

Marilee, a pretty quarter-Cherokee woman of twenty-two, was a high-school dropout and former drug abuser. She had turned her life around with the help of counselors at the Cherokee Nation's Job Corps Center in Buckskin. After earning her GED, she'd enrolled in the Job Corps' medical-assistant course and graduated with the highest grades in the class. She'd been working at the clinic for three months now.

"Sorry to cut short your break, Marilee, but I need some X rays on the patient in two. Right-side, upper-body AP and lateral and both obliques."

"Jessie Hatch?"

Rhea nodded. "That maniac worked her over again."

"Yeah, I noticed she was bunged up when she came in." Marilee sighed and got to her feet.

Rhea suddenly remembered that Tyler Hatch was the director of the Job Corps Center. "You must know Jessie's husband. Did you ever suspect him of battering his wife when you were at the center?"

Marilee shook her head. "Not in a million years. When I first went to the center, I was a total wreck and he was incredibly kind and understanding. I used to get severely depressed and want to quit going to class, but he wouldn't let me. He helped me a lot." She frowned in perplexity. "He's kind of a woman chaser, but he was a real friend when I needed one badly."

Big of him, Rhea thought sourly. "You say he chases women? Does he go out with students from the center?"

She shrugged. "He hit on me at first, but when I found out he was married, I let him know I wasn't interested. He probably does it with other girls too. I never asked." She dropped her gaze. When she looked up, her eyes narrowed. "Tyler helped me stay straight, Rhea, him and the counselors. He seemed"—she paused, searching for the word—"well, nice. He may run around on his wife, but I never saw any violence in him. Even now . . ." She frowned and drew her brows together. "Are you *sure* he's the one who's beating her?"

Rhea nodded. "She as much as admitted it to me the last time she was here."

A few minutes later, after looking at Jessie's X rays, Rhea was able to tell her, "No broken ribs. They're just badly bruised. I'll have to tape them. I'll be as gentle as I can." Rhea worked in silence for several moments, remembering Marilee's doubt. She said, "You're about the most accident-prone patient I've ever seen, Jessie."

"I've always been clumsy," Jessie mumbled.

Rhea managed to keep her mouth shut until she finished taping. But then she walked around to face Jessie. Rhea herself had no doubt, but she wanted Jessie to say it. "When are you going to stop lying for him?"

Jessie's head was bowed. When she finally looked up, her eyes were rim-full of tears. "What choice do I have?"

"There are always choices, Jessie."

She shook her head. "If I leave him, he'll find me. He says he loves me too much to ever let me go. He says I nag him, that it's my fault when he has to hit me."

"That's what all batterers say. It's sick!" Rhea tried to rein in her anger. "You know I have to report this to the police, just like last time."

"It's no use. I wouldn't press charges then, and I won't now."

"Why, Jessie? One of these days he's going to kill you if you don't put a stop to it."

"The police can't help me. All they can do is get a restraining order."

"That's a start. It would at least get your complaint on record, and if it happened again, maybe they could charge him with defying the order as well as battering."

Jessie shook her head. "It's a piece of paper. It wouldn't keep him away from me. It'd just make him madder. He— he'd kill me for sure then." She shuddered.

Rhea could see remnants of a youthful prettiness in Jessie Hatch's face, but it was obscured now by her shrinking manner and tendency to stoop, as though she were trying to fold in upon herself and disappear. Jessie had long ago lost whatever ability she'd once had to stand up for herself. She was defeated and helpless. It was the most frustrating thing Rhea had to deal with in patients, this attitude that they were at the mercy of the negative forces in their lives—whether it was an addiction to nicotine or alcohol, or a husband who hit them. "Think about your boys, Jessie."

Jessie looked at Rhea, her dark eyes like a wounded deer's. "I am. I'm really worried about them," she admitted, "especially Jason—he's the oldest, fifteen. He's been getting in trouble at school. He seems so angry all the time."

Seeing your father beat up your mother on a regular basis will do that to you, Rhea thought.

"Tyler's had a cold and sore throat for a week. He saw a doctor and got some pills, but they don't help. He feels achey all over, he says, so he's been real touchy. At breakfast, I said something that made him mad and he started yelling, woke up the boys, and . . . well, you see what happened. After he left, Jason got all worked up and said he was going to kill his dad if he ever hurt any of us again. I don't think he meant it but— I—I'm afraid he might really try to stop Tyler the next time he goes into one of his rages, and Jason would be the one to get hurt."

"Your son has reached an age where he feels he has to protect you. No fifteen-year-old should carry that burden. If you won't leave for your own sake, Jessie, then you have to do it for the boys. Don't you have relatives you can go to until you get on your feet?"

She sighed wearily. "An aunt, but that's the first place he'd look." Jessie slid off the examining table carefully and eased out of the gown.

Rhea helped her fasten her bra and get into her clothes. Then, gripping Jessie's shoulders, she turned her around. She was about to do something she'd sworn she'd never do, get too involved in a patient's personal life. "Look, I have a spare bedroom. You can stay with me until you decide what to do. The boys can come too, if you want."

Fresh tears filled Jessie's eyes. "That's so sweet of you, Doctor Vann. But I can't let you do that." Rhea pulled a tissue from a box on the cabinet and handed it to her. Jessie wiped her eyes.

"Why not?"

"He knows I had an appointment with you this afternoon. I left word for him at the center, in case he called while I was gone. He—he gets upset if he calls and I'm not home—"

God in heaven, Rhea thought. "Don't worry about me. I'm not afraid of him."

"He might come here, looking for me. He could get violent."

"I doubt it." Characteristically, men like Tyler Hatch took out their frustrations on their wives and kids, not on outsiders, who weren't apt to be cowed into protecting them. "And if he shows up here, I'll say I don't know where you are."

Jessie stared out the window, her brow furrowed with thought. "The boys could stay with my aunt. I don't think Tyler would care. But he wants *me* there when he's home. Oh, I just don't know . . ."

Rhea watched hope flicker in her expression, but it was quickly doused by ingrained resignation. "Don't even go back home," she urged. "Did you drive yourself here?"

"No, Tyler has the car. I didn't want to ask him to bring me, so I got a friend to drop me off. I'm supposed to call her when I'm ready to leave."

Rhea was thoughtful for a moment. "My next patient isn't due until four-thirty. I'll take you to my house and get you settled in. What time does your husband get home from work?"

"A little after five, usually."

"We've got time then. You can call your boys from my house and ask them to bring whatever you'll need. What do you say?"

Jessie took a shallow breath, met Rhea's gaze. "Well . . ."

"For the boys, Jessie."

"I'm so afraid to cross him!" she burst out.

"I know you are," Rhea said calmly, "but try to think about yourself now instead of Tyler. You at least need some time alone to think."

"Maybe he'll miss me so much he'll agree to counseling."

Yeah, sure, Rhea thought, and the sun's going to set in the east today. "So you're going to my house?"

Finally, she nodded, took a deep breath. "All right, Doctor."

Rhea smiled. "Good. And since we'll be housemates for a while, you'd better make it 'Rhea.' "

She gave her a puffy-lipped smile. "Okay, Rhea, and thank you."

4

It was ten after five and Rhea's last patient had left the clinic. She was in her office catching up on paperwork, when Marilee pushed open the door and said in a rush, "Tyler Hatch just drove up. He was going so fast when he hit the parking lot, I thought he was coming right through the front door."

Rhea rose from her chair. "Lock the door and close the blinds. I'll get the back door." As Marilee scurried away, she hurried down the hall, locked and bolted the back door, then went to the reception area. Marilee was closing the last venetian blind.

"He's talking crazy." Marilee's voice shook.

Tyler Hatch banged on the front door. "Let me in! I know she's in there! Filthy whore's gonna pay for ruining my life! I'll kill her! Let me in!"

Marilee had taken refuge behind the counter in the office section of the reception area. She was as pale as her uniform.

"Call the police," Rhea said.

As Marilee snatched the phone off the hook, Tyler Hatch's booted foot crashed through one of the big front windows, spraying shards of glass into the reception room. One of them barely missed Rhea's face. She jumped back and yelled, "Stay out of here!"

Two big hands grabbed the venetian blind and ripped it away. Marilee screamed and dropped the receiver.

"Call the police!" Rhea said again, looking around for

something with which to defend herself and Marilee. The Formica-topped tables in the waiting room had legs that screwed into the tops. They had come disassembled and Rhea had assembled them herself. She raked the magazines off the nearest table, flipped it over, and unscrewed a leg. In the background, Marilee was shouting into the phone for somebody to hurry. When Rhea turned around, Tyler Hatch's head and shoulders were coming through the window. She drew the table leg across her right shoulder in batting position.

"You can't come in here! I'm warning you, back off! The police are on the way here right now."

Hatch ignored Rhea and lunged toward Marilee, jerking the receiver from her hands. "I'm gonna kill you, bitch!"

Rhea took one long step and brought the table leg down on the side of his head. It sheered off and banged down on his shoulder hard enough to lift her heels off the floor. He staggered backwards, addled, then regained his balance and made another lunge across the counter. Rhea hit him again.

"How many times did you hit him?" Mitch asked. He and Virgil Rabbit, who'd come on duty at four o'clock, had arrived at the clinic to find a gaping hole in one of the clinic's front windows and Dr. Rhea Vann comforting her assistant, Marilee Steiner. Broken glass had been swept into a pile against the wall.

Now Marilee was seated on a green vinyl couch. The doctor had given her a paper cupful of water. She was clutching it in hands that shook so badly she kept sloshing water on her white uniform. Rhea Vann sat beside her, perfectly calm, or so Mitch would have thought if he hadn't noticed how tightly she was gripping the arm of the couch.

"I think I hit him twice," she said.

"You don't know?"

"It all happened so fast." She seemed to make a conscious effort to relax the fingers that gripped the arm of the couch. She gestured toward a piece of wood propped against the wall. "I hit him with that table leg. It was the only thing handy. I took it off that." She indicated a three-legged table which was turned on its side. "He kept trying to get over the counter to Marilee and prevent her calling for help. She'd already reached the police station, though."

"And after you hit him the second time, he decided to leave?"

Rhea nodded. "He threw his arms over his head and turned and jumped back through that hole in the window, the same way he came in. He got in his car and drove away."

"Was he drunk?"

"I don't know."

Virgil was peering at the jagged edges of glass left in the window frame. "Looks like he cut himself, Chief. There's a little blood here."

"You must pack a powerful punch," Mitch said, trying to imagine the doctor, who couldn't weigh more than a hundred and twenty pounds, fighting off a big man like Tyler Hatch. Pure adrenaline, he thought.

"I was fighting for our lives," Rhea said. "He was totally irrational. I didn't doubt for a moment that he meant to hurt us. When he saw Marilee on the phone with the police station, he said he was going to kill her. Now that I think about it"—for the first time, she looked shaken—"it's a wonder he didn't attack me after I hit him the first time."

"Why was he after you two?"

"He didn't come here for us, we were just in his way. He was looking for his wife. She'd been in to see me earlier in the day with a black eye, swollen face, and severely bruised ribs. He kept yelling something about her ruining his life. Oh, and he threatened to kill *her* too." The corners of her mouth turned down in disgust. "He said she'd ruined his life. Typical abuser. She made me do it."

"Were you and Miss Steiner the only people in the clinic?"

She nodded. "The receptionist had left a few minutes earlier. Marilee was in the waiting room, I was in my office, making out an abuse report for your department, when she came in and told me Tyler Hatch was outside."

Mitch had followed up on a previous abuse report from the clinic, but Jessie Hatch had insisted she'd cut herself when she fell against a door frame, her husband had nothing to do with it.

"I'd just locked the front door," Marilee said shakily, "when he started banging on it." She set the paper cup on a table and hugged herself and shivered, although it was comfortably warm in the room. "I never saw him like that before. It was terrifying."

"You know him?" Mitch asked.

Marilee nodded.

"How well?"

"Pretty—well," she said haltingly, "or I thought so before today. He's the director of the Job Corps Center, and I was a student there for two years."

Mitch asked them to repeat what had happened with as many details as they could recall and took a few notes. Then he said, "We'll pick him up, but if we don't find him right away, you probably shouldn't open the clinic until we do."

"I can't close the clinic," Rhea said.

Mitch saw the stubborn set of her jaw. "Then get that window replaced or boarded up first thing tomorrow morning and keep the doors locked."

Rhea thought about it. "We can put up a sign, instructing patients to ring the bell to be admitted."

"When did his wife leave here?"

"More than an hour ago," Rhea said.

"From what you told me about her injuries, I would've thought she'd go straight home. She wouldn't want to be seen. I wonder," Mitch said, frowning, "why he thought she was still here." He looked at Rhea. "Maybe it was you he wanted, after all. Maybe his wife told him you were going to file another abuse report."

Rhea thought about it. "No, he was looking for his wife." She stood, glancing at Marilee and then Virgil. "Chief Bushyhead, may I speak to you in private?"

"Sure." Mitch followed her down the hall to her office,

where she closed the door. He had met Rhea Vann several months ago while he was investigating the murder of a student at the tribal boarding school. She'd been with her grandfather, an old medicine man called Crying Wolf. Since then, he'd only seen her a few times from a distance.

She had high cheekbones and chocolate-colored, almond-shaped eyes, the lashes so thick and long they might have been fake, but there was nothing artificial about Rhea Vann. Her long black hair was pulled straight back in a single French braid, exposing small, well-formed ears with plain gold studs in the lobes. If she'd started the day wearing makeup, it was gone now, not that that face needed any—it would be sort of like painting a beauty mark on the Mona Lisa. Even though she wore a hip-length lab coat over white pants, it was open in front and didn't completely conceal her trim body or the fact that she had curves in all the right places. Mitch was suddenly too aware of how attractive she was.

"I wanted to tell you," she said, "that I convinced Jessie not to go back home. That's why I know her husband came here looking for her. He must think we know where she is."

"Do you?"

She nodded. "I took her to my house." She hesitated, walked to her desk, picked up a glass paperweight, put it down. "That may have been unwise, but she had nowhere else to go. Neither Robin, my receptionist, nor Marilee knows where she's hiding. The fewer people who know, the less likely her husband will be to track her down."

"You better hope he doesn't find out where she's staying. As you saw, Tyler Hatch can get violent, and if he learns she's with you . . ."

She folded her arms and her dark eyes flashed angrily. "I have a good security system, and I own a handgun."

He lifted a brow. "Do you know how to use it?"

"Yes, and I have a license to carry it too. Before I came back to Buckskin, I was almost killed by a drugged-out kid who broke into a clinic where I was working late. After that,

I got the gun. I haven't been carrying it since I moved back. It seemed unnecessary—until today."

So she'd been attacked by a strung-out addict. It explained why she hadn't hesitated to fight off Tyler Hatch with such ferocity. After today, she'd be carrying again. Mitch understood, but guns in the hands of private citizens made him nervous. Half the country was walking around armed, nuts buying bloody bazookas and machine guns. Things had come to a pretty pass when even the Kirkwood sisters were threatening to get a gun.

"Did Mrs. Hatch say anything about Henderson Sixkiller?" Mitch asked.

Her brow furrowed. "Who?"

"Henderson Sixkiller, Jessie Hatch's brother."

"No. She mentioned an aunt who lives in town, but not a brother."

"He doesn't live here at the moment, but he broke out of the Delaware County Jail Saturday morning and may have come this way. If he's in the area, he may try to contact her."

She thought about it and shrugged. "Since she's not at home, he won't know where to find her."

"Do her kids know where she is?"

Rhea hesitated. "I think she called them from my house. She needs clothes and toiletries."

"Then Sixkiller could catch one of them at school and get word to her that way."

For the first time, Rhea actually looked worried. Maybe it hadn't occurred to her before that Hatch, too, could force his sons to tell where their mother was staying. Nor had she planned on having to deal with Jessie Hatch's convict brother. "If I hear anything about Jessie's brother," she said, "I'll let you know."

He studied her. "Do I have your word on it?"

She bristled and dropped her arms to her sides. "Absolutely," she said shortly.

Mitch hesitated, wondered if he should apologize for insinuating she couldn't be trusted, then decided to let it go. "Officer Rabbit and I will be leaving now. You aren't planning to stay around here much longer today, are you?"

"No. I can finish that report tomorrow. I'll send Marilee home, then go straight to my house and see if I can get the lumberyard to send somebody out this evening to fix that window."

"Good." Mitch paused. "Miss Steiner's still pretty shaken. Does she live far from the clinic?"

"A couple of miles. I can drive her home if she's not feeling up to it."

Marilee was consulted and insisted that she could drive herself.

"My roommate will be there," she said, "and my boyfriend's due back in town today. We'll probably go out to dinner tonight. I'll be okay once I get home."

Mitch said he'd follow her, to be sure she made it there without incident. She got her purse and went out to her car, an economy-model Chevrolet, several years old.

In the clinic's open doorway, Rhea Vann smiled briefly, revealing perfectly even white teeth, and extended her hand.

"Thank you for responding to our call so promptly, Chief Bushyhead." Her grip was warm and firm. "I'll lock my office and the supply room and leave by the back door."

Mitch and Virgil got in the Landcruiser and circled the clinic, watched Rhea Vann get into her dark-blue Oldsmobile, lock the doors, and wave. Mitch accelerated and followed Marilee Steiner's slowly moving taillights. He was glad to see she was driving cautiously. He followed her to a duplex on the other side of town.

Then they went to the Hatch house. The lights were on but nobody was home, or if they were, they weren't answering the door. The attached garage was empty and no car was in the driveway.

"Where could Hatch be?" Virgil asked.

"He's probably still looking for his wife," Mitch said. "Think I'll run by the doctor's house, see if she got home okay."

"That's one good-looking woman," Virgil observed.

"Oh?"

"You didn't notice?"

"Not really."

Grinning, Virgil gave him a long, sideways look.

Wanting to distract Virgil from that line of thought, Mitch told him about having to drag Amos Flycatcher from under the Kirkwoods' porch. "He didn't want us to take him home. He kept saying he'd seen the fire carrier. Ever hear of anything like that?"

Virgil looked at him and laughed. "Every Cherokee in eastern Oklahoma has. Except for a few outlanders, like you."

Although half Cherokee, Mitch had been raised by his white mother in Oklahoma City. Even though he'd lived in Cherokee County for more than ten years now, he was still considered something of an outsider by many traditional Cherokees. Virgil, a full-blood, had managed to plant a foot in both worlds. He was a member of the Nighthawk Ketoowahs, a secret society dedicated to preserving the old ways; but he was also a representative of the white man's law.

"For a couple of years I didn't hear of any sightings, but lately they've started up again," Virgil went on. "If it was just Amos, I wouldn't put much stock in it, but I've heard it from other people."

"So?" Mitch asked. "What's a fire carrier?"

"That's a matter of some dispute. The Fire Carrier is the name the Cherokees give it. Some of the traditionalists believe it's an evil spirit who followed their ancestors here from the old Cherokee country back East. When I was a kid, my granddad scared the crap out of me with stories about people who were out at night and had the misfortune to meet up with the Fire Carrier."

"Such as?"

Virgil leaned forward and turned the heat down a notch. "For example," he said, settling back, "according to my granddad, an old man he knew turned white-headed overnight after an encounter with the Fire Carrier, but he never would talk about what had happened. Slept with the lights on, though, and he wouldn't go out at night for a long time after that."

"In other words, it's a legend that's grown over the years," Mitch inserted.

Virgil paused, then said judiciously, "Personally, I never knew anybody who claimed to have seen the Fire Carrier up close. It's a mysterious light that has appeared from time to time, usually east of Buckskin—that's what most people mean when they say they've seen him. The light is probably what Amos saw. Sometimes the light rests just above the horizon, glowing. Other times it dances and moves all over the place. I've also heard it called the Spook Light."

Mitch turned down the street where Rhea Vann lived. Her car was in the driveway. Lights shone dimly behind closed blinds. The neighborhood was quiet.

"Looks like the doctor got home okay," Virgil observed.

Mitch drove slowly past the house, then turned back toward the station. "Hasn't anybody ever tried to find out what that light really is?" he asked.

"If you believe it's an evil spirit, you're not going to mess with it."

Mitch noticed that Virgil hadn't said whether he was in that camp. "I mean more, uh, skeptical observers."

Virgil chuckled. "Oh, sure. People have tried to chase it in their cars, especially kids on Halloween. It might look to be a few yards away, but, when they go after it, it disappears and reappears somewhere behind them. Sometimes it breaks up into several lights."

"Sounds like moonlight reflecting off fog or something," Mitch mused.

"That's one theory. A few years back, a crew from the U.S. Army Corps of Engineers camped out where there had been several sightings, but they couldn't determine its source. One guy set up a telescope to watch it, claimed he saw it climb a fence and disappear into the blackjack trees on the other side. Dottie Horn swears it came right through her car once and lit up the whole inside." He laughed. "But then Dottie's a little dotty."

"A genuine mystery," Mitch mused.

"As you said, the stuff of legends," Virgil added, perhaps facetiously. Perhaps not.

Henderson Sixkiller had been watching his sister's house for several hours. He'd almost had a heart attack when the police showed up, but they just knocked on the door, walked around and looked in the garage, and left.

When he'd arrived, he'd knocked on the door too and, like the police, got no response. From his hiding place in a toolshed in the side yard, he'd seen the boys come home from school and had thought Jessie could surely not be far behind. But fifteen or twenty minutes after his nephews had appeared, they'd left again, carrying two gym bags and a paper sack. They must have gone back to the school for ball practice.

It was almost dark by five o'clock when Tyler Hatch came home. Neither the boys nor Jessie had returned, but the mere sight of that no-good brother-in-law of his made Sixkiller clench his fists hard and curse under his breath.

He'd wanted to follow Hatch inside and beat the hell out of him, see how he liked it. But he thought better of it. He knew if he got hold of his brother-in-law he might do great bodily harm before he could stop himself. And if he did, Hatch would take it out on Jessie after he'd called the law on Sixkiller.

He would probably have only one chance to rescue Jessie, so he'd better make a plan. But he'd wanted to catch her alone at home and talk to her first. Where was she?

Sixkiller had seen lights going on as Hatch went through the house. Then he heard the telephone ringing. Moments later, Hatch came out of the house in a hurry, leaving all the lights on. He'd looked mad enough to commit murder. He'd spun his tires in the snow and, when he got some traction, burned rubber as he drove away.

A short while after that, the police showed up. They'd probably been notified of Sixkiller's jailbreak and wanted to ask Jessie if she'd heard from him.

Sixkiller waited a half hour after the cops left, but it was getting colder by the minute in the shed. Hatch had probably gone to pick up Jessie, wherever she was, so Sixkiller wouldn't be able to talk to her today.

He felt frustrated. Circumstances had conspired to keep him away from Jessie's house longer than he'd planned, and then he had felt such a sense of urgency about getting there. It hadn't occurred to him that Jessie might not be at home.

Last night, he'd broken into an isolated cabin half a mile from Tenkiller Lake, wrapped himself in a blanket he found in a closet while his clothes and the double wedding-ring quilt dried, and helped himself to a couple of cans of soup from the kitchen cabinet. The electricity had been left on, but there was no propane in the tank out back, so there was no heat, except for what little came from a small electric heater in the bathroom. There wasn't even a fireplace where he could burn wood, if he'd had the strength to go in search of some.

His stomach full, he'd stretched out on a sofa with nubby upholstery worn smooth as glass in places, a castoff from somebody's house in town, and fallen asleep, awaking in the night with a raging fever. He'd stumbled to the tiny bathroom, rummaged through the medicine cabinet, and found half a tube of toothpaste, some cotton-tipped swabs, a jar of petroleum jelly, bobby pins, a nail file, several empty prescription pill bottles, but no aspirin.

Finally, he'd stood, naked and shaking, in front of the electric heater and splashed cold water on his face and chest. He'd dried himself with a thin towel, clutched the blanket around his shoulders again, and stumbled back to the sofa, where he'd drifted in and out of consciousness, dreaming feverish dreams about the Fire Carrier. Once he thought he was at a window, looking out. He saw a light bobbing through the black woods and knew it was the Fire Carrier. But, later, he wasn't sure if it had happened or he'd only dreamed it.

When he'd come fully awake again, sometime around midday, his fever had dropped but he was as weak as a newborn baby. He'd found a coffee can about a quarter full and boiled some grounds in a pan on the electric stove. He'd eaten a can of pork 'n beans and sipped strong coffee, after which he'd been totally exhausted again. He'd slept until three in the afternoon, feeling somewhat stronger and free of fever.

He'd dressed and come to Jessie's house, taking a roundabout way through the woods. After two hours in the shed, he felt weak and trembly again. And he was freezing. He'd better move while he could still make it back to his hiding place.

He'd get to the cabin, make coffee, and open another of the few cans of food remaining in the cabinet. Then he'd make a plan. There was a flashlight in the shed and he decided to take it with him. With the flashlight, he could find his way around without risking turning on lights in the cabin.

His strength seemed to come back as he walked and got the blood pumping through his body. He picked up his pace when he entered the woods and was practically running by the time he reached the cabin, his footsteps dogged by irrational fear, his dream about the Fire Carrier vivid in his mind. Or had it been more than a dream?

Gasping for breath, he stumbled from the woods up the path to the cabin's back door. It opened at his touch; he'd broken the lock to get in last night.

Stepping into the dark cabin, he closed the door and stood in the blackness, listening to the thunder of his heart. He was reminded of when he was a kid, afraid of the dark, sure that the minute he turned off the bedroom light a big, hairy hand would shoot out from under his bed and grab him. He hadn't felt like this in years. He wanted to switch on the flashlight and look through the cabin, but he stifled the need, determined to conquer his childish fear. He stood where he was for several minutes, listening, until he was convinced he was alone in the cabin.

Before turning on the flashlight, he laid it in the kitchen sink where the light would be trapped in a small space. He left his coat on as he made coffee and ate spaghetti and meatballs from a can.

Fortunately there was plenty of water, since the well pump operated on electricity. After eating and finishing the coffee, he ran water in a big roasting pan and set it on the stove. When the water finally began to boil, he carried the pan to the bathroom, emptied it into the tub, and added enough water from the tap to drop the water's temperature to a tolerable level.

He stripped and crawled into about two inches of warm water in the tub. There was no soap in the cabin, so he scrubbed himself roughly with a piece torn from the ragged towel he'd been using to dry with, letting the warm water trickle over his goose-pimpled flesh.

And he thought about how to rescue Jessie. Where could he take her that Hatch wouldn't find her? The lifelessness he'd seen in her eyes when she visited him in jail worried him. She seemed to have accepted that she'd never be free of Tyler Hatch. What if she refused to go with him? Even supposing he took her away, what would happen to her if he was apprehended? She might go back to Hatch.

Better think about a backup plan. Everything would be simpler if Hatch was gone. Then he wouldn't have to take Jessie away and leave her to fend for herself with strangers if the law caught up with him. In Buckskin, at least, she had a few friends and Aunt Sophie.

He made himself face his thoughts squarely. Was he contemplating murder here? Sixkiller, he asked himself, could you really go through with it?

Dawn was graying a narrow strip of sky at the horizon when Bob Strain and his son, Greg, heard Dixie, Bob's blue-tick hound. They'd already rounded up Greg's two redbones and put them in the cage on the back of Bob's pickup. The Strains, who worked a five-hundred-acre family farm near Buckskin, had spent most of the night engaging in their favorite pastime, coon hunting.

Rex and Buster, Bob's redbone hounds, began howling in response to Dixie.

"Shut up!" Greg shouted at the dogs, and they subsided, except for a few nervous moans.

Dixie was starting to make Bob nervous too. The sound of the hound's frenzied barking seemed to come from near the lake.

Bob grabbed a leash from the back of the pickup and the two men headed east, Greg in front with the flashlight. He'd left his shotgun locked in the cab of the truck, but Bob was carrying his.

"Wonder what Dixie's into?" Greg said. "That's not a tree bark, and it's not a trailing bark."

"She must've bayed one," Bob said.

"Or she's fighting one."

"I hope it's not that old boar that took her on a few months back. That was the biggest and meanest dadgummed raccoon I ever saw." A coon could do serious damage to a dog in a fight.

The shrill, panicked barking continued. They walked a little faster, encumbered by heavy hiking boots and insulated coveralls over thick long johns. They wore fleece-lined caps with the ear flaps pulled down and heavy gloves. Inside the gloves, the ends of Bob's fingers were beginning to lose sensation.

Now that the hunt was over for the night, Bob noticed how tired he was, He wanted nothing so much as his bed, cozy with his wife's body heat. He stumbled over a root. His feet in the heavy boots were beginning to drag.

"You all right, Dad?" Greg asked over his shoulder.

"Yeah."

They trudged on through the black woods, bits of frozen snow dropping on them from the bare trees. As they drew closer to the lake, fog lay among the trees so thick the flashlight beam could penetrate only a few steps in front of them.

Dixie's barking was louder now and rougher. She was getting hoarse. Bob gave a shrill whistle and yelled, "Here, Dix! Come on, girl!"

There was hardly a pause in the barking.

"She's got her bowels in an uproar about something," Greg said.

"If that boar coon's after her again," Bob said grimly, "I'm gonna blow him away."

The flashlight beam flickered dimly through the fog. "I think I see her," Greg said and pointed. "Over there."

As they came closer, Bob could see Dixie's hindquarters, tail in the air, back legs rigid. There was no coon in sight. Bob walked up to the hound and ran his hand over her neck and back. Her coat was damp, and he could feel her trembling beneath the thick hair. "Hey, girl. What's the trouble?"

Dixie looked up at him and barked sharply, then stretched her neck and stuck her nose to the ground near a thicket of brush.

Bob felt for her collar and snapped on the leash. "It's okay, girl. Whatever you've got bayed in there can wait till another time." He tugged on the leash. Dixie resisted, her feet scrabbling for purchase on the hard ground. Bob pulled harder, lifting the dog's front legs off the ground and forcing her head around.

Greg stepped in front of his father and turned the flashlight on the thicket. Tendrils of white fog drifted in the beam of light. "Wait a minute, Dad." He bent down. Dixie resumed barking, fast and shrill, and lunged against the leash. Greg pushed a tangle of branches aside with his arm, exposing a man's head and shoulders.

"Oh, my God!"

Bob stopped trying to pull the hound the other way and ran to Greg's side. Dixie sniffed the man's head and backed off, her hackles rising.

Squatting down, Bob pulled off a glove and placed two fingers under the man's jaw. His fingers were so cold, it was several moments before he could be sure.

Then he stood and pulled Dixie away. "Dead," he said.

*   *   *

Mitch and Roo Stephens, the officer whose turn it was to take calls from midnight till 8:00 A.M., when the station wasn't manned, saw the ambulance parked on the edge of the lake road as they came around the curve about a mile past Eagle's Nest Lodge. The lake community east of town had been brought into Buckskin's city limits by a vote of the people. Mitch had campaigned to have the area left in the county sheriff's jurisdiction, but the city fathers had wanted the additional tax base, and they'd gotten it. An example of the futility of fighting city hall.

On the other side of the road, opposite the ambulance, a silver veil of fog lay over gray water. A car was parked in front of the ambulance. Mitch recognized Ken Pohl's new white Buick. He parked the Landcruiser in front of the Buick, noticing a pickup parked even farther down the road ahead. He could see the outlines of two people sitting in the truck. Must be the hunters who found the body. He got out of the Toyota, hesitated, then decided to get to the hunters after he'd talked to the medical examiner.

Dr. Pohl, the medical examiner for Cherokee and Adair counties, and two ambulance attendants, in white trousers and heavy down jackets, huddled close together about a hundred yards into the trees. Wordlessly, they watched Mitch and Roo approach.

"Morning, Chief," Pohl said when they reached him. "Out for a brisk morning stroll?"

Mitch didn't smile. "Right. How are you, Doc?"

"Can't complain—I didn't see my name in the obituary column this morning. But I'd rather be in the Bahamas."

"Wouldn't we all."

"Hello, Officer Stephens," Pohl added. "Hear you're getting fitted for a double harness."

"Huh?"

"Hear you're getting married."

"Oh." The end of Roo's pale, freckled nose was red with cold. His Adam's apple bobbed. He stuffed his hands into his coat pockets and ducked his head bashfully. "Yeah, but not till next summer."

"We all gotta walk down that long aisle sooner or later, I guess," Pohl said. "That Laura Tucker's a fine young woman, and summer will be here before you know it. Then you can get you a mortgage and payments on a second car, like the rest of us suckers."

Mitch glanced at Roo, who was not amused. In fact, he was looking glum. Roo had told him that Laura, outwardly a shy, retiring young woman, could be as stubborn as a mule. Mitch was pretty sure the summer wedding was Laura's idea and that Roo wasn't ready to even think about matrimony yet. Mitch had advised him not to let himself be talked into something he didn't want, but Roo had insisted that he loved Laura, and they'd get married sooner or later, so it might as well be sooner. Roo was barely twenty-two, and a late bloomer. Laura was the first serious girlfriend he'd ever had. How could he be sure Laura was the woman he wanted to spend the rest of his life with? But Mitch had said all he felt he could say on the subject.

He turned to Ken Pohl. "What've we got, Doc?"

"Guy who made somebody mighty mad."

The ambulance attendants stepped away from a man's body, making room for Mitch and Roo. "We had to pull him out of the brush," one said, "so Doc could make his examination."

Mitch looked down into the dead face of Tyler Hatch and heaved a silent groan. "Looks like we finally found our man, Roo," he said grimly.

Roo's Adam's apple bobbed. "Lordy," he breathed. All at once, the blood left his face.

Mitch grabbed his arm. "You okay?"

"Yeah." Roo pulled out a handkerchief and mopped up the sweat that had popped out on his forehead.

"You've been looking for this man?" Pohl asked. "Is there a warrant out on him?"

"We hadn't gotten that far yet," Mitch told him. "We just wanted to talk to him."

"He's done talking now. What's his name?"

"Tyler Hatch."

Pohl looked startled. "I know that name. Isn't he the director of the Job Corps Center?"

"Was," Mitch said. "He broke into the Cherokee Nation's clinic yesterday afternoon, looking for his wife. She'd been at the clinic earlier for treatment after Tyler beat her up. When he got home after work she wasn't there, and he went ballistic."

"Hmmm," Pohl murmured. "The Tahlequah paper just ran a story on how dedicated he is to the kids at the Job Corps Center. Quoted some of 'em. All very complimentary." He shook his head. "So he went home and beat up his wife? Imagine. You never know about people, do you?" He sucked in his cheeks. "Well, maybe the worm turned."

Mitch looked at him sharply. "Could be."

Mitch had returned to the Hatch house a second time the previous evening, after he'd had dinner with Emily, but again the house was empty. Before going off duty at midnight, Roo and Virgil checked out a few places Hatch had been known to frequent. They didn't find anyone who'd seen Hatch after he left the clinic at roughly five-twenty.

"Maybe she saw one of those battered-wives-fight-back programs on *Oprah*," Pohl mused, still on the worm-turning line of thought.

"You made a preliminary diagnosis, Doc?" Mitch asked.

"Well, there's a cut on his arm received before he died, but that wasn't life threatening."

He cut himself when he broke the clinic's window, Mitch thought. Virgil had noticed traces of blood on the glass.

"Hatch suffered a blow to the back of the head," Pohl went on. "Several blows, in fact, on the back and left side of the cranium, and on his left shoulder. Don't quote me yet, but unless something else shows up on autopsy, the head injuries will be the probable cause of death."

I think I hit him twice.

"You said several blows. Does that mean more than two?"

"I'd say three, at least. Could be more." He lifted an eyebrow. "That's what I call fighting back. I can probably give you the exact number of blows he received after I've examined him at the morgue."

Doc was still thinking about Hatch's wife, but Mitch was thinking of Rhea Vann, who he knew for a fact had hit Tyler yesterday afternoon.

I think I hit him twice. . . . It all happened so fast.

"How long do you estimate he's been dead?" Mitch asked.

Pohl pursed his fleshy lips. "Hard to say, the temperature being below freezing. Postmortem changes are slowed by cold." He shook his head. "Did you know that bodies of explorers have been found under the polar ice, preserved as if they had died the day before they were discovered?"

"That's what I was afraid of," Mitch muttered. Unless they located a witness who'd seen Hatch after he left the clinic, death could have occurred anytime between approximately five-thirty the previous afternoon and about six this morning, when the call had come in from a man who'd found a body while coon hunting with his son in the woods.

One of the attendants stamped his feet to encourage circulation. "Damnation, it's cold," he said. "Can we take him now?"

"Be my guest," Pohl said. "Mitch?"

"He's all yours, men," Mitch said. "That pickup on the road, Doc—are those the men who found the body?"

Pohl nodded. "Bob and Greg Strain. I told 'em you'd probably want to talk to 'em." They watched the ambulance attendants carry the body out of the woods. "Whoee," Pohl breathed. "Hell of a way to make a living, eh?"

"Who're you trying to kid?" Mitch asked. "You wouldn't do anything else."

Pohl shrugged. "If you boys'll meet me at the Three Squares, I'll buy your breakfast."

The words proved Mitch's point. A man whose first

thought after examining a murder victim was food *had* to like his work. "Give us twenty minutes to look around here and talk to the Strains," Mitch said, "then we'll be along."

"I'll tell 'em to keep the coffee hot," Pohl said, trudging toward his car.

Mitch bent down to examine the thicket of brush where the body had been found.

"What're we looking for, Chief?" Roo asked.

"Evidence that he didn't get here under his own steam."

"You mean like he was killed somewhere else?"

"Maybe." Mitch wasn't sure what he was looking for. Yesterday afternoon Hatch had left the clinic, alive and able to drive. If Hatch had died from the result of the blows administered by the doctor, then he'd collapsed sometime after leaving the clinic. If that were the case, then who had moved the body? Mitch had seen no vehicle but Pohl's and the Strains' on the lake road, so Hatch didn't drive himself to the lake to collapse and die. Besides, why would he have come out there after dark? He couldn't have expected to find his wife in the woods. Unless Pohl was right, and Mrs. Hatch had lured him there to kill him.

The ground around the thicket yielded no clues. Mitch rose and expanded his search to the surrounding area.

Roo had been working his way back to the road, searching the ground. "Come here, Chief," he called. "These dead leaves look like something heavy's been dragged over 'em."

Mitch went to where Roo was standing at the edge of the woods. Leaves covered the ground for the space of a few feet. From there to where the body was found, the ground was bare and hard. Mitch examined the spot and agreed that a body could have been dragged over it. On the other hand, five men, not counting the two coon hunters who'd found the body, had tromped through there. The marks Roo had found could have been made by heavy shoes and boots kicking and scattering the dead leaves.

"We need to find Hatch's car," Mitch said. "I'll get Duck and Shelly on that. Let's hear what the Strains have to say."

The two men got out of the pickup when Mitch and Roo walked up, leaving the cab door open to keep the dome light on. The younger man had a fleshy face with a deep crease over the bridge of his nose between his dark brows. The older one had a face that looked like a granite outcropping, weathered, hard, and angular.

A dog barked and the smell of wet hounds wafted from the cage in the back of the pickup.

"Shut up, you rascals!" the younger Strain ordered, and the dogs grew quiet.

Mitch introduced himself and Roo, adding, "I understand you found the body."

"It was my coon hound," the older man said. "We couldn't call her up with the other two hounds when we were ready to go home. We were looking for her when we heard her barking."

"We could tell by the sound of Dixie's bark that she hadn't just treed a coon," Greg Strain explained. "She was real upset about something."

"We figured maybe she was in a fight," Bob said. "Sometimes a coon will jump on a dog. They can be vicious. But when we got to her—" He shook his head sadly. "She had her nose stuck in that thicket and she didn't want to leave."

"We didn't see the body at first," Greg said, "but I knew it was something real bad."

"Because of Dixie's barking?" Mitch asked.

"That and Dixie's hackles were standing up and she was shaking."

Mitch nodded.

"So," Greg said, "I pushed aside some limbs, and that's when we saw him. Talk about a shock!" He took a deep breath, went on, "I stayed with the body. Dad took Dixie to the truck and drove to the lodge to call the police station, then came back here. Then a man in a white Buick drove up, said he was the medical examiner. He told us we should wait for you in the truck where it was warm."

"Do you know what time it was this morning when you first heard Dixie barking?" Mitch asked.

The two hunters looked at each other. "Not exactly," Greg said. "Between five and five-thirty, I'd say."

"That sounds about right," Bob agreed.

"Okay. I'll have to ask you both to come down to the station later today. We'll rough out your statements and you can check them for accuracy and sign them."

"Do you know who the dead man is?"

"Tyler Hatch," Mitch said.

Greg thought a moment, then shook his head. "Didn't know him. What happened to him? Was he shot? I didn't see any blood."

"He wasn't shot," Mitch said.

"Then, what—"

"Can you be at the station about one this afternoon?" Mitch interrupted.

Greg frowned, obviously wanting more details about the body, and then said, "I guess so."

"We'll be there," the older man said.

"Thanks for your help," Mitch said. He and Roo walked back to the Landcruiser. "Let's go get some breakfast," Mitch said.

5

The Three Squares Café fronted on Highway 10, which inter-sected Buckskin's main street, Sequoyah, four blocks to the east. Most of the town's businesses were either on Sequoyah north of the highway or strung out for eight or nine blocks along Highway 10. West of the last business on the highway, a trailer park and a few scattered houses on small acreages marked the western outskirts of the town. Even farther west an industrial park contained a tire factory, where they'd laid off so many workers they were down to a skeleton crew; a more prosperous plant which produced small electric motors; and a factory that manufactured steel shopping carts.

Steamy warmth and the smell of fresh coffee, baked bread, and frying bacon greeted Mitch and Roo as they entered the café. At seven-thirty in the morning, the place was packed.

Herschel Lee, owner of the Three Squares, stood in the doorway leading to the kitchen in back, one hand braced against the facing, the other holding a coffee mug. His rust-colored polyester trousers hung precariously low on his hips beneath a protruding stomach. Herschel was short and bald with drooping eyelids that made him look as though he might burst into tears any minute. He waved at Mitch and Roo with his mug.

"Hey, Herschel," Mitch called. "What's happening?"

"Nothing I'd talk to the police about," Herschel said and cackled. When he laughed, his eyes closed completely. Mitch had heard the waitresses say that when Herschel laughed he looked just like a cute kewpie doll. Mitch couldn't see anything cute about Herschel.

Dr. Pohl called to Mitch and Roo from a booth on their right as he gathered up the newspaper scattered across the table. They returned several greetings as they made their way to the booth. Pohl folded the newspaper and placed it on the seat beside him. "Sit down, gentlemen," he said as Mitch and Roo slid into the booth across from him.

Mitch eyed Pohl's half-eaten breakfast, the remains of fried eggs, gravy, and biscuits. For a doctor, Pohl was surprisingly unconcerned about fat and cholesterol. "I see you waited for us," Mitch observed.

"Like one dog waits for another," Pohl said.

Mitch removed his coat, folded it on the end of the seat.

"Learn anything useful from the Strains?" Pohl asked.

Mitch shook his head, glanced around, and said quietly, "I'm eager to get your report. Any possibility you can tell me something today?"

Pohl lifted one bushy brow. "I can probably do Hatch this afternoon, but I've already told you what I expect to find."

"Death from a blow or blows to the head," Mitch murmured.

"That's right." Pohl glanced at Roo. "Maybe we better not talk about corpses while we're eating. Believe it or not, some people find it uncouth." Roo was shrugging off his coat, unaware of Pohl's perusal. Obviously the medical examiner had a cast-iron stomach—he'd have to, in his line of work. Mitch had seen milk, fruit juice, and sandwiches in plastic bags right alongside body parts in the refrigerator at the morgue. But evidently Pohl was concerned about Roo's stomach, considering his reaction to the first sight of Hatch's body. Mitch wasn't inclined to temper his conversation for Roo's sake. A weak stomach was a detriment to a law officer, and Mitch thought the sooner Roo got over it the better.

Geraldine Duckworth, Duck's chunky, gossipy wife, came to the booth with two mugs in one hand, a pot of coffee in the other. She had a round nose that looked like a ball of dough stuck on her face, and her dark hair was pulled back in a bun that was covered by a hair net.

"Hi, guys. Who wants coffee?"

Roo nodded and Mitch held up two fingers and said, "Times two."

Geraldine poured, eyeing the medical examiner curiously, no doubt wondering what he was doing in Buckskin so early on a weekday morning. "What's going on, Mitch?"

Mitch grinned. "I hear we're due for a break in the weather later today. Supposed to get up to forty-five degrees."

Geraldine looked nettled. "Very funny. You know that's not what I meant. You and Roo came in here to meet Dr. Pohl. It has to be police business."

Pohl looked amused, but remained silent. "A mere chance encounter," Mitch said. "I haven't even been to the station yet today." Clearly Geraldine hadn't heard about Tyler Hatch's death, and he wasn't going to enlighten her and then have to fend off her questions as to all the grisly details. The waitresses at the Three Squares were a clearinghouse for the rumors and gossip that circulated through Buckskin. They'd learn about Hatch too soon, as it was. If word hadn't already reached the café by the time Duck came in for his morning coffee break, he'd tell them.

Mitch ordered a short stack, and Roo asked for scrambled eggs with biscuits and gravy. The morning's experience had evidently not affected his appetite, Mitch was glad to note. Frustrated by Mitch's stonewalling, Geraldine stalked off with the order.

"Now you went and made her mad, Chief," Roo said.

"Better her than me."

"Small towns," Pohl observed.

"Yeah," Mitch said. He leaned toward Dr. Pohl. "Let me ask just one more question about Hatch."

Pohl mopped up some gravy with half a biscuit and popped it in his mouth. Glancing at Roo, he chewed slowly, then swallowed. "Shoot," he said.

"Could Hatch have received those blows to his head some time before he died?"

"By some time, you mean—?"

"Say, an hour or two—or more," Mitch said. Roo gave him a puzzled look.

Pohl thought about it. "Possibly. The wounds were nonpenetrating, but that type of injury can cause internal bleeding that can be as dangerous as penetrating wounds. I felt for a skull fracture at the scene. Couldn't find one, but I'll do a more thorough exam at the morgue. Internal bleeding or a blood clot could have been caused by a fracture. A hematoma from torn veins will cause bleeding too, but it might occur slowly, over a period of several hours."

Mitch expelled a deep breath. "In the meantime, could Hatch have been walking around, talking—driving?"

"It could happen. A subdural hematoma compresses and compromises the brain because of the confined space within the skull, but it can take a while." He looked at Mitch reflectively. "Do you have reason to believe that a considerable time passed between Hatch's receiving the blows and dying?"

Roo continued to look at Mitch with a perplexed expression; then, suddenly, Roo became tense and alert. When Virgil returned to the station the previous afternoon, he must have told Roo what had happened at the clinic. Evidently Roo had finally put that together with what Mitch was saying.

"Chief—" Roo said.

Mitch shook his head, then replied to Pohl's question. "Maybe, but I don't want to say any more about that until I get the autopsy report."

Pohl studied him as he sipped from his coffee mug.

"How often does it happen, Doc," Mitch went on, "that somebody receives a blow to the head but has no serious symptoms immediately?"

Pohl shrugged. "Often enough, I guess."

Pohl wasn't being a lot of help. Mitch thought for a minute while Roo watched him closely.

Pohl mopped up the last of his gravy. "A friend of mine,"

he said, becoming expansive, "an internist, sometimes works weekends in a Tulsa hospital emergency room. A couple of months ago, a woman was brought in after a fall." He ate the bite of gravy-soaked biscuit, washing it down with coffee. He set his mug down. "She'd been painting her house, fell off a tall ladder and banged her head. She got up, convinced her husband she wasn't hurt, said she felt fine, and went back to work. More than an hour later, she said she was feeling dizzy and shortly thereafter collapsed. Her husband rushed her to the emergency room, but it was too late."

"She died?" Mitch asked.

Pohl nodded. "A hematoma."

"Would somebody," Roo put in impatiently, "please tell me what in heck's a hematoma?"

"A swelling filled with blood," Pohl said, adding, "according to my internist friend, if that woman had seen a doctor immediately after the fall, the hematoma could have been corrected. I ran across an interesting statistic in a medical journal just recently. More than half the patients who were still conscious and able to talk after their head injuries, but later died, could have been saved if they had received treatment immediately."

Pohl fell silent as Geraldine brought Mitch's and Roo's food and set it down. "Don't mind me," she sniffed, then hurried off to answer a summons from another customer.

"That's Duck's wife," Roo said to Pohl.

"I know," Pohl said. "And she's still put out with you, Mitch."

Mitch shrugged. "She's got this weird idea that she should be kept up to date on police business because she's married to an officer. She'll get over it."

As the three men ate, Mitch reflected on what Pohl had been saying when Geraldine interrupted, but they talked of other things. Then Pohl paid the check and left for the morgue in Tahlequah.

As they watched him go, Roo took a deep breath and asked,

as if he would explode if he didn't get it out, "You think Dr. Vann killed Tyler Hatch, Chief?"

"Keep your voice down!" Mitch looked around to see if Roo had been overheard, but no one was paying any attention to them. Mitch answered quietly, "I don't know yet, Roo. It could be just a coincidence." He didn't add that he always distrusted coincidences. "I sure don't want word to get out that a highly respected physician is a suspect in a murder investigation." He looked at Roo sternly.

"Well, *I* won't breathe a word of it, Chief." Roo sounded a bit indignant. He slid out of the booth and put on his coat. "I'm going home now and get some rest before I have to go on duty."

Mitch followed Roo from the café and drove to the Hatch home. There was still no car in the driveway or in the garage, so he headed toward Rhea Vann's house. As he'd hoped, the doctor's Oldsmobile was gone; she'd already left for the clinic. He parked in the driveway, glad for a chance to talk to Jessie Hatch alone.

All the blinds were closed. Mitch knocked on the front door of the neat, red-brick house. Leaning closer to the door, he heard faint sounds of movement from within. He waited, knocked again, then saw two slats in a venetian blind open a crack, as someone peeked out.

"Who is it?" a woman's voice asked.

"Mitch Bushyhead. Chief of police."

He waited. After several moments, the door opened. Jessie Hatch was a thin, tall woman, probably about five-eight, though a tendency to stoop made her seem shorter. She wore a velour robe over pajamas. Her normally narrow face was swollen and bruised, and her eyes darted anxiously.

"Mrs. Hatch?"

"Yes." She sighed. "I guess Dr. Vann told you where to find me."

"Yes, ma'am."

"You're here about her report."

"Report?" She'd lost him.

"She said she had to file a report —" She touched the purple skin beneath her right eye. "About this."

"Uh, no, ma'am. It's about your husband, Tyler Hatch."

Her expression shifted, became wary. She didn't move for a moment and then fear flickered across her face. "Tyler sent you here? How did he find out where I was?" Either she didn't know what had happened to her husband or she was a good actress. But, then, Mitch supposed battered women learned to play roles, in self-defense.

"I haven't spoken to your husband, ma'am. It's you I need to talk to. May I come in?"

"Oh," she said, becoming flustered. "All right." She opened the door wider and Mitch stepped into a large room with gray carpeting and walls and white woodwork. Several large, framed prints by Indian artists hung on the wall. Mitch recognized a couple by the noted Cherokee painter Murv Jacob, done in dark colors, depicting wolves dancing around Rabbit, a great trickster according to numerous Cherokee folktales.

Two couches faced each other, separated by a large, low pickled-pine table. The couches were upholstered in a bright plaid of mauve, gray, and white. The swags over the room's windows were of the same plaid fabric. There were other light-wood tables in the room, and several chairs upholstered in shades of blue and mauve.

"Would you like to sit down?" she asked tentatively.

Mitch hesitated, then decided to sit so that she would. He took a chair and she lowered herself to a couch. She was slow and deliberate, as though sudden movements were painful for her.

"Mrs. Hatch . . ." He hesitated again. He never had figured out a gentle way of telling a person that someone close to them was dead. As usual, he felt hopelessly inadequate to the task. "Your husband died last night," he said finally.

She stared at him for a long moment, as though she suspected this was some kind of trick he was playing on her. She clutched her robe together beneath her chin. "Tyler?"

"Yes, ma'am."

"He's dead?"

Mitch nodded. "A couple of coon hunters found his body in the woods east of town."

She blinked rapidly. "In the woods? He's been sick, strep throat, maybe, but I never thought——"

"As far as we know right now, he didn't die of an illness, Mrs. Hatch."

She seemed incapable of taking it in, her eyes looking everywhere but at Mitch. He saw her expression change the moment it sank in. Suddenly, she was agitated and, oddly, frightened again. "Oh, please, no. Did Jason——" She halted abruptly and pressed both hands to her mouth. She squeezed her eyes shut. She was clearly in great distress, and when she opened her eyes, tears spilled down her cheeks. After several moments, she composed herself and dropped her hands. "How did he die?"

"We're not sure yet. There will be an autopsy."

She winced and stared at her hands lying palms up in her lap. "I don't understand. What was he doing in the woods?" She wiped her cheeks with the back of her hand and looked up, frowning. "Was—was he shot?"

"The medical examiner found no gunshot wound during his preliminary examination. He'll do a more thorough exam later today."

"I see. Oh . . ." She cleared her throat. "Has anyone told my boys?"

"We thought you'd want to do that."

"They're at school." Her hand fluttered in midair as if she didn't know what to do with it. "I don't have any way to go there."

"I could pick them up," Mitch offered, "bring them here."

Her head bobbed. "Yes, would you do that, please?"

Mitch asked to use the telephone and was directed to the front bedroom, which was decorated in melon and white, a puffy white comforter covering the dark walnut queen-size bed. Mitch wondered fleetingly if Rhea Vann always slept there alone. The phone sat on the bedside table.

When he returned to the living room, Jessie Hatch was still sitting where he'd left her, on the edge of the couch, shoulders slumped, head bowed. "They'll be waiting for me in the principal's office," he told her. "I just said there was a family emergency and their mother needed to see them."

She nodded and mumbled thank you.

"Before I go, I have to ask you a few questions, Mrs. Hatch."

She lifted her head, the frightened-animal look back in her eyes.

"What kind of car does your husband drive?"

She swallowed. "It's a Blazer. Black."

"Do you know the license-plate number?"

She shook her head. "No, I'm sorry."

He could get the tag number from the driver's license bureau. "Do you know where we could find the Blazer?"

Confusion clouded her eyes. "It wasn't—I mean, didn't you find the car with Tyler?"

"No, ma'am. At least, it wasn't on the road near where he was found. We'll find it, though." He paused, let the silence hang for a moment. Then, "When was the last time you saw your husband, Mrs. Hatch?"

Dry-eyed now, she searched his face before she replied. "Yesterday morning, when he left for work."

"Is that when he hit you?"

She dropped her gaze, stared at her hands, which were clutching her robe. "Yes," she whispered.

"Did you come here to Dr. Vann's house directly from the clinic yesterday?"

"Yes, she brought me and then went back to the clinic."

"And you stayed here until she came home for the evening?"

She nodded dully.

"From then until she left this morning, were you and Dr. Vann here together?"

She looked at him with a frown. She pressed her swollen lips together and sighed. "She went to the supermarket."

"Alone?"

She nodded.

"What time was that?"

"I don't know," she said with a helpless shrug. "About six-thirty, I guess. She bought a two-weeks' supply of groceries. She was gone for quite a while."

"And after that?"

"What do you mean?"

"Did either you or the doctor leave again after she returned from the supermarket?"

She squeezed her eyes closed for a moment and nodded in resignation. "She let me use her car to go to my aunt's house. That's where the boys are staying. I wanted to be sure the boys and Aunt Sophie were getting along all right together."

Mitch took down Aunt Sophie's full name and address. Re-calling Jessie's question as to whether Tyler had been shot, he said, "One more question, if you don't mind. Do you own a gun?"

She stiffened. "Oh—no." Her look was troubled. "I hate guns. Tyler keeps—kept a shotgun, for hunting, but I never liked having it around. Why are you asking me about guns?"

Good question, Mitch thought. He had gotten a bit off track, but when he'd told her about her husband, she'd specifically asked if he'd been shot. But maybe she'd known already how Hatch had died, maybe she'd been there and the question was an attempt to muddy the waters. Yet she'd seemed almost relieved when he'd said the M.E. had found no evidence of a gunshot. "When you learned your husband was dead, you asked if he'd been shot, as if that's what you expected."

"But, I didn't—" The hand fluttered again. "I don't know why I said that. It was just—well, when you said Tyler was found in the woods, I thought maybe he'd gone hunting."

The explanation didn't ring true. She was hiding something. He'd find out what it was eventually.

"What kind of hunting did your husband do?"

"Doves. He only hunted doves." She evidently didn't know it wasn't dove season.

Mitch excused himself and went to pick up the Hatch boys.

They sat, side by side, in oak armchairs in the principal's outer office. The principal's secretary, who'd shown Mitch in, said, "Jason, Harry, this is Chief Bushyhead. He's going to take you to your mother."

As they stood, Mitch watched the older one, Jason. He wore his dark hair in a style that Mitch had seen other teenage boys in town sporting: cut short on top, shaved at the sides, with a ponytail in back. Jason moved with an awkward grace. About fifteen, Mitch judged, but close to six feet tall already, all arms and legs and big hands. A good athlete, Mitch guessed. The expression on the boy's thin, angled face was stoney.

Oh, please, no. Did Jason— Did Jason what?

Harry, the younger boy, who looked to be about thirteen, was a head shorter than his brother, with finer features, an almost-pretty face. Harry looked bewildered. He fell into step beside Mitch. "Why does mom want to see us?" he asked as they left the high school.

"I think she'd prefer to tell you herself," Mitch hedged.

The boys crawled in the back seat of the Landcruiser. "Your mother says you're staying with an aunt," Mitch said, trying to get a conversation going as he drove away.

"Just for a little while," Harry said.

"I'm sure you'd rather be with your mother," Mitch said.

"Yeah," Harry agreed, "I wish it could always be just mom and me and Jason. I don't like to sleep over at Aunt Sophie's, but when mom decided to stay with Dr. Vann, she said we should—" The words ended with a grunt. Mitch glanced in the rearview mirror as Harry was straightening up and scowling furiously at his brother. Jason had jabbed his elbow in Harry's stomach to shut him up.

After a moment, Mitch said, "Your dad's car seems to be missing."

Nobody said anything.

"You haven't been driving it, have you, Jason?"

Jason snorted. "I'm not old enough to drive," he muttered shortly.

Nobody spoke again until they'd reached Rhea Vann's house. Mitch had hoped the boys would be more talkative.

He left them at the front door, saying to Jessie, "I'll be back a little later, after you and the boys have had a chance to talk."

During his absence, she'd changed into a blue sweat suit. Looking confused, she sent the boys to the den, which was beyond the kitchen, then asked Mitch, "Why do you need to come back?"

"I'll have to ask the boys a few questions."

She searched his face and appeared to sense determination; it seemed to alarm her. "Why? They had nothing to do with this."

"We have to talk to all family members in these cases," Mitch said.

"But they're only children."

"You can be present when I talk to them." He knew he'd learn more if he could question the boys alone, particularly Harry, but, the rules of evidence aside, he couldn't justify the ethics of that to himself. Unless she offered . . .

She didn't. "Well . . . what time do you think you'll be back?"

Mitch looked at his watch. "Will ten-thirty be all right?"

She nodded once and shut the door.

6

When he got to the station, Mitch informed Duck and Shelly of the discovery of Tyler Hatch's body and told Duck to get Hatch's automobile license tag number, then check around town and the area between town and Lake Tenkiller for the Blazer.

While Duck got on the phone with the motor-vehicle bureau, Mitch said, "Shelly, I want you to go with me to question Hatch's two sons. Their mother is telling them about their father right now. I said I'd be back at ten-thirty." It had occurred to him that another woman's presence might ease Jessie Hatch's anxiety a little. He probably should let Shelly handle most of the questioning too. The boys might see him as just another father figure, so maybe he should stay in the background.

He phoned the clinic and made an appointment to talk to the doctor at four-thirty that afternoon, assuming he'd have heard from the medical examiner by then.

Before going to Rhea Vann's house, Mitch and Shelly talked to Sophie Beard, Jessie Hatch's aunt. Mitch had had a high-school teacher in Oklahoma City named Sophie Wiggs. She'd been short—all the boys had towered over her, and most of the girls—and slender with delicate features, a cheerful disposition, and a sweet smile. As a sophomore, he'd been half in love with her. He'd never known anyone else named Sophie, so he still associated the name with small, cheerful, delicate women. In the case of Sophie Beard, he could not have been more wrong, as was clear the moment she opened the door to her old-fashioned frame house in one of Buckskin's older neighborhoods. Words like *small, cheerful,* and *delicate* fit Sophie Beard the way ballet slippers fit a rhinoceros. And, like a rhino, Sophie Beard was large and slow. She wore a loose cotton dress that must have required a bolt of fabric to make.

"I'm busy," she yelled over the sounds coming from the television in the background. "What'd you want?" Not only was she fat and slow, she had an attitude.

Mitch introduced himself and Shelly and said he wanted to ask her a few questions about a police matter.

"My niece called and told me Tyler died," she snapped. She said it as though reporting the death of a neighbor's troublesome dog. "That what this is about?"

Mitch admitted that it was. "What's it got to do with me?" she demanded.

"You're related to the dead man's wife."

She thought about it and said sullenly, "I guess you can come on in."

She lumbered to a sagging recliner placed squarely in front of a color television set, where an attractive young couple were kissing passionately. A soap opera, Mitch deduced. On one wall was a photograph of the Dionne quintuplets as babies; Mitch hadn't seen one of those in twenty-five years. Another wall sported an embroidered sampler with the words, "Fear God and Keep His Commandments," sewn in red. Beneath the sampler was a boxy couch upholstered in purple velvet. Beside the recliner was a three-legged end table with an empty sour-cream-and-onion potato-chip sack and an empty Poppycock caramel-corn can, the large size.

On the television screen, to which Sophie's eyes were glued, the attractive young woman was saying to the craggy young man with a dimple in his chin, "Oh, Damien, of course I love you, but if my father finds out about us . . ."

Sophie Beard had not offered her visitors a seat, so Mitch and Shelly remained standing. "Mrs. Beard—" Mitch said.

She tore her eyes from the screen. *"Miss* Beard. I'm not married, never have been, and glad of it, after what I've seen." She snorted contemptuously. "Marriage. You can have it."

"Excuse me. *Miss* Beard—uh, would you mind turning the volume down a little?"

She squinted at him, heaved a sigh, picked up the remote control from the floor beside her chair, and turned the volume off, leaving Damien and his lover with their mouths moving soundlessly between episodes of trying to swallow each other's tongues.

"As if Jessie and those boys didn't already have enough to deal with," Sophie muttered, her eyes shifting back and forth between the television and Mitch, "now that worthless Tyler has gone and left 'em without any savings and no insurance. He died selfish, just like he lived." She sighed heavily, pausing to watch Damien leave his lover and the camera zero in on the young woman's tear-streaked face. When a commercial came on, Sophie continued, "Well, I don't suppose she's that much worse off. Tyler treated them like dirt. Many's the time I tried to get Jessie to leave him, but she wouldn't. I hate to say it, but my niece isn't very"—she seemed to search for the right word—"strong," she finished finally.

"Physically, you mean?" Mitch asked.

She shook her head. "Emotionally. No backbone. If she'd had one, she'd have left that sorry excuse for a man years ago. He used his fists on her."

"The battering has gone on for a long time?" Mitch inquired.

He had become aware that Shelly had tensed beside him. She was hearing about the battering for the first time; he hadn't yet had a chance to fill her in.

Sophie Beard snorted angrily. "Years." She shook her head. She pointed a pudgy finger at Mitch. "One time, that's all it'd take for me to kill anybody who beat me up. I know the Bible says it's wrong to hate, and may the Lord forgive me, but I pure-dee hated that man! He wasn't worth the powder it'd take to blow his brains out. Every time he beat her, I told Jessie she and the boys could move in with me—I have three bedrooms, though they're small, but it would've been better than staying with *him.* Poor Jessie always had an excuse for him, though. Now the boys are teenagers. I just hope they're not scarred for life."

"Did Tyler beat them too?" Mitch asked.

She gave an impatient sigh, her eyes wandering back to the TV screen where a woman appeared to be extolling the virtues of a laundry detergent. "Does a dog have fleas? Why, he'd sock any of them who happened to be around when he got mad. He needed killing! That man was as mean as a snake. And that's not all."

Watching her, Mitch believed Sophie's claim that she wouldn't have put up with Tyler Hatch's abuse for a minute. She might be fat and slow, but she was spunky. Too bad Jessie hadn't inherited some of her spunk. "Oh?" Mitch said encouragingly.

Her round face flushed. "He was an adulterer!" She spat the word out as if it were contaminated, and her hands gripped the arms of the recliner so hard the fingers turned white.

"How do you know that?" Mitch asked.

She frowned at him. "Jessie told me. I don't guess he tried to hide his nasty little flings. He'd taunt Jessie with it. Proud of it, you know?"

Her eyes were now fixed on the TV screen, where an older woman was talking to Damien. Mitch waited. "Do you know the names of any of the women Tyler Hatch had affairs with?"

"Hmmph! Who cares about the names of harlots? Women he worked with at the Job Corps Center, probably." Intent on the television screen, she sat forward as if she were trying to read the actors' lips.

Mitch cleared his throat. "Can you tell me what time the Hatch boys arrived here yesterday?"

The scene on television ended. She looked around and

blinked. She had little piggy eyes in a round face. "It was about five-thirty. After school, they went home first and Jessie called them and told them where she was, said they should pack a few things for her and them and come here. I fixed dinner for them."

"Did they see their father after school?"

"No, thank goodness he wasn't home."

"They told you this?"

"That's what I said, isn't it? If he'd been home, he would never have allowed them to leave again. And he'd probably have beat them until they told him where Jessie was."

"He didn't come here looking for his family?"

"No." She hesitated. "That's odd, now you mention it. This would have been the first place he thought of."

Mitch thought so too, and wondered what had diverted Hatch from coming there. "Did either of the Hatch boys leave the house anytime after dinner?"

She frowned. "Jason wanted to go to a friend's house, but I told him I'd rather he stayed in. He accepted that without much fuss. Jessie may put up with back talk from those boys, but they know I won't tolerate it. Then Jessie came over to get her things and see the boys. She only stayed about fifteen minutes. After she left, the boys and me watched a movie on TV. John Wayne and Alexis Smith." Her expression became wistful. "I love John Wayne. He was a *real* man." She seemed to shake herself. "Anyway, both boys went to bed when I did, about ten. I keep the back bedroom ready for them, anytime they want to sleep over."

"And what about you, Miss Beard?"

"Excuse me?"

"Did you leave the house last evening?"

She stared at him with her piggy eyes. "Never stepped foot outside this house yesterday."

On the drive to Rhea Vann's house, Mitch filled Shelly in on the incident at the clinic the previous day and what had precipitated it. "Hatch beat his wife yesterday morning, and when Jessie went to the clinic, Doctor Vann talked her into going home with her," Mitch summed up. "Tyler Hatch came there looking for his wife. Kicked out a window." He paused, thinking, then decided not to mention the blows administered by Rhea Vann until after he'd talked to the medical examiner.

"At least his family can come out of hiding now," Shelly said, her voice sharp, "and not have to live in daily fear of being hurt again." Mitch glanced over at her. She'd worked for a suburban Tulsa police force before coming to Buckskin seven months ago. At five feet, nine inches, she was boyishly thin in her khaki uniform. Short sandy hair framed her angular face. She wasn't pretty in the traditional sense, but brilliant green eyes made people look twice. At the moment, the eyes were narrowed and her jaw was clenched.

Though childless and unmarried, Shelly seemed to have an uncommon empathy for mistreated children. Mitch had first noticed it during the investigation of the murder of an eight-year-old girl the previous spring. He was very glad he'd brought Shelly along.

"The cases involving kids are always tough," he said.

"Sophie Beard might be a slob, but she's right about one thing. Tyler Hatch deserved to die."

Mitch was surprised by the heat in her words. "Well . . ."

She looked at him. "For five years, I lived with a stepfather who abused me. I know what I'm talking about, Mitch."

Mitch didn't know what to say. It was the first time he'd ever heard Shelly mention her childhood, though he had suspected her affinity for mistreated children had its source in something personal. It explained a lot about Shelly.

As Mitch had expected, Jessie Hatch was not pleased to see them. "I hope you don't upset my boys any more than they already are," she said as she admitted them.

"We'll try not to," Mitch told her. "It'll only take a few minutes."

Clearly not reassured, she went to the kitchen, returning with Jason and Harry. Jason was sullen; Harry seemed merely subdued.

Mitch had told Shelly to take the lead in the questioning. When the boys and their mother were seated, he took a chair in the corner and nodded at Shelly.

She pulled a chair close to the couch where they were sitting and said, "Boys, I'm Officer Pitcher, and I need to ask you a few questions."

Harry glanced at his mother anxiously. Jason stared sullenly at his knees.

"Let's see now," Shelly said with a smile, "you're Harry, right?" Harry nodded. "And you must be Jason." Jason wouldn't meet her gaze. Shelly looked at Mitch and he nodded again encouragingly.

"Harry, when was the last time you saw your father?"

Harry swallowed. "Uh—yesterday morning before I went to school."

"You didn't see him after school?"

Harry glanced quickly at Jason and shook his head. "No, ma'am."

Shelly shifted her eyes to Jason. "Jason, do you have any idea who might have wanted to kill your father?"

The boy lifted his head. His dark eyes were blazing. "How the hell should I know?"

"Jason!" Jessie cried.

He shook off his mother's hand. "He's dead and I don't care! He was always yelling at us and hitting us. Big man!" He jabbed a thumb in his mother's direction. "Look at her. He did that."

Shelly kept her voice low. "When your father hit you, Jason, did you ever fight back?"

"Of course he didn't!" Jessie interjected, her voice breaking. "It would only have made things worse."

Shelly continued to look at Jason. He shrank back against the couch and the rage went out of his eyes. Perhaps it had just dawned on him that his answers to Shelly's questions could be incriminating. "No," he said, shaking his head. "I didn't fight back."

"But you wanted to," Shelly said.

Jason shrugged and dropped his eyes.

"Jason," Mitch said from the corner of the room, "if you and your father got into a fight and there was an accident . . . say, he fell or something——"

At the sound of Mitch's voice, the boy jumped, as though he'd forgotten for the moment that Mitch was there. "There wasn't any fight," he muttered. "I know I should've taken up for my mother, but I didn't."

"Sweetheart," Jessie said, rubbing his back, "you did the best thing."

"So," Mitch said, "none of you has any idea who might've been mad enough at your father to kill him?"

Both boys shook their heads. Jessie sat forward, hands on her knees. "Tyler never told us much about his life away from home but—well, he might have made some enemies."

"Who, for example?" Mitch asked.

She hesitated. "Men whose wives . . ." She halted abruptly. "Could the boys leave the room now?"

"Oh, Mom," Jason groaned. "You don't need to protect us. We know dad screwed around."

"Jason," Jessie said sharply, "that's enough."

"Why don't you boys go out to the kitchen," Mitch suggested. They left without another word, though Jason shot a scowl at his mother.

Mitch waited until the boys had walked through the dining room and disappeared into the kitchen. "We've heard from other people that your husband had affairs, Mrs. Hatch. But we need names."

She glanced toward the kitchen to reassure herself that the boys were out of earshot. "After the first time or two, when the boys were small, I didn't try to find out their names. I suspected several times that he was seeing someone from the Job Corps Center. There was a secretary named Hannah . . ." She thought, shook her head. "I can't remember her last name, but she was married. She doesn't work there anymore, so maybe her husband found out about her and Tyler." She was nervously rolling and unrolling the ribbing at the bottom of her sweat shirt, watching her hands instead of Mitch. "He may have slept with some of the students too," Jessie went on as she continued to roll and unroll her sweat shirt. "Tyler liked them young. A couple of weeks ago, I came out of the grocery store just as Tyler drove by. There was a redheaded girl with him, sitting so close they looked like they were glued together. He had his arm around her." She looked up finally. "I'm sure I saw her at the Job Corps Center, but I don't know her name."

"Can you think of anyone else?" Mitch asked.

She shook her head. "There could have been others, but I don't know who they were. I learned early in our marriage not to question Tyler about where he'd been or who with."

"Thank you for being so candid, Mrs. Hatch. You've been very helpful." Mitch stood.

"Can we go back home now?" Jessie asked.

"Sure. Would you like us to take you?"

"No, thanks. I'll call Aunt Sophie."

Walking back to the Landcruiser, Shelly muttered, "Tyler Hatch was a real prince. There could be more than one angry husband around town whose wife had an affair with Hatch."

They got into the Toyota. "Maybe," Mitch said.

"Jessie Hatch said—" Shelly began, buckling her seat belt.

"I heard her," Mitch interjected, "but I got the impression her main concern was to divert suspicion from herself and her sons."

Shelly shook her head. "The woman was too cowed to oppose her husband. My mother was like that, so I know what I'm talking about. I can't see Jessie Hatch getting up the nerve to kill him. Now, Jason . . . well, maybe."

"Yeah," Mitch agreed. "He's angry. And Harry's scared, which might mean he knows his brother did it."

"Could be," Shelly said.

"When I told Jessie Hatch her husband was dead, she said, 'Oh, please, no. Did Jason—' She didn't finish, but then she asked me if her husband had been shot. And, get this, her husband had a shotgun."

"Sounds like she thought Jason might have used it on him."

"Yeah, only he wasn't shot."

Shelly was thoughtful for a long moment. Finally, she said, "I'd put Sophie Beard near the top of the suspect list too."

Mitch nodded. "That woman could kill and convince herself she was wreaking God's vengeance."

"I can see that."

"I don't know, though," Shelly said, sighing. "An angry husband still might be our best bet. Do you want to swing by the Job Corps Center—see if we can find that redhead?"

"No. We'll wait till we have the autopsy report before we question anybody else."

7

Back at the station, Helen greeted them with, "Oh, good, you're back, Mitch. I was just wondering whether to try to get you on the radio."

"Chief," Shelly interjected, "I'll try to find Duck. I can help him look for Hatch's Blazer."

"Good idea," Mitch said, and Shelly left the station. Mitch turned back to Helen. "You were saying?"

"There's somebody waiting for you in your office."

"Who?"

"Lex Burnside." She glanced at the office's closed door and lowered her voice. "He's fit to be tied."

Mitch studied the closed door. "What about?"

"I couldn't tell at first. Not till I could get him calmed down enough to understand what he was saying. His place was burglarized. Wanted me to page you and say it was an emergency. I managed to put him off."

"So you determined it's not an emergency?"

Helen frowned. "It didn't take a nuclear physicist. He's been out of town for five days. When he got back, he discovered some things were missing." She tapped her forehead. "Putting two and two together, I deduced they could've been taken right after he left town or anytime while he was gone."

"Hmmm. I see your point. Thanks, Helen." Mitch went into his office, shutting the door behind him. "Hey, Lex," he said heartily. "It's good to see you."

Lex Burnside, a leather-skinned, wiry little guy who'd sustained so many broken bones and torn tendons rodeoing that he now had arthritis in most of his joints, was pacing the office. Actually, he was physically incapable of pacing—rather, he was hobbling from one side of the office to the other, his gator-skinned Tony Lamas clunk-clunking on the tile floor. Burnside had made a living rodeoing for years, had won the coveted professional title of National All-Around Cowboy more than once. Broken-down and arthritic, he'd retired from the arena about five years ago.

The little man's mouth drooped and his eyes were red-rimmed. He grabbed Mitch's arm. "Thank God, you're back! You gotta catch 'em, Mitch," he said fervently. "Catch the sneakin' possums red-handed. Before they get shed of my stuff."

"We'll do our best, Lex."

Burnside lowered himself into a chair, grunting as his joints cracked in protest. He patted his shirt pocket, which clearly revealed the circular outline of a can of chewing tobacco, as if to assure himself it was still there. Then he snatched the felt cowboy hat off his head and jammed it down on a knee. "Damn thieves," he sputtered, his face flushed a dangerous-looking bright red. "Cleaned out my tack room." Burnside lived on five acres at the edge of town but within the city limits, where he kept a couple of horses. "Anybody that'd steal a man's tack would take money from his own mama's purse and then lie about it!"

Mitch hung his coat on the rack beside Burnside's fleece-lined, Western-style denim jacket, then pulled out the creaking swivel chair behind his desk and sat down. "Did you have it locked?"

"Hell, yes!" He held up two crooked fingers. *"Two* locks. They used bolt cutters, snapped 'em right in two."

Mitch picked up a pen and a memo pad. "When did it happen?"

"Sometime between last Thursday morning and last night." The tack thieves had been busy last weekend, Mitch thought.

This was the second break-in reported, bringing the total of such burglaries to ten. "I took the wife to Vegas," Burnside said. "Got back late, so I didn't check the tack room till this morning. A neighbor fed the horses for me, but he had no reason to go into the tack room, so he never noticed the locks were broke. Oh, shoot!" He slammed his hands down on the wooden arms of his chair and winced at the self-inflicted pain.

"It's a darn shame, Lex."

"They didn't just steal some tack, Mitch. They took my life!" He muttered a curse as his gnarled fingers worked at loosing the top pearl button of his Western shirt, which was clearly too tight at the neck. Burnside had put on some weight since he stopped rodeoing. Finally, he got the button undone and stretched his wattled neck while running a finger down between shirt and skin. Then he jerked on his string tie. "Those gravy-sucking hogs are cleaning out all the horsemen around here. Why can't you people catch 'em?"

"We're trying, Lex," Mitch said. "Most of those burglaries happened outside the city limits. They're in the county sheriff's jurisdiction. This is the first one in Buckskin. But I know law-enforcement officials across the state are keeping a close watch on auctions and farm sales."

"Have they recovered any of the stuff?"

"Not the last I heard," Mitch said. "But the Equine Association is offering a reward, so maybe that'll entice somebody to come forward with information."

"Shoot, why didn't they just rip my heart out and be done with it?" Burnside's face was still as red as a vine-ripened tomato. Mitch was afraid he might keel over with a stroke right there in his office.

"Calm down, Lex. Aren't you insured?"

"Yes, but that stuff can't be replaced with money." He jerked on his string tie again and, suddenly, his eyes filled with tears. It was the second time this week Mitch had seen a grown man cry. Of course, Amos Flycatcher had been blind drunk. Burnside wasn't drunk, but he was beside himself with outrage. "I'd give my new filly colt to catch those lowlifes!"

"We'll catch 'em, Lex. It's just a matter of time."

"But will you catch 'em in time to recover my stuff? I tell you, hanging's too good for 'em. If I ever get my hands on 'em, I'll nail their hides to the barn door!" He'd grabbed his hat in both hands and was unconsciously squashing it between his gnarled hands.

Mitch pointed with his ballpoint pen. "Your hat, Lex."

He looked down. "Oh, hell, I'm so worked up I don't even know what I'm doing." Scowling, he straightened the hat back into a semblance of its former shape and hung it on his knee. "There's two things I can't stand, Mitch, and a thievin' lowlife is both of 'em. I'd like to hog-tie those suckers and drag 'em a mile through a blackberry patch!"

Before Burnside could think up any more fiendish punishments for the tack thieves, Mitch prompted, "I'll need a detailed list of the missing items, Lex."

"Right here." Burnside reached in his shirt pocket and pulled out a folded piece of paper. He unfolded it and consulted the scrawled notes it contained.

"Thirty-three engraved belt buckles," he read, "fifteen of them were silver, and two were fourteen-carat gold. I won most of 'em rodeoing. Some of 'em have my name engraved on the back with the date and what I won it for. I had a special velvet-lined case made to keep 'em in." His voice broke. He swiped at his eyes angrily with the back of his hand as Mitch made a note about the buckles. "I wore calluses on my butt as thick as a boot heel winning them buckles, Mitch. And then to have some lazy no-account rip 'em off—" He shook his head helplessly.

Before Burnside could go off on another tangent of threats, Mitch asked, "What else is missing?"

Burnside wiped his nose with an index finger and consulted his notes again. "There's the saddles." He paused, took a deep breath, and winced as though it was physically painful even to think about the saddles. "O Lord, it pure breaks my heart. Everything from Corduras to show saddles. Here." He reached in his pocket and pulled out another piece of paper. "I got 'em itemized on this." There were tears in his eyes when he handed the paper to Mitch. "Some of 'em were awards for winning the all-'round title at big rodeos. Two of 'em are silver-plated and engraved. Real fancy. They came with the National All-'round Cowboy title in '78 and '81." He leaned forward with a grunt of pain, extracted a handkerchief from a back pocket of his Levi's, and wiped his eyes.

Mitch glanced down the list of saddle descriptions, twenty-three in all. "I see what you mean, Lex, about the saddles being irreplacable. Most of these are one of a kind."

"And worth thousands, all told. I don't even know how to put a dollar value on 'em. Far as I'm concerned, a million wouldn't be enough. But I don't want money. I want them saddles back. The buckles too. The blankets and bridles, other stuff—they can keep it, if I could just get my saddles and buckles back. Left 'em to the Cowboy Hall of Fame in my will. I can't hardly go in the tack room without crying like a baby."

Mitch managed to get a description of the missing saddle blankets and bridles between further bursts of outrage.

"I'll get this list out to every law-enforcement agency in the state, Lex. I'll let you know the minute we hear anything."

"Okay," he said morosely. He levered himself painfully to his feet. "Wish I'd never let the wife talk me into going to Vegas," he mourned, settling his hat on his head. "They just practice another kind of thievery out there." It sounded as though Lex had lost money at the tables. "And if I'd been home, I'da heard 'em breaking in my tack room." He extracted the can of Skoal, opened it, took a pinch of tobacco, and tucked it in his jaw.

Mitch came around the desk and helped Burnside into his jacket, then gave him an encouraging pat on the back. "Try not to think about it too much, Lex. Leave it with us." He walked Burnside to the door of his office. Burnside was wiping his eyes with his handkerchief as he left the station.

"That's downright pitiful," Helen said sorrowfully. "Poor old broken-down cowboy."

Mitch handed her the list he'd made. "Get the word out on this."

"Will do, Chief." Helen glanced down the list. "Oh, shoot, no wonder old Lex was bawling." The phone rang and she turned to answer it. "Hello, Emily. How are you, hon? Great. Yes, he's here." She handed the receiver to Mitch.

"What's up, sweetheart?"

"Daddy, I *have* to have my car. It's majorly important. The guy at the Texaco station is giving me the runaround."

The streets were mostly clear of snow and ice, but Mitch had forgotten to notify the mechanic that it was okay to release the Mustang. "I'll take care of it, honey." He handed the receiver back to Helen. "Would you call the Texaco station, Helen, and tell them to leave Emily's car at the high school before three-thirty?"

"Sure, Chief." As she reached for the phone again, it rang. "Hi, Duck. Just a sec." She handed the receiver back to Mitch.

"Yes?"

"I found the Blazer."

"Good job. Is Shelly with you?"

"She just got here. We're about two miles from Eagle's Nest Lodge on the lake road, Chief. The Blazer's in the woods about five hundred yards off the road. Somebody hid it real good in a bunch of cedars. If I hadn't noticed the sunlight reflecting off a little-bitty corner of a taillight sticking out of the brush, I don't know when we'da found it."

"Did you touch anything?"

"Of course not! What do you take me for?"

Mitch wasn't about to comment on that. "Wait right there. I'm on the way."

Mitch pulled off the shoulder and parked the Toyota behind two patrol cars. After raising Duck on the radio and getting his location, Shelly had taken the patrol car Mitch ordinarily drove, the only patrol car they had that was equipped with a cellular phone. Already, the temperature was above freezing, and Duck and Shelly were standing at the edge of the woods, waiting for Mitch.

They walked into the woods together. "The keys are still in the ignition," Duck said, leading the way.

The Blazer was well concealed from the road by several fat cedar trees. Mitch used his arm, protected by his coat sleeve, to push aside the brittle limbs of a thorn bush and peered into the Blazer. "Did you check the license plate?"

"Yep," Duck said. "It's Hatch's, all right."

So Hatch had driven himself out there, after all, and apparently somebody had been waiting in ambush for him or had followed him from town. "Let's dust the door handles for fingerprints before we get inside," Mitch said. Shelly ran back to the patrol car she and Duck usually shared and got the fingerprint kit and camera.

Unfortunately, the handles on all four doors had been wiped clean. As had the steering wheel and ignition key, they discovered in a careful examination of the interior of the Blazer. In fact, they found not a single clue to who might have driven the Blazer off the road and behind the line of cedar trees.

"I'll get the guys at the Texaco station to come get it," Mitch said, his disappointment palpable. "They can leave it at the Hatch house. I'll see you two back at the station after lunch." He trudged back to the Landcruiser.

After a burger at the Sonic Drive-in, Mitch went back to the station. The Strains showed up at one, as promised. Shelly and Duck, who were leaving for lunch, stayed long enough to have them sign their statements.

Mitch checked in with the sheriffs' departments in Cherokee, Adair, and Delaware counties. Even though they'd sent deputies to various livestock auctions in their jurisdictions, not a single item from the tack burglaries had been found.

"Heard anything from the Equine Association?" Mitch asked Bo Zickenfoose, a sheriff's deputy in Delaware County.

"They've been getting some calls," Bo said, "people trying

to implicate their brother-in-law or some neighbor they're mad at. One old gal said she thought her husband did it. Seems he's been getting home late. The sheriff talked to him, he broke down, admitted he was getting some nooky on the side. That's why he's keeping such late hours. We've learned a lot about the callers, but nothing helpful on the thief or thieves."

Mitch hung up, shucked his uniform shirt, and climbed on the exercise bike he kept in his office. Some days he got some of his better insights while pedaling. Where were the thieves disposing of all those saddles and tack? Ranch and farm auctions were the logical places, and they were probably hauling the loads to sales run by several auction companies so as not to arouse suspicion. He was still convinced they were taking the stuff out of state, and, if so, they'd wait till they got a good load before transporting it.

Where were they storing it in the meantime? The burglaries had occurred in five counties, but half of them took place in Cherokee County. Which could mean the thieves lived in Cherokee County. They wouldn't want to haul the loot far to store it, so they could be hiding it inside the county. Not a particularly helpful thought. Cherokee County covered a lot of territory.

And now he had a probable murder to solve. He got a bad feeling in his gut when he thought about his scheduled interview with Rhea Vann that afternoon. Maybe Pohl would come up with some other cause of death, something besides a blow to the head.

Uh-huh, and maybe Duck would turn into the Thin Man overnight.

I think I hit him twice . . . It all happened so fast.

If she really had hit him only twice at the clinic, then she or somebody else had had another go at him later. Jessie Hatch? Aunt Sophie? A jilted lover?

Thinking about that led nowhere. He didn't have enough facts. From what he'd heard so far, there was no shortage of people who might have wanted to kill Hatch, but not one scrap of evidence to put any of them with Hatch after he left the clinic yesterday afternoon.

Clearly, it wasn't one of his insightful days.

He put Hatch on the back burner and started thinking about Lisa and wondering why she hadn't called. When he began to rationalize calling her at the college where she taught, he got off the bike and busied himself with paperwork.

First he went through the case reports covering the past month, which he'd let stack up on his desk, and filed them in the cabinet in his office. Then he got out the file on the tack burglaries and checked the dates. They had all occurred within the past six weeks. Checking the calendar hanging on the wall, he noted that all of them had happened on weekends. Which probably meant the thieves were gainfully employed during the week. He went through the file several times and finally put it away, little wiser than before.

When Dr. Pohl hadn't called by three-thirty, Mitch phoned him at the morgue.

"I was going to call you before I went home," Pohl said. "I know you're in a rush."

"As a matter of fact, I am."

"Hurrying shortens the life span, Mitch. Makes you constipated too."

Mitch wasn't in the mood for Pohl's weird sense of humor. "What do you know about Hatch, Doc?"

"A few things. I can tell you he was hit four times. Somebody really wanted him dead. It was a blow to the base of the skull that did it. There's a skull fracture I missed before. There was internal bleeding from that and a big hematoma to boot. Both resulted from the same blow, I'd say. I can give you all the medical mumbo-jumbo if you want it."

"That's not necessary," Mitch said. He'd been hoping he could cancel his appointment with Rhea Vann, but he'd have to talk to her now. "Anything else of interest?"

"Not yet. I won't get the results on all the blood and tissue tests for a few days."

Mitch felt a flicker of hope. "So it could be something else that killed him?"

"No way. Most of these tests are routine. One thing, though."

"What?"

"I hesitate even to mention it becuase I can't be sure."

"Mention it, Doc," Mitch said impatiently.

"Well, I measured all the welts left by the blows. Two of them are wider than the other two."

"Which means?"

"It doesn't *mean* anything. But it raises an interesting question. Maybe the difference is only because those blows were harder than the others. On the other hand, it's remotely possible they could have been made by a second instrument."

"Is that the one that killed him?"

"Yep."

"You said a second instrument is remotely possible. How remote?"

"Tsk, tsk, Mitch. I hear that note in your voice, and I must caution you. Don't jump to any conclusions here. I said *remotely* and I mean *remotely*. There *may* have been two weapons, that's all. Under oath, I'd have to say I can't be sure."

"Okay, what about the time of death?"

"Sometime in the twelve-hour period before he was found."

"We already knew that."

Mitch could sense Pohl's shrug. "You asked. The weather makes it impossible to get closer than that. I'm not a psychic, Mitch, just a lowly pathologist."

"What about the blow that killed him? Could he have gone on walking around, driving, for a while before he died?"

"I really doubt it, but I can't be absolutely sure. If he did, it could only have been for a very short time."

"Can't be sure, huh? That's becoming your favorite phrase, Doc," Mitch said disgustedly.

Pohl chuckled. "We physicians have learned to cover our backsides."

"Let me see if I've got it. Hatch was hit four times, but the blow that killed him is the one that cracked his skull. There may have been two instruments, which might indicate two different attackers, but that can't be proved. He may have lived for an indeterminate length of time after the death blow. That can't be proved, either. He died sometime between the time he was last seen at the clinic and when he was found this morning. Is that about it?"

"Couldn't have summarized it better myself, Mitch."

8

Melted snow dripped from trees and ran off roofs in streams as Mitch drove through town to the clinic. The temperature had reached forty-nine degrees during the day, but it was starting to edge down again as evening approached.

He parked beside Rhea Vann's Oldsmobile, noticing that the broken window had been replaced in the square, buff-brick clinic building. The only other cars in the lot were Marilee Steiner's Chevy and an old Ford pickup, which evidently belonged to the young Cherokee woman behind the counter in the reception room. Her name tag read Robin. She was plump with coppery skin, a wide mouth, and slightly crooked teeth that somehow gave her a gamine look.

She smiled at him. "How may I help you?"

Marilee Steiner, who'd been out of sight, bending down behind the counter, her attention on the shelves near the floor, stood up. "He's here to see the doctor," she said.

"Could I have a few words with you first, Miss Steiner?" Mitch asked.

"Sure." He took note again of her beauty—classic bone structure, smooth skin, big brown eyes beneath perfectly arched black brows, hair as black as a crow's wing, caught at the nape of her neck in a clasp, the ends reaching halfway to her waist. But today her beauty was marred by dark shadows beneath haunted eyes and stress lines in her forehead and on either side of her mouth.

"We can go back to the lounge," she said, leading the way down the hall to a small room containing several steel-framed brown-vinyl chairs, a small refrigerator, and a corner table on which sat a coffee maker and a microwave oven.

She went to the table. "Would you like a cup of coffee?"

"No, thanks."

She poured a cup for herself, then lowered herself into the nearest chair with a sigh. "It's been a long day," she murmured. "Jessie Hatch called the clinic this morning to tell us that her husband died last night. I'm still trying to take it in." She tested the coffee, found it still too hot, and rested the Styrofoam cup on the arm of her chair.

Mitch took a chair near hers. "You told me yesterday that you knew him pretty well."

She nodded. "He was a real friend to me, and I needed friends when I went to the Job Corps Center. All my old friends, even my family, had washed their hands of me. I'd pretty much hit bottom, and it was Tyler who picked me up and made me believe I could make something of myself. I never saw the violent side of him until yesterday when he broke into the clinic." She shook her head in bewilderment. "And then to learn he's dead . . ." She took a tissue from her uniform pocket and blotted her eyes. "Jessie didn't know much beyond the fact that his body was found by hunters out in the country somewhere."

"In the woods," Mitch said, "near Lake Tenkiller."

She took a deep breath. "I just don't understand it. Jessie said he'd been sick—flu or something—but she said you told her he didn't die of that." The lines in her brow deepened.

"That's right. He was killed by a blow to the head."

Her pretty face creased in horror. "Oh, how *awful.*" She stared at Mitch in stunned concern.

"Yes," he agreed. "According to the medical examiner, he was hit four times."

"Poor Tyler," she breathed. She raised the cup to her mouth. Her hand trembled slightly. She sipped and grimaced

at the taste. "This is old," she said distractedly and bent to set
the cup on the floor beside her chair.

"We know that at least two of the blows to his head were
received when he broke in here," Mitch said.

She looked up sharply. "Oh, you can't think Dr. Vann—"
She gave a small shake of her head. "She hit him, yes, to
make him go away—but he was all right when he left here."

"Are you sure about that?"

"Of course." Her expression was one of confusion. Her
hands rose in dismay. They were slender hands, the fingers
long and elegant, the nails a soft pink. "I saw him get in his
car and drive away."

"Now that you've had time to reflect on what happened
here yesterday," Mitch pressed, "can you remember how
many times Dr. Vann hit Tyler Hatch?"

She wadded the tissue she still held in one hand. "Let me
think," she murmured. "I was so terribly frightened." She
smoothed back her shining hair. "Two or three times, I think."
She seemed a little vague about it. "I'm sorry, it's sort of a
blur. I was intent on getting out of Tyler's reach. I was looking at him, not Dr. Vann. His eyes were"—both her hands
were shredding the tissue in her lap—"they were glazed. I remember thinking, He's lost his mind, he doesn't even know
who I am."

"When he went to his car, did he stagger or seem disori-
ented?"

She frowned. "I wouldn't call it staggering. There was
snow on the ground, you'll remember. He was hurrying, so he
slipped once or twice, getting to his car." Her eyes flicked to
the open door and back to Mitch. "I don't understand why
you're so interested in Dr. Vann. Tyler didn't die here. He died
out in the woods, miles from here."

Mitch thought she'd probably studied head injuries in her
M.A. course and knew exactly why he was interested. She
wanted to protect Dr. Vann, who'd hired her straight from the
Job Corps Center, after her friends and family had given up

on her. She must feel as indebted to Rhea Vann as she did to Tyler Hatch.

Instead of replying to her implied question, Mitch said, "I know that Tyler Hatch didn't show up at Jessie's aunt's house or at Dr. Vann's last night, looking for his wife. Did he come to your place?"

She swiftly shook her head. "No." She shivered involuntarily. "It never even occurred to me to think he would. Anyway, I went out again, to have dinner with my boyfriend."

"And you didn't see Hatch's Blazer anywhere?"

Her eyes were somber. "No, and I knew his car. I'd have noticed if I passed him." Her brow knitted tightly.

"What time did you go to dinner?"

She thought for a moment. "I left home about seven and met my boyfriend at the restaurant. Charlie and I—that's Charlie Handler, my boyfriend—we were probably there for an hour, an hour and a half at the most. Then we went back to his place to watch a movie. It was well after midnight when I got home. But my roommate was there all evening. That's how I know Tyler didn't go there."

"You said you met your boyfriend at the restaurant. Why didn't he pick you up?"

"He was running late. He was coming from his parents' house. They live on an acreage several miles out of town, near Lake Tenkiller. He'd made reservations for seven-fifteen, so he called and asked me to meet him." She swallowed and leaned back in her chair. "Is that when Tyler was killed? While Charlie and I were eating our dinner?"

"We're not sure yet." He leaned forward, bracing his hands on his thighs. "It's strange," he mused. "Hatch didn't show up at any of the places he would logically have gone to find his wife."

"That is strange," she murmured. She gathered up the shredded pieces of tissue and tossed them in the wastebasket, which was against the wall a few feet from her chair. She fished a fresh tissue from her pocket and wiped away a tear. "Could he have just gone home?"

"He might have gone there to see if Jessie had returned, but once he knew she wasn't there—considering his state of mind when he left the clinic—he'd have gone out again, looking for her."

She nodded. "Yes, you're probably right."

"We'll keep digging," he said. "Eventually, we'll find out where Hatch went, who he saw, between the time he left the clinic and when he ended up in those woods." They'd better find out, he thought morosely; it was the key to solving the puzzle of Hatch's death. "If you hear of anyone who saw him, you'll let me know?"

"Of course."

His hands still planted on his thighs, Mitch pushed himself to his feet. "Thank you, Miss Steiner. I'll talk to Dr. Vann now."

"Her office is at the end of the hall, on the left."

"Thanks. I know the way."

She was wiping her eyes when he left.

The office door stood open. Rhea Vann sat at her desk, head bent over a thick medical file, half-glasses perched on her short, straight nose. Sunlight fell through a window onto her hair, making it shine like onyx. Mitch tapped with his knuckles on the door facing.

She glanced up and smiled.

"Hi," he said.

She looked tired. "Come on in." She removed the glasses and a pencil that was tucked behind her ear, laid them on the desk, and closed the file.

Mitch took off his coat, threw it over the back of a chair. She leaned forward with her elbows on the desk, fingers laced together under her chin. Her expression was only mildly curious.

"I've been talking to Miss Steiner," Mitch said. "She tells me you've known about Tyler Hatch's death since this morning."

She nodded. "Jessie called the clinic right after she talked to you. Marilee took the call. She was pretty broken up over the news. She credits Hatch with helping her stay off drugs and get her act together at the Job Corps Center."

"She was an addict?"

Rhea nodded. "Hard-core. Started when she was fourteen. Crack, heroin, you name it, Marilee has tried it. After her last rehab program, she ended up at the Job Corps Center and managed to stay clean, with the help of Hatch and the counselors. If you've ever dealt with addicts, you know that getting them to stay off is no small feat." She lowered her hands, clasped them together on the desk. They were competent hands, the nails filed short and left unpolished. "Apparently Hatch was two different people, one at work, the other at home."

"Did you talk to Jessie Hatch yourself when she called the clinic?"

She nodded.

"How did she sound?" Mitch asked.

"Shell shocked. It'll all hit her later, probably already has. Tyler may have battered her, but he paid the rent and bought the groceries." She watched Mitch shift in his chair. "Jessie said you didn't know how he died."

"I do now," Mitch told her. "I talked to the medical examiner before I came here."

He paused, watching her, and she lifted her dark brows questioningly. Mitch went on, "Hatch was hit on the head and left shoulder four times. The blow that killed him landed at the base of his skull and cracked it."

She digested this, her dark eyes fixed intently on Mitch's face. "You knew this when you made the appointment to see me, didn't you?"

"I knew he'd received several blows, but I wasn't sure that's what killed him."

"Sure enough to want to talk to me again," she said, her face expressionless and very still. "Let's put all the cards on the table, shall we? You're working on the theory that he left here, after I hit him with that table leg, drove out to the lake, got out of his car, and died." Her dark eyes challenged him.

"That's one scenario," Mitch admitted, though he was fairly sure it hadn't happened exactly like that. It made no sense for Hatch to have driven the Blazer into the woods and hidden it from the road. Somebody else did that. So somebody had been with Hatch or had met him at the lake. And if they'd met on that country road, had the meeting been planned or accidental?

Her eyes searched his face. "Only one problem," she said. "You said he was hit four times. I only hit him twice." Marilee had said two or three, but then she'd admitted she hadn't been looking at Rhea at the time.

"When I was here before, you said you weren't sure how many times you'd hit him."

"Well, I am now," she said flatly. "I've given it a lot of thought, and I'm sure neither of my blows connected with the base of his skull. He had his left side to me as he came through the window. I hit him on that side of his head and on his left shoulder."

But she'd also said that he lunged for the telephone as Marilee Steiner was calling the police. The reception counter and telephone would have been on Hatch's right, which meant he was between Rhea and Marilee. If he lunged for Marilee, he'd have been looking at her—he *had* been, in fact, because she'd noticed that his eyes were glazed—and the back of his head would have been to Rhea. Had she struck both blows before that moment?

He cleared his throat. "If he went after the telephone, as you said yesterday, he'd have turned the back of his head to you."

"I hit him only twice," she said, enunciating the words clearly, "and neither blow was to the back of the head." She didn't look worried, confirming the impression that Mitch had of her during his first visit to the clinic. Rhea Vann was a strong, self-assured woman. She'd had time to come up with her story and he wasn't going to shake her from it. Maybe, upon reflection, she really had remembered exactly how many times she'd hit Hatch. But Mitch regretted revealing, so early in the interview, the number of blows Hatch had received. He switched course.

"When I told Jessie Hatch her husband was dead, I had the distinct impression she thought her son Jason was involved. Any idea why she might have thought that?"

She picked up the glass paperweight, held it in both hands, looked at it for a moment. Expelling a long breath, she set it down. "Yesterday morning, after the beating and after Tyler left the house, Jason threatened to kill his father the next time he hit any of them."

"Did he mention a gun?"

She thought about it. "Jessie didn't say anything about a gun, just that Jason was very upset and threatened to kill his father."

From what Jessie and her sons had told him, Hatch hadn't hit any of them after beating Jessie yesterday morning, but Jason might have decided not to wait for the next time. Clearly, Jason felt guilty for not having protected his mother from Hatch. Had he brooded on it all day and decided, finally, to take action? Sophie Beard claimed that Jason hadn't left her house last evening. But she'd gone to bed at ten. Jason could have slipped out after she was asleep. He could have tricked his father into driving out to the lake by saying Jessie was staying at the lodge. If that's what happened, Jason had somehow gotten his father to leave the car short of the lodge, killed him, and dragged the body into the woods. Then he'd hidden the Blazer. He wouldn't have risked trying to hitch a ride back to town, leaving a witness who could place him in the vicinity of Hatch's body. He'd have walked.

Jason was strong and physically fit, but that was a six- or seven-mile walk in near-freezing weather. Maybe he'd hoofed it, but wouldn't it have made much more sense to drive the Blazer back to town before abandoning it?

Well, maybe the kid had panicked.

"According to Jessie Hatch," Mitch said, "you went grocery shopping last night, and when you returned home, you let her use your car to go to her aunt's house."

"Yes?" She sounded faintly puzzled.

"What time did Jessie leave your house?"

She frowned. "It was a little before eight, I think."

"How long was she gone?"

"About an hour . . . but, you're not suggesting that Jessie killed Tyler?"

The drive from Rhea Vann's house to Sophie Beard's would have taken less than five minutes. According to Sophie, Jessie was at her house about fifteen minutes. Add five minutes driving time both ways and it still added up to only twenty-five minutes. That left thirty-five minutes unaccounted for.

"Who had a better motive?" Mitch asked.

She shook her head. "Tyler Hatch had Jessie so frightened, she could never have raised a hand to him."

"If she believed he would kill her if she didn't fight back, she might have. He was driving around town last night, looking for her, and he was in an irrational state of mind. You said so yourself. Maybe he saw her in your car and followed her. Maybe she headed out of town, trying to lose him. Maybe he forced her off the road and she grabbed something—whatever was handy to protect herself."

"There's nothing in my car she could have used as a weapon."

"Don't you have a tire iron and other tools for changing a flat?"

She hesitated for a long moment. "A tire iron and several wrenches," she said carefully, "in the trunk—but she would have to get out, unlock the trunk, and find the tire iron or a wrench before Tyler reached her. If he forced her off the road, Jessie would never have been able to think so logically, act so quickly. She would have been too frightened." She hesitated again. "At least, that's my take on Jessie."

Shelly Pitcher would agree, Mitch mused. But everybody has a breaking point, and when it's reached, adrenaline and the survival instinct take over. Then the worm turns, to use Dr. Pohl's phrase.

He would have to talk to Jessie Hatch again. But there was no rush. He'd wait until after the funeral. Now that the M.E. had released the body, the service would probably take place tomorrow or the next day.

"How did she seem, when she got back to your house last night?"

"Seem?"

"What was her state of mind? Was she agitated? Afraid?"

She shrugged. "She seemed a little anxious. She was worried about her situation, probably wondering how she'd support herself and her sons if she didn't go back to her husband."

"And she didn't mention that she'd seen Hatch, even from a distance, while she was gone?"

"No." She pushed her chair back from the desk, pointedly looked at her watch. "If there's nothing more, I'm expecting a patient shortly." She stood.

Mitch had been thinking that Tyler Hatch could have seen Rhea Vann driving through town as easily as he could have seen his wife, and, by that time, he'd probably focused on the doctor as the cause of his wife's leaving him. "Just one more thing."

She eyed him thoughtfully. "Yes?"

"While you were away from your house last evening, did you go anywhere besides the grocery store?"

She looked at him sharply, but her reply was swift. "No. I drove straight to the Super Mart on Sequoyah, did my shopping, and drove straight home. And, before you ask, I didn't see Tyler Hatch after he drove away from the clinic yesterday afternoon."

Mitch rose. "Thank you for your time, Doctor." He opened the office door and walked out.

A pair of dark, smoldering eyes watched him go.

After leaving the clinic, Mitch talked to the manager at the Super Mart. He confirmed that Rhea Vann had been in his store the previous evening, though he couldn't say how long she'd stayed.

"I do remember that her shopping cart was piled full when

she got to the cash register," he said. "I remember that because she usually buys only a few items at a time. Eats out a lot, I guess. I kidded her about buying so many groceries, asked if she expected to be snowed in."

"How did she respond?"

"She just said she would have a houseguest for a while and she was out of everything."

Mitch returned to a former question, rephrasing it. "What's your best guess as to how long it would take to fill a shopping cart with groceries?"

He scratched his head. "Some people know what they want when they get here, have a list, whiz right through, you know. Others dawdle along, read labels, check prices. Since Dr. Vann isn't used to buying so many groceries at one time, I'd say she was probably here close to an hour."

Henderson Sixkiller stood in the deep shadows behind the Hatch house. Several times he saw Jessie or Jason or Harry walk past a window. He was waiting for a chance to catch Jessie in a room alone. He didn't want the boys to know he was anywhere around until he'd talked to Jessie. He saw the light go on in the den. From where he stood, he could tell that somebody had turned on the television, but he couldn't see the couch where they sat to watch TV, so he didn't know which of them was in the den.

He continued to wait, growing more and more impatient. Finally, he saw Jessie walk into the kitchen and sit at the table next to a window. She was drinking from a cup—coffee or tea. Her face was bruised and she looked haggard, worse than she had the last time she visited him in jail.

He cursed Tyler Hatch under his breath and ran quickly across the yard to the window. He put his face up to the glass and tapped with his finger. She started and jerked toward the pane. When she saw him, her eyes widened until he could see white all the way around. Her hand flew to her mouth.

He put his finger to his lips, warning her to keep quiet, and pointed toward the back door, then ran around the house and waited for her to let him in.

It was a few moments before he heard the bolt being turned. The door opened. "Henderson!" she whispered, "What are you doing here?"

"Shhh," he cautioned as he stepped inside. "Don't let the boys hear you." Once he was inside, he could see the purple and yellow bruises around her eye. "Ah, Jessie." He put his arms around her and hugged her close.

Her arms remained at her sides, her body was stiff, unyielding. "You're hurting me," she gasped. "My ribs."

"I'm sorry." He released her.

She stepped back. "You're in big trouble, Henderson. The police called here, looking for you. Breaking out of jail was a stupid thing to do. When they catch you—and they will catch you, Henderson—they'll give you more time."

"I'll worry about that later."

"Typical." She sighed, went back to the table, sat down. She picked up her cup, clutching it in both hands. "Did you ever wonder how a ma like ours could have two such losers for kids?"

"Aw, Jess . . ."

She looked at him. "Why did you come to Buckskin, of all places?"

"Because of you, Jess. I had to save you from Tyler."

She stared at him as if she couldn't believe her ears. A soft moan escaped her. "Save me? Oh, Henderson . . . oh, my God, you didn't—" She broke off, clapped a hand to her mouth. "What on earth are we going to do?"

When Mitch got home, he found a note from Emily attached to the refrigerator with a red heart magnet: *I'm at Temple's. Cheerleader meeting to decide on shoes. Be home by nine.*

Ah, yes, the majorly important cheerleader shoes. Mitch crumpled the note and threw it in the trash basket under the sink. He didn't feel like cooking. He rummaged through the refrigerator, found a small portion of leftover stew, and heated it for his dinner.

He was hungry, and the stew tasted even better the second time around. Spooning up the first bite, he reflected upon his meeting with Rhea Vann. Had she told him the truth about how many times and where she'd struck Tyler Hatch? He mulled it over and was inclined to believe her, especially now that it was possible Hatch had been hit with two different instruments. Pohl had warned that he couldn't swear to it, but it felt right to Mitch.

Two instruments almost certainly meant two people had attacked Hatch. Taking into account the fact that he liked Rhea Vann and would hate having to arrest her for murder, two instruments still made sense. Rhea had hit him twice at the clinic, and, sometime later, a second person gave him another couple of blows, including the one that killed him.

After finishing the stew, he rinsed his bowl and set it and the glass and spoon he'd used in the dishwasher. When his wife died, he'd been a novice at keeping house and cooking. Not that he was ever going to give Julia Child any competition, but he'd become competent at preparing simple meals. He even enjoyed cooking when he had the time for it.

Keeping house had been harder to come to terms with. There was nothing enjoyable about it. At first, he'd let it go, let things pile up until something had to be done. Then he and Emily would spend all day Saturday putting the house to rights again. A few times, when he just couldn't face it, he'd hired a neighbor woman to clean. Finally, he'd realized that he had to get organized. He'd assigned certain chores to Emily and others to himself. Now, one of the house rules was that they place dirty dishes in the dishwasher after every meal and run the dishwasher once a day.

He poured detergent in the pocket in the dishwasher door, set the machine to *wash,* and turned it on. He was still hungry. He opened the freezer and took out a carton of vanilla ice cream. As he was reaching into the cabinet for a clean bowl, the telephone rang.

"Mitch?"

At the sound of her voice, his heart took a nose dive, then lifted again dizzyingly. "Well, hi," he said as casually as he could manage, "I'd begun to think I was leaving messages on the wrong machine." Too late, he wondered if that sounded like criticism.

"I'm sorry to take such a long time getting back to you. I've been so busy, you wouldn't believe it."

"I understand." He didn't understand at all. "Did you have a nice Christmas?"

"Yes, and thanks for the perfume. Did the shirt I sent fit?"

"Like a glove." The silence that followed made him apprehensive. "How's the job?"

"Fine. Wonderful, in fact. And I'm enrolled in a doctoral program at the university. I'm teaching five classes and taking two evening courses." She couldn't have earned a doctorate while living in Buckskin, which was the main reason she'd wanted to move. He knew that, but irrationally he resented her obvious excitement over her new life.

"Sounds like a heavy load."

"It is, but I'm enjoying it. I really am."

"Well, that's good."

"How is Emily?"

"She's well. I got her a car for Christmas, so I see even less of her than before. And she's on the cheerleading squad this year."

"Good for her." He could hear the smile in her voice. She and Emily had hit it off, once Emily had gotten over the idea of a new woman in her father's life. At first, Emily seemed to miss Lisa as much as Mitch, but school and extracurricular activities took up most of Emily's time and she hadn't said much about Lisa lately. "Emily is such a sweetheart, Mitch," Lisa was saying, "but you know that, don't you?"

"Yeah."

"Give her my love."

"I will." What was going on here? They sounded like

strangers, struggling to keep a conversation going. Well, to hell with it. "Lisa, I miss you. I—"

She cut him off. "Mitch, I called to tell you something."

In the silence that followed, he leaned back against the counter, dragged a hand through his hair. Here it comes, he thought.

"I'm seeing someone."

And there it was. The reason she hadn't come to Buckskin for Christmas, the reason she hadn't returned his calls. She'd been working up the courage to tell him. Well, hadn't he known it all along, somewhere deep inside himself? How long had she been 'seeing someone'? It was probably bound to happen sooner or later, but so soon after she left Buckskin—and him? "Oh," he said inanely. "I see."

"It's not that I haven't missed you too," she said in a rush. "I've missed you terribly. I still do. But this long-distance relationship just isn't working." Her assertions were so much air, meaningless, considering what she'd just told him. He said nothing. "Mitch?"

"Yeah, I'm here."

"He's an administrator at the college. He's a nice man. You'd like him."

Right. He'd probably take the SOB fishing with him. "Well, thanks for telling me," he said stiffly. "I won't make an even bigger fool of myself by leaving more messages on your machine."

"Mitch, don't be like that. Talk to me. Please."

"Are you sleeping with him?"

"Mitch, please."

"I'm sorry. That was out of line." He was gripping the receiver so tightly, his hand hurt. "I have to go now. I think I hear somebody at the door. Good-bye, Lisa."

He hung up and turned around to face the counter. He bowed his head, bracing himself with both hands on the counter edge. He felt as though he'd been slugged and the blow had bruised his chest. It hurt to breathe. On the cabinet top, the ice cream had begun to sweat with tiny beads of moisture. The ice cream had softened, the way he liked it. He straightened, took down a bowl. He stared at it for a moment, then put it back. Something seemed lodged in his throat. He didn't feel much like eating any longer.

106   Fog, Tony, Lora, and Gregory...with me then. It
on of, and be down, and throwing a gust of wind
up right when she realized something in the office. He
so. He's must be this, the way said it.

9

Tyler Hatch's burial service at eleven the next morning was held at the cemetery. Fortunately, the day was windless and the temperature hovered near fifty by the time people began to gather. There was no music, not even a cappella singing. The minister from the local Presbyterian church spoke briefly in general terms. Mitch had the impression he hadn't even known Tyler Hatch. The funeral home must keep a list of ministers willing to preside at the funerals of people who have no church affiliation. It was simply the Presbyterian minister's turn.

He spoke quietly of death being merely a prelude to another, better life. He asked Tyler Hatch's family and friends to cherish their loving memories of the departed and look forward to meeting him in the heavenly kingdom someday. Mitch guessed he had no idea of the kind of memories Hatch's family members were left with. They would be hard pressed to recall one worth cherishing. And he doubted that any of them would look forward to meeting him again in the afterlife.

About forty people were gathered around the blue funeral canopy. The silver-gray casket rested above the newly dug grave. Seated in the line of chairs beneath the canopy were Hatch's wife and sons, Sophie Beard, an older white man and Cherokee woman, whom Mitch didn't recognize, and Dr.

Rhea Vann, who sat beside Jessie and held her hand through much of the service.

Harry, red-eyed and anxious-looking, sat on the other side of his mother. Watching him, Mitch was reminded that he needed to talk to Harry again and try to find out what he was so worried about. Jason, seated between Harry and Sophie Beard, was stone-faced and dry-eyed. For most of the short service, he stared at his shoes.

Marilee Steiner and the clinic receptionist, Robin, stood behind Rhea's chair. About a dozen solemn-faced young people, most of whom looked to be in their late teens or early twenties, stood together at the back of the small gathering. Probably from the Job Corps Center, Mitch thought. One young woman, with hair too red to be natural, wept silently through much of the service.

After a final prayer, most of those present passed down the line of chairs, reaching out to clasp Jessie's and the boys' hands, bending to murmur condolences.

Mitch stayed where he was for a few moments and looked at faces. And he wondered which one of them was the killer. Rhea Vann's face was calm, her eyes unreadable.

I only hit him twice . . . neither of my blows connected with the base of his skull.

Jessie, in a plain black dress and coat, touched a handkerchief to her eyes. The facial bruises were no longer discernible to an unknowing eye. Her face was bleak, but her eyes were dry. Her other hand clung to Rhea's as though to a lifeline, as she nodded in response to expressions of sympathy. The overall impression she gave was of a person who desperately wanted to be somewhere else.

I learned early in our marriage not to question Tyler about where he'd been or who with.

Jason, in khaki trousers and a navy sport jacket that was too large for him—his father's?—sat stiffly in his chair, barely looking up as one after another bent to pat his shoulder or take his hand.

He's dead and I don't care!

Harry's arms were clasped tightly across his chest. His face was drawn. He wore jeans and a black imitation-leather jacket. He kept glancing toward his mother and brother.

I wish it could always be just mom and me and Jason.

Sophie Beard sat swaddled in a purple wool cape, her heavy face grim, her mouth set in a straight line, as though glued shut.

I pure-dee hated that man!

Mitch studied the face of the older man seated next to Sophie and, for the first time, saw his resemblance to the deceased. The plump Cherokee woman beside him was weeping into a handkerchief. Tyler Hatch's parents, Mitch guessed.

Harry suddenly bent over to say something to his mother. Then he stood, stepped between two of the young people from the Job Corps Center, and, once in the clear, raced toward the black limousine which had brought the family to the cemetery.

Mitch followed him to the car and tapped on the window. Harry fumbled with the buttons beneath the window, realized he couldn't lower it when the motor wasn't running, and opened the door. A scowl twisted his drawn face.

"You okay?" Mitch asked.

"Yeah." His voice was flat.

"How's your mother doing?"

"Okay, I guess." He wouldn't meet Mitch's eyes.

Mitch glanced over his shoulder, saw the group beneath the canopy breaking up, some already walking along the path through the cemetery toward their cars. He looked at Harry, who had slid down in the soft leather seat with his hands stuffed in his jacket pockets.

"Look, Harry," Mitch said, "I think you're trying to protect your brother, but the truth usually comes out in the end." The boy didn't speak, didn't look at him. "The other night, when you and Jason stayed overnight with Sophie Beard, did Jason slip out of the house after she was asleep?"

His head shot up. "No!"

He met Mitch's gaze just long enough for Mitch to see the fear and deep desperation. He was lying.

"How long was Jason gone?" Mitch asked quietly.

Abruptly, he sat forward and held his face in his hands. "Just a little while," he muttered miserably. "Honest. He went across the alley to his buddy Matt Corn's house. They listened to music, then Jason came back." He lifted his head, his eyes pleading. "You won't tell anybody I told, will you?"

"No," Mitch said and stepped back as Jessie and Jason approached.

Ignoring Mitch, Jason went around the car and got in on the other side. Jessie paused beside the limo, her eyes questioning. Before either of them could say anything, they were joined by the older couple who had sat at one end of the line of chairs under the funeral canopy. Jessie introduced them as Tyler's parents, said they'd arrived yesterday from Omaha and would return home tomorrow.

Mitch shook hands with Tyler's parents, murmured, "My condolences," and hastily excused himself.

After a steak sandwich and fries at the Three Squares Café, Mitch drove out to the Job Corps Center. Once a reportedly unprosperous motel run by the Cherokee Nation, the two-story red-brick building was built in the shape of an *L*. Offices and classrooms now occupied the short end of the *L,* the former guest rooms now housing Job Corps students.

The receptionist watched him curiously as he approached the desk. "Yes?"

Mitch introduced himself. "I'd like to speak to whoever's in charge."

"That would be Mrs. Downing." She reached for the phone, murmured a few words into the receiver, hung up. "Her office is one-oh-three, down the hall to your right. Go on back."

The plaque on the door said: Earlene Downing, Assistant Director. A large portrait of the current principal chief hung on one office wall. On the opposite wall was a framed list of the names of current council members, done in calligraphy.

Earlene Downing was a fiftyish woman with coppery skin and gray-streaked black hair cut in a short cap with bangs across her forehead. He'd seen her at the funeral, standing alone, a little apart from the group of Job Corps students. She invited Mitch to be seated, then leaned back in the chair behind her desk and looked at him with interest. "How may I help you, Chief Bushyhead?"

"I'd like to talk to you about Tyler Hatch."

Her eyes narrowed thoughtfully, and she glanced toward a photograph of herself and a Cherokee man, presumably Mr. Downing, on the desk, as if seeking guidance on what her attitude should be. She looked back at Mitch. "I still can hardly believe what happened to Tyler."

"Yes, ma'am. How well did you know him?"

She shrugged. "He was my boss."

"Did you like working for him?"

She shrugged again. "He treated me all right. I had no complaints."

"Did he have much contact with the students?"

She hesitated. "That's unavoidable. Most of our students live here. They stay anywhere from six months to two years, depending on what course they've enrolled in. We get to know them all pretty well." Mitch thought she knew what he was driving at, but she wasn't going to volunteer the information without prompting. She squinted at him and her next words confirmed what he was thinking. "If I knew exactly what you're getting at, maybe I could be more helpful."

"Do you know of anyone who had a beef with Hatch?"

Creases appeared in her forehead as thick black brows rose. "Not specifically, but I can't say he hadn't made somebody mad sometime. I imagine there were people who didn't like Tyler much."

"Why do I get the feeling you were one of those, Mrs. Downing?"

She gave an impatient sigh and arched a dark brow. "I did my job, he did his. We didn't have to be pals."

Mitch realized he'd have to be frank. "I've been told that Tyler Hatch had affairs, with women he met here."

She met his gaze steadily. "I've heard those rumors too."

"There was a secretary named Hannah . . . "

She hesitated, then nodded reluctantly. "Hannah George. She hasn't worked here in nearly three years, though. I'd heard the gossip about her and Tyler, of course, but all I know for a fact is that Hannah left her job without notice, and she and her husband moved away."

"Do you know where she is now?"

She shook her head. "I've no idea."

"What about students? I was told Hatch could have been involved with some of them."

She gazed at the ceiling for a moment, then at the photograph of her husband as if for moral support. "Tyler was a flirt. He came on to all the female students. Frankly, I found it unprofessional, even disgusting. I tried to talk to him about his too-familiar behavior with the girls, but he always said he didn't mean anything by it. He claimed he just wanted to be a friend to the students." She hesitated. "In all honesty, I have to say that he was friendly with the male students too. I think he really wanted to help them get their lives on the right track. Most of the people who come here are high-school dropouts. Some have been drug and alcohol abusers. A few even have police records. This isn't a private prep school, Chief Bushyhead."

He nodded his understanding.

"Right now, for example," she went on, "we have two brothers enrolled in our diesel-mechanics course. Tim and Martin have been arrested several times, for stealing cars. The last time they were arrested, the judge gave them one last chance to stay out of jail. He put them on probation with the stipulation that they get job training. Tyler took a real interest in them. Even took them camping a couple of times, and I'm sure he paid for their bus tickets to Dallas. They go there a couple of weekends a month to see their mother. They're really going to miss Tyler. I just hope they don't drop out of their classes." She paused and seemed to shake herself. "But to get back to your question, there were frequently rumors floating around about Tyler and one or another of the female students, but I couldn't tell you if there was any substance to them. Frankly, I didn't want to know."

What she said jibed with what he'd heard from others. Tyler Hatch seemed to be one person at work with the students, and another at home with his wife and sons.

"There was a redhead at the funeral who cried a lot."

She shifted uneasily in her chair. "That would be Alice Browne. She's only been here about a month. She's a computer-programming student."

"I'd like to talk to her. Where could I find her?"

Another pause. She looked at her watch. "She'll be in class until four."

Mitch remained seated and looked at her expectantly. "I'd like to talk to her now, please."

She pushed back her chair. "I'll see if I can find her," she said, flushing with irritation. "Wait here."

She was back in a few minutes. "Alice didn't show up for her afternoon classes. She's probably in her room. That's two-fifteen."

Mitch thanked her and left. He walked back across the foyer and went through a back door and along a sidewalk that ran the length of the wing containing the students' rooms. He saw no one. The students would be in class. Halfway along the length of the sidewalk, a stairway led up to the second floor.

Room 215 was the first room to the left at the top of the stairs.

He knocked and waited several moments before Alice Browne opened the door. She'd changed from the brown dress she'd worn at the funeral to jeans and a gray sweat shirt. Her feet were bare. She probably had some Indian blood—most of the Job Corps students did—but she couldn't have much. Her thin face was pale and freckled, with dark circles beneath her brown eyes, which were bloodshot but dry. "Yes?"

"I'm Mitch Bushyhead with the Buckskin Police. May I come in and talk to you for a few minutes?"

His appearance at her door clearly baffled her. "What about?"

"Tyler Hatch."

"Why me? I mean, I haven't been here long. I—I hardly knew him."

He watched her carefully as he said, "Miss Browne, you were seen riding around town with Hatch. He had his arm around you."

Her face flushed. She caught her breath. "Who—?" Then she heaved a sigh and said, "He was just comforting me. I've been having trouble in one of my classes."

"May I come in, Miss Browne?"

She hesitated. "I guess so."

The room contained twin beds, a double dresser, a desk, and two chairs. Neither of the beds was made. As Mitch entered, she picked up several items of clothing from the floor, tossed them into the adjoining bathroom, and closed the door. She sat on one of the beds, her back against the headboard, her knees drawn up to her chest. Mitch pulled a chair out from the desk, turned it to face the bed.

"When was the last time you saw Tyler Hatch alive, Miss Browne?"

She picked at a hole in the knee of her jeans. "The day before he was—before he died. In the morning, as I was going to my first class. He was in a hurry to get to his office. He said hi, but he seemed"—she frowned—"like his mind was on something else. He wasn't in a very good mood."

No doubt, Mitch thought. He'd just punched out his wife.

"I don't think he was feeling very well," she added.

"You didn't see him after that?"

She shook her head. "I was in class all morning." She picked at the hole in her jeans. "At lunchtime, I went to look for him—" She glanced up quickly and down again. "I wanted to talk to him about a part-time job. He'd said he'd help me find one. But he wasn't in his office, and the receptionist said he'd gone to town for lunch. I never got another chance to talk to him." She swallowed. "I never even saw him again."

Mitch watched her pick at her jeans for a few moments. "How often did you see him away from the center?"

Red crept over her freckled cheeks. "We met a few times. For coffee, once for dinner." She met Mitch's eyes with an effort. "I needed someone to talk to and—well, so did he."

"Why didn't he talk to his wife?" Mitch asked dryly.

She flushed redder. "He said he couldn't talk to her. She didn't understand him."

Gee whiz, how original, Mitch thought. "Were you aware that he made a habit of beating his wife?"

Her eyes widened, locked with his. She swept tangled red hair from her eyes and shook her head. "If she told you he did, she lied. Tyler would never do anything like that. He was the sweetest, most understanding man I ever knew."

Mitch let it go. It wasn't important if she believed him or not. "Were you sleeping with him, Miss Browne?"

Tears sprang suddenly to her eyes. She grabbed a corner of the sheet and wiped them. "No," she said and threw him a look of intense dislike. "I know that's what everybody said about Tyler, that he got it on with the girls, but it wasn't true. He was a friend, that's all."

Maybe she was telling the truth, Mitch thought, but if she was, and Hatch hadn't died, he guessed it would have been only a matter of time until the friendship progressed to something more. That was probably Hatch's modus operandi.

"You have any idea who might have killed him?"

She paused a beat. "Well," she said finally, "what about his wife? If she is spreading lies about him . . . " She shrugged, leaving the sentence unfinished.

When Mitch reached the large reception area, on the way out, students were milling around or clustered in groups, talking. Evidently they had a break between classes.

Two young men who were standing near the door to one of the classrooms caught Mitch's notice. They spoke in low voices, but there was an urgency about it. They seemed to be arguing and didn't notice Mitch as he approached.

"That's crazy, Marty!" the shorter one was saying. "Why take any more chances? Forget it. It's over."

The one called Marty jutted his head forward, getting in the other one's face. "Forget it? Not hardly!"

"We screw up one more time, we're in jail. That what you want?"

"We ain't gonna get caught. We're—" He saw Mitch and halted, backed off a step.

"Hi," Mitch said, extending a hand. "I'm Mitch Bushyhead."

Marty scowled at the hand, making no move to accept it. It was plain he wanted no contact with a cop. After a brief hesitation, the other one shook Mitch's hand. "I'm Tim Kramer. This is my brother, Martin."

They had to be the brothers Earlene Downing had mentioned, the ones Hatch had taken a special interest in. The car thieves. Mitch could see the family resemblance in their wide foreheads and square jaws. Muscles rippled beneath their knit shirts when they moved, the result of some pretty serious body building. Had they chosen another path in life, they might have been college football players. They were near the same age, nineteen or twenty; Mitch couldn't have said which was the older.

"Could I ask you a few questions?"

Martin kept on scowling. Again, it was Tim who answered. "We have to be in class in a couple of minutes." He glanced nervously past Mitch to a group of six or seven students who were watching them.

"We could go down to the station, if you prefer," Mitch said.

Martin broke his silence. "Right here is okay," he growled. "What'd you want?"

"I understand Tyler Hatch was a good friend to you."

"Where'd you hear that?" Martin demanded.

"Mrs. Downing told me. Are you saying he wasn't a friend?"

Martin glanced quickly at his brother, who shuffled his feet and looked at the floor. "That ain't what I said," Martin contradicted. "Hatch treated us good."

"Took you camping, I understand," Mitch said, "bought you bus tickets to visit your mother."

Martin was losing what little patience he had. "What's your point, copper?"

Mitch dropped the friendly act. "My point is, somebody close to Hatch killed him. Where were you two Monday night?"

Tim looked alarmed. "We went to Dallas last weekend, didn't get back till about two o'clock Monday morning. Check the log. We signed out Friday and back in Monday."

"I said Monday night."

"Yeah, like I said, we were bushed. So we went to bed early Monday, about eight, I guess."

"You share a room?"

Tim nodded.

"No other roommates?"

"No," Tim said. "The rooms aren't big enough for more than two people."

"Do you own a car?" Mitch asked.

The brothers exchanged worried glances. "An old Ford," Martin grumbled. "It gets us around town, but that's about all."

It must be galling, Mitch thought, for a couple of car thieves to be reduced to driving a clunker. Martin and Tim could have left their room Monday night, taken their car, found Hatch, killed him, and returned to the Job Corps Center with no one the wiser. But why would they kill a man who had befriended them?

A bell rang, signaling time for the next class. "Wait a minute," Mitch said when Martin started to leave. "Did you ever hear Hatch mention a beef he was having with some-body?"

"Nobody but his old lady," Tim replied. "He griped about her all the time. Said she was lazy, never wanted to go out and have any fun. Stuff like that."

"Fortunately, he had his girlfriend to have fun with," Mitch remarked dryly.

"Who?" Tim asked.

"Alice Browne."

"Oh, Alice." Tim shrugged. "I thought he was just trying to help her."

"Like he helped you?"

"Yeah—I guess."

Mitch let them go, watched them walk toward a classroom, their heads together, mumbling.

10

"Mrs. Corn confirmed what Harry told you, Chief," Shelly said.

When Mitch had returned from the Job Corps Center, he'd sent Shelly and Duckworth to question the mother of Matt Corn, Jason's friend, and to have another go at Jessie Hatch. They'd just come back to the station and were reporting to Mitch in his office.

"Jason showed up at their house a little after ten," Shelly went on. "He told Mrs. Corn his mother was visiting Sophie Beard and had given him permission to come over. She thought it was kind of late for a visit, but she had no reason to doubt him."

Duckworth sat hunched forward in his chair, hands planted on his thick thighs, elbows thrust out as though he expected to take flight any minute. "He's got her snowed," he stuck in. "The kid's a slick little customer. Real polite around adults."

"Funny, I didn't notice that," Mitch muttered.

"Yeah, well, I guess he makes an exception for cops," Duck said. "But Mrs. Corn thinks Jason is a good influence on Matt. When he's there, it's yes-ma'am and no-ma'am and thank you-ma'am all over the place. She said other kids could take a lesson in politeness from Jason Hatch." He snorted. "We didn't tell her he'd crawled out the bedroom window. We sure didn't tell her he'd threatened to kill his dad."

A good influence? Polite? Mitch hadn't seen *that* side of

Jason. Like his father, Jason had two very different personas, depending on the particular situation. "Sounds like the kid's a con artist."

"Like I said," Duck added, "a slick little customer."

"Don't be too hard on Jason," Shelly said, glancing imploringly from Mitch to Duckworth. "He's had a lot to deal with in his short life, but I don't think he's a murderer."

"That's not what you said after we talked to him," Mitch reminded her. "What changed your mind?"

"I'm not sure," she said, sighing. "I just can't believe he'd suddenly up and kill his dad."

Duckworth snorted. "You feeling maternal toward this kid? Like maybe the alarm on your biological clock is going off?"

Shelly's face got red. "Don't be stupid, Duck! You have no idea what it's like to be fifteen years old in a family like Jason's."

"Look," Duck retorted, rolling his eyes, "you don't even know this boy. Besides, when a kid kills somebody, people always say stuff like that, people who know him a lot better than you know Jason Hatch. Why, he was always such a *nice* boy. Yeah, right."

Shelly gave Duckworth an impatient glare, though she didn't argue, which she clearly knew was pointless. But Mitch was inclined to take Shelly's assessment of Jason with a grain of salt too. Because of her own childhood with an abusive stepfather, she found it easier than Duck to excuse the behavior of mistreated kids. "How long did Jason stay at the Corns?"

"Mrs. Corn said about thirty minutes," Shelly replied. "The boys went to Matt's room, shut the door, and listened to Matt's boom box. Then Jason said good-bye to her and went back to Sophie Beard's."

"That's where Mrs. Corn assumed he was going," Duck muttered. "He could easily have gone looking for his dad, and found him."

"Harry said he wasn't gone from Sophie Beard's house long," Mitch told him. Jason was at the age when kids resented being told what to do. So when Sophie Beard told him he couldn't go out, he waited till she was asleep and went out, anyway. A few minutes would have been enough to prove his independence to himself.

"Kids lie for each other," Duckworth said, eliciting another frown from Shelly.

"What about Jessie? Did you find her at home?" Mitch asked.

"Yes," Shelly said. She hesitated, ran a hand through her sandy hair, and glanced at Duckworth, as though she wondered if their takes on the mother were as opposed as those on the son. "She seemed real nervous to me."

"At first," Duck added. "But when we asked where else she'd gone besides Sophie Beard's house the night her husband was killed, she seemed kind of relieved."

Shelly nodded a puzzled agreement. "Like she thought we'd come to talk to her about something else, something worse. She probably figured we were going to grill her about Jason."

"Hmmm," Mitch mused, "maybe. How did she answer your question about the night Hatch was killed?"

"She claims after she left her aunt's house she drove a couple of blocks and parked in front of a vacant lot," Shelly said. "Said she needed to be alone to think."

Mitch grunted. "She saw nobody who could corroborate her story, I'll bet."

"Got it in one, Chief," Duckworth said.

"Yeah, that's what she told us," Shelly agreed. "According to her, no other car even came down that street while she was parked there."

So neither Jessie nor Jason had an alibi that stood up to close scrutiny. But then innocent people often didn't. As for Hatch's murder, Mitch had no strong gut feel for whether either Jessie or Jason was the murderer. If he had to pick one of the two as a potential killer, though, he'd go with Jason. The kid was carrying a load of guilt for not having protected his mother from Hatch in the past. Killing his father might have seemed the only way to stop the abuse. Even if he'd planned it, he might not have thought to set up a good alibi. He would have been scared and, afterward, in a panic to get back to Sophie Beard's house.

"You better write up reports on the interviews," Mitch said, signaling the end of the session.

As Shelly and Duckworth left Mitch's office, Lex Burnside dragged in. He looked as low as a snail's belly. "Hey, Lex," Mitch greeted him.

"Wanted to see if you had any leads on my saddles and buckles," Burnside said. He'd removed his cowboy hat and held it against his chest, as though he could hear the strains of the national anthem in the distance. Maybe it was Burnside's praying position, Mitch thought. The ex–rodeo star might be calling on the divinity to make Mitch give him the answer he wanted.

Mitch hated to disappoint him. "Sorry, Lex. Wish I had better news for you, but nothing's changed."

"Damn." Burnside dropped his arm, slapping the hat against the side of his leg. "I been all over my end of town, asking people if they noticed any suspicious goings-on at my place over the weekend. People, cars, lights, whatever. Nobody saw a thing."

"Tough," Mitch murmured, thinking that Burnside had saved him the trouble of canvasing the neighborhood.

Burnside went on, "The Kirkwood sisters' yard is sort of catty-corner to our acreage, you know, and Millicent heard a car late Saturday night, after midnight. Something she ate disagreed with her and she couldn't sleep. She said the car was loud, like the muffler was faulty or something. So it could've been a truck. You couldn't haul all the stuff they stole from me in a car."

"This vehicle was at your place?" Mitch asked.

His shoulders sagged. "She couldn't be sure. She got up and looked out her bedroom window. She didn't see anything, but with all those trees between our place and hers . . ." His voice trailed off as he made a helpless gesture with his arthritic hands.

"Well, Lex, you know the Kirkwood sisters. They're kind of paranoid about people breaking into their house, wanting to jump their bones. Millicent could have imagined it."

"Yeah, I know." He was still standing, clutching his hat at his side, but he seemed reluctant to leave.

"If I hear anything, I'll get in touch with you right away."

"Maybe you could talk to Millicent," he said. "If you asked the right question, she might remember something else."

Burnside was grasping at straws, and Mitch was not particularly in the mood to drop in on the Kirkwood sisters. But this morning Emily had said she was having dinner with Temple's family. Afterward, the girls would take the pep-club bus to an out-of-town basketball game. Mrs. Roberts would meet the bus when it got back to town, and Emily would spend the night with Temple.

Mitch didn't relish sitting in the house all evening with nothing but thoughts of his late romance to keep him comapny. *Lisa—God, how he missed her.* The thought of Lisa summoned a new wave of sadness. He swallowed hard. He definitely didn't want to spend all evening at home, alone. "Tell you what, Lex. I'll stop by there when I leave the station."

"Why, Chief Bushyhead," Polly Kirkwood trilled, her eyelids flapping flirtatiously, "we didn't expect you. Come on in. Millicent, just look who's here."

Steps sounded from somewhere in the back of the house—the kitchen, Mitch deduced, since he could smell something baking. Polly insisted that he sit down, but she remained standing in the center of the living room, smoothing stray wisps of gray hair off her face and beaming at him. Every piece of furniture in the room was adorned by at least one crocheted doily. Millicent's handiwork, Mitch guessed. Polly liked to be active. She took daily walks, weather permitting, and collected rocks. Occasionally she invited children from the tribal boarding school over for a party. Mitch couldn't see her being content to sit in a rocking chair, crocheting.

"We'd be delighted if you could stay for dinner," Polly cooed. "We're having meat loaf and baked potatoes and apple pie. There's plenty for three people."

"No, thank you, Miss Polly," Mitch said. "I have to get on home."

Millicent entered the room. An apron was tied over her dark-green dress and there was a smudge of flour on her thin, pointed nose. She peered down at Mitch quizzically through her rimless spectacles. Mitch stood hastily and moved away from the sofa, deciding not to sit down again. This shouldn't take long. "Good afternoon, Miss Millicent."

"I was asking him to stay for dinner," Polly said with a giggle, waving her hands.

"That's real nice of you, Miss Polly, but I can't."

"Do stop fluttering, Polly," Millicent said dampingly. "Now, how may we help you, Chief Bushyhead?"

"Lex Burnside came by my office this afternoon," Mitch said, glad to get down to it. "He says you heard a car that might have been at the Burnsides' house late Saturday night, Miss Millicent. I guess Lex told you his place was burgled sometime over the weekend, while they were out of town."

"Yes, he told me," Millicent said.

Polly gasped. "They had a burglary?"

Millicent ignored her. "I'm afraid Lex exaggerated a bit. Poor man's grieving so over his loss. I didn't say the car was at the Burnside house. I'm not sure exactly where it was. I did hear a car, though. I wasn't asleep—I had an upset stomach—"

"She *will* eat cucumbers," Polly inserted.

Millicent dismissed the interruption with a scowl. "As I was saying, I wasn't asleep, but if I had been, that car would have awakened me. The motor was quite loud."

"It wasn't a car," Polly said.

Both Mitch and Millicent turned to look at her. "Oh, how would you know, Polly?" Millicent inquired. "Have you suddenly developed psychic powers?"

Polly lifted her plump chin and said indignantly, "I saw it. It was a truck."

Millicent shot Mitch a deliver-me-from-my-sister's-silliness look. "I hate to say it, but she likes to call attention to herself."

"Do not!" Polly cried. Mitch would not have been surprised if she'd stamped one of her small feet, which oddly were encased in white crew socks and blue Keds. Now that he noticed them, he realized how comical they looked with her prim, button-down-the-front, brown-and-white striped dress. But she didn't stamp her foot, she planted her hands on her round hips. "It woke me and I got up and looked out. My room is at the back of the house, Chief, so I had a better view than Millicent." She flashed a triumphant look at her sister. "I saw a truck backing off the Burnside property. I didn't know the Burnsides were out of town, so I assumed it was Lex."

"After midnight?" Millicent asked disbelievingly.

Polly sniffed. "I didn't know what time it was."

"Miss Polly," Mitch said tactfully, "with the woods behind your house, I wouldn't think you could see the Burnsides' driveway from here." The Burnside property joined that of the Cherokee Nation's boarding school on the east, and it was impossible to see any of the school buildings from the Kirkwood house.

Polly frowned thoughtfully. "You're right." She tapped her chin with an index finger. "The truck wasn't in the driveway. That's on the south side of the house and we can't see it. But we can see a little of the north side of the Burnsides' property from here. The truck was on that side."

Mitch recalled that the north side was where Lex's horse barn, which also housed the tack room, was located.

"I remember wondering if the Burnsides were moving," Polly added.

Millicent sighed loudly. Clearly she suspected Polly of making up her story as she went along to keep Mitch interested and, therefore, to keep him from leaving. Mitch was beginning to suspect that himself.

"Why did you assume they were moving?" Mitch asked. "It was the middle of the night."

She thought about it, then smiled at him coquettishly. "Now I know why that occurred to me. The truck, it looked like one of those moving vans. You know, with a big, rectangular back end."

"You couldn't have seen it that well," Millicent protested. "It was too dark."

"I did too! The Burnsides have that bright outdoor light on their barn. I know what I saw, Millicent. I still have very good eyesight. I only need my glasses for reading, unlike some people I could mention." She gave a little toss of her head and turned back to Mitch. "I wasn't privileged to be included in the conversation my sister had with Mr. Burnside, Chief. If Millicent had bothered to tell me the Burnsides had had a burglar, I would have come straight down to the station and reported what I saw."

Of course she would have, Mitch thought. Opportunities to add a spark of adventure to her life did not come along that often.

"I didn't tell you about the burglary, Polly, because I didn't want to upset you," Millicent said. "You know how overwrought you get."

"Pooh. You just didn't want to share the neighborhood news with me," Polly retorted. "You can be downright stingy sometimes, Millicent."

Mitch inserted hastily, "Did you notice the color of the van, Miss Polly, or if there was any lettering on the side?"

Polly shook her head regretfully. "There wasn't *that* much light. Oh, dear, I saw the truck used to haul the stolen goods, didn't I? If only I had known!"

"Did you see who was driving the van?"

"No. The truck was backing into the street when I saw it. Imagine, I went straight back to sleep, never dreaming I'd witnessed a crime."

Mitch was beginning to believe her. Polly's description of the truck jibed with his own speculations. A moving van would hold a lot of loot, and one could be rented in almost any town.

"You've been a big help, Miss Polly. I appreciate it."

Realizing he was about to go, Polly said, "Have you caught the vile animal who murdered poor Tyler Hatch yet?"

"No, ma'am."

"Buckskin used to be safe," Millicent mused. "Our parents never even locked their doors, but now . . . " She clicked her tongue. "I swear, I don't know what the world is coming to. The things they show on TV! Dope fiends everywhere. Pillaging hordes of teenagers. Children with guns." She looked at Mitch expectantly. "I suppose you at least have a murder suspect."

Sensing she was about to deliver one of her pungent quotations, Mitch said quickly, "I'm afraid I can't discuss an ongoing investigation with you, Miss Millicent."

Millicent nodded sagely. " 'Nothing is hidden that will not be revealed.' "

"In due time, ma'am," Mitch said. "Now, I'd better be on my way."

Polly put out a plump hand to touch his arm. "You wait right there, Chief. I'm going to get you a piece of apple pie to take home with you." She started toward the kitchen, but turned back to add, "I'll bring two pieces, one for your daughter."

"Just one piece will be fine, Miss Polly. Emily's eating at a friend's house this evening."

Mitch carried the still-warm piece of pie to his car on a china plate. Polly had used the good china, Mitch suspected, so he'd have to come back to return it. Well, he told himself, he shouldn't begrudge the sisters a few minutes of his time. They were lonely and bored with each other's company, which made them quarrel like children. He didn't have to go in. He'd just swing by in the next day or two and deliver the plate at the door.

After smelling the apple pie all the way home, he took it straight to the kitchen, added two big scoops of vanilla ice cream, and ate it at the kitchen table. It was delicious. If Emily had been there, he'd have felt duty-bound to eat something else first so as not to set a bad example. But Emily wasn't there, so the pie and ice cream served as his dinner.

He washed the china plate, wrapped it in a brown grocery sack, and set it on a living-room table where he'd see it the next morning as he left the house.

In one of Oklahoma's swift weather changes, the temperature had hit sixty-three degrees that afternoon. It had dropped back into the high fifties after the sun went down, but it was still mild for January. Tomorrow it could turn frigid again.

The dead silence in the house was oppressive. Mitch decided to take advantage of the break in the weather and go for a walk. He changed to civilian clothes—jeans, sweater, and his New Balance running shoes, bought a year ago when he had thought he'd take up running. He never had; he used the stationary bike at the station instead. Physical activity helped him think, and pedaling was a dual-purpose way to occupy himself during lulls at work. He grabbed a windbreaker and took off walking briskly.

As he walked, he made a mental agenda for the next day. That van Polly Kirkwood saw was probably rented—how many people owned a moving van? If he could find the agent who'd rented it, he should remember somebody who'd taken out a van for five of the past six weekends. The only place in Buckskin that rented trucks was the Chevrolet dealership. He'd go by there on the way to work in the morning.

Then he tried to decide what his next move in the murder investigation should be. Rhea Vann was no longer a suspect. And he'd checked out the remaining suspects' alibis, to the extent that they could be checked out, and there was no evidence that Jason or Jessie Hatch had been anywhere but exactly where they'd told him they were last Monday evening and night. Jessie or Jason *could* have done it, but he'd pursued that about as far as possible, for the moment.

He slowed his pace as a new thought struck him, something Duckworth and Shelly had said that afternoon. Something about Jessie Hatch. He pursued the elusive memory until he had it. According to Duck and Shelly, Jessie Hatch had been relieved to be questioned about her whereabouts the night of her husband's murder. As though that was better than being questioned about something else, maybe Jason. But what about Jessie's brother, Henderson Sixkiller? Since checking with the Delaware County Sheriff's Department and alerting his officers to be on the lookout for the escaped convict, Mitch had given little thought to Sixkiller. But they'd received no report that Sixkiller had been apprehended. What if he was in Buckskin?

Was he in town the night Hatch was killed?

If he was here, Sixkiller would probably have been in contact with his sister. Jessie Hatch could even be hiding him in her house. If so, when Shelly and Duck arrived, she might have assumed they knew she was harboring a criminal, and she would certainly have been relieved when she realized that wasn't the case.

Hmmm. An intriguing possibility.

Assume Sixkiller *was* in town. He'd surely seen his sister, had seen the evidence of Hatch's abuse. Maybe he'd decided to stop it once and for all. By killing Hatch. Could be, but so far there was no evidence to support the theory.

As for other suspects, Mitch hadn't turned up any angry husbands. Hannah George's affair with Hatch had evidently ended three years ago. Her husband might have been enraged enough to kill Hatch then, but not after three years. The only recent dalliance Hatch seemed to have had was with Alice Browne, who wasn't married. To cover all the bases, though, he'd better find out where Alice was Monday night.

And what about Tim and Martin Kramer? He wished he'd overheard more of their odd conversation at the Job Corps Center. Tim had said something about not taking any more risks, and that it was over, but what was *it?* Hatch's life? No, because Martin had insisted it wasn't over.

The Kramer brothers had acted uneasy, guilty almost, when they saw Mitch. With their arrest records, it could've been just a general distrust of the police. But maybe they were nervous that he had overheard an incriminating conversation. Too bad he hadn't heard enough to figure out the gist of it. Could the Kramer brothers be involved in something illegal? Earlene Downing had said that Hatch befriended the brothers, so he must have kept close tabs on them. Surely he'd have known if they had gone back to their old ways and would have stopped them. Or tried to. Well, maybe that's exactly what happened, and they'd killed him for his pains. Another theory with nothing to back it up.

What about Earlene Downing herself? She had clearly disliked Hatch, and his death made her the most obvious person to take over as director of the center. A pretty flimsy motive for murder. Still, maybe he'd better find out where she was Monday night too.

Absorbed in his thoughts, he hadn't paid close attention to where he was going. Suddenly, he realized he'd walked to Virgil Rabbit's neighborhood. If Virgil wasn't at work, he'd have stopped for a while. Through a lighted front window, he could look through the living room and into the Rabbits' big kitchen. Trudy, Virgil's wife, and five of Virgil's kids were at the dinner table. The oldest boy, Donald, was away at college.

The warm family scene touched Mitch. He used to wish he and Ellen had more kids. After Emily's birth, Ellen had had two miscarriages, so they'd given up. When she died of cancer, he discovered it was difficult enough raising one teenage daughter alone. He wondered how he would have coped if he'd had more kids, but he knew he would have, somehow. You did what you had to do. Money had to be tight at the Rabbits' house, but still he couldn't help envying Virgil a little.

He thought about his house, empty and silent with Emily away. He'd never minded being home alone when Ellen was alive or when he and Lisa were together. Unbidden, Lisa's face appeared in front of him, beautiful, smiling, surrounded by a cloud of golden hair. With a force of will, he dismissed the vision, tried to clear his mind and think of nothing at all as he continued walking.

He didn't exactly decide to head down Rhea Vann's block, not consciously, anyway. But when he found himself in front of her house and saw the light in the window, he halted.

The last time they'd talked, he'd left her with the clear impression that he suspected her of killing Tyler Hatch—accidentally, but still . . . He remembered how she'd gone all stiff and how her eyes had burned. He remembered, too, the smooth curve of her cheek, the way her black hair shone.

Maybe he should tell her he'd eliminated her from the suspect list. Maybe she'd offer him a cup of coffee and he could kill some more time before going home.

Suddenly something yowled and streaked across the sidewalk in front of him. He jumped back, reflexively reached for his gun which wasn't there, before he realized it was only a cat.

He continued to hesitate, staring at the house. Do it, man, he told himself, or get on down the road. He walked up to the front door.

11

"If you've come to give me the third degree," Rhea said, "you'll need an arrest warrant." Mitch didn't know her well enough to tell if she was serious. He did notice a sparkle in her dark eyes when she said it, though. She could be daring him, or teasing him. He couldn't tell which.

"Nothing like that," he said. He felt a little silly, now that he was there. Maybe he shouldn't have stopped. "I happened to be in the neighborhood and saw your lights."

She cocked her head and took her time looking him over. Made him want to squirm. She had on jeans and a black sweat shirt with Oklahoma/Southwest Celebration of Books in red script across the front. The book festival was held annually at the University Center at Tulsa. Emily and Temple had gone the previous year with Lisa, their English teacher at the time, who gave extra credit to students who attended. Later, Emily had said she'd really enjoyed it, as though the fact surprised her. She had especially liked hearing the science-fiction writers speak, she'd said.

Freed of its French braid, Rhea's hair was parted on the left and fell loose and shining around her shoulders. She combed back the right side with her fingers, tucked it behind her ear, and said, "Come on back to the kitchen. We're just finishing dinner."

We? Great, she had a man back there. Now Mitch *knew* he shouldn't have stopped. And why did he feel so disappointed?

Had he thought she had no personal life? He'd probably interrupted a romantic tête-à-tête. He expected to find some guy eating by candlelight, but he couldn't very well leave now. He'd stay a few minutes, he thought as he followed her to the kitchen, and then make his excuses.

"You know my grandfather, I believe," Rhea said.

The old medicine man Crying Wolf stood up as they entered. He wore his long gray hair in two braids that hung halfway down his back. His khaki shirt and trousers looked nearly new. They were probably his best clothes, Mitch thought as he shook the old man's hand. "Don't let me interrupt your dinner, Grandfather," he said, the address of respect for elderly Cherokee men coming naturally. "I'm not staying."

"He's checking up on me," Rhea said with a smile and a lift of dark brows for her grandfather. "I think he wanted to make sure I hadn't skipped town."

Crying Wolf stared at Mitch, unblinking, his black eyes sorrowful. "Rhea has told me about the man who beat his wife and broke into her clinic so that she had to protect herself." His voice was rough and guttural, the words enunciated with precision, the words of one who spoke Cherokee more often than he spoke English. "In the old days, the tribe would have taken care of such a man."

Mitch did not wish to pursue the methods that might have been used. "The main reason I stopped," he said to Rhea, "was to tell you the manager of the supermarket remembers seeing you at the store Monday evening. He says you were there at least an hour."

"So you've decided I didn't have time to track down Tyler Hatch and bludgeon him to death?" Rhea asked. Her eyes were definitely challenging this time.

"Uh, well . . . " Mitch stammered, feeling that she was being unfair. He had never thought that. What he had thought was that *possibly* one of the blows she'd delivered at the clinic had eventually killed Hatch.

Before he could explain that, she asked, "I don't suppose you know who did kill him?"

"Not yet," Mitch admitted. "We're still following up several leads."

She waved a hand over the table, which held the remains of a pot roast and vegetables. "Sit down. Have you had dinner?"

"Yes." He hesitated.

"Would you like a cup of coffee? Or fry bread. I have to make fry bread for Grandfather to get him to have dinner with me. Of course, tonight's a special case. We're going somewhere later."

Mitch wondered where, but she didn't elaborate. He pulled out a chair. "Coffee would be fine, thanks." He shrugged off his jacket, letting it fall over the back of the chair. The kitchen was an efficient U of oak cabinets, with copper-bottomed pots hanging from a ceiling rack. The walls were papered in a bold hunter-green-and-white check, and pots of greenery were scattered around.

Rhea placed a cup of coffee in front of him and poured another for herself. Crying Wolf already had a cup, in addition to a half-full glass of milk. The cups were white, with vines of green dotted with red berries curling around them.

"Amos Flycatcher was in the clinic today," Rhea said to Mitch with a wry smile. "He didn't have many kind words for you. He says you roughed him up, shoved him into your car, and took him home when he didn't want to go, made him walk more than a mile to his son's house."

Mitch sighed. "He was hiding under somebody's porch, wouldn't come out, so we had to drag him. He didn't mention that he wanted to go to his son's, and I had to take him somewhere. He was drunk."

Crying Wolf nodded gravely. "Amos can't leave liquor alone."

"I treated him for a cough and chest congestion," Rhea said. "I also gave him the schedule of local AA meetings, but I doubt that he'll go. He's not ready. He was feeling sorry for himself, still blaming other people for his drinking. His wife left him, he told me."

Mitch nodded. "And he kept saying he saw the Fire Carrier. Virgil Rabbit says other people have seen it lately too."

Crying Wolf went very still, his hand curled around his glass. *"Atsil'-dihye'gi'* may have come back," he said finally, "but I don't think so. Two years ago we made powerful medicine to drive him away."

Mitch knew little about Cherokee medicine, but he respected the old man too much to make light of it. Even though he tended to be a skeptic about supernatural intervention in the affairs of men, he'd seen too many unexplainable things to dismiss the possibility completely. "You're sure he left then?"

Crying Wolf nodded. "For a long time, nobody saw lights out there where *Atsil'-dihye'gi'* roamed."

"Until lately," Mitch said.

He nodded again. "I do not believe it is *Atsil'-dihye'gi'*. If he was back, he'd be looking for the ones who drove him off. He knows who we are. Before we did that, about a year before, *Atsil'-dihye'gi'* came right up to my door. Trying to scare me, you see. I made medicine to protect myself and then I went out to the woods and faced up to him."

Mitch glanced at Rhea, who was watching her grandfather, her expression one of deep affection. "Tell him about that, Grandfather."

The old man looked at Mitch doubtfully. His face was like soft brown leather that had been wadded in a fist, leaving fine, wandering wrinkles all over it. "Maybe he doesn't want to hear."

"Yes, I do," Mitch said. "What happened when you faced up to the Fire Carrier?"

He considered Mitch for another moment, perhaps to judge if he seriously wanted to hear or was merely humoring an old man. Finally, he said, "I took a black scarf with me. People said if you looked through a black scarf, you could tell what the light really was." He drew in a deep breath, as though the memory still had the power to affect him. "It was true."

"You actually *saw* him?"

He nodded gravely. "I went with a friend, another *didahn-vwisgi*, in his car."

"Dick Cornsilk was the other medicine man, wasn't he, Grandfather?" Rhea asked.

"Yes. Dick had a black scarf too, but he stayed in the car. I got out and stood where the Fire Carrier had been seen and I put the black scarf over my face." He paused, drawing out the suspense like a true storyteller. Rhea caught Mitch's eye and smiled. Mitch's attention returned to the old man. One thing he was sure of, Crying Wolf wasn't the least bit senile. Clearly, he'd seen *something*. Mitch wanted to prompt him, but he'd had dealings with Crying Wolf in the past and knew that patience was required.

Crying Wolf picked up his glass and took a swallow of milk before continuing. "What I saw was this. In front of Dick's car was a big, long black car. I don't know what kind. Later Dick said it was a Pierce-Arrow, but I don't know about cars." He paused to finish off a piece of golden fry bread. Mitch sipped his coffee and kept quiet. He felt Rhea's eyes on him. She had a way of seeming to look right into your mind that made him want to fidget.

Crying Wolf looked up. "A skeleton was sitting in the car. He had on a big black hat and a black coat buttoned up all the way to his chin."

"What did he do?" The question slipped out. Mitch couldn't help himself.

"He stared at me. His eyes were black holes. I took off the scarf and walked back to Dick's car." He chuckled suddenly. "I wanted to run, but I made myself walk very slow. When I got in, Dick was shaking so bad he could not drive for a while. He'd seen the skeleton too. Dick would never talk about it, after that night. He didn't go out there with the rest of us when we drove *Atsil'-dihye'gi'* away."

Mitch didn't much blame Dick. "So you're sure the light Amos Flycatcher saw was not the Fire Carrier?"

He hesitated briefly, then shook his head. "Maybe he saw

car lights," he said hopefully, "or a flashlight." Was he really afraid that the Fire Carrier had come back, but didn't want to admit it? To admit it would be to recognize that the Fire Carrier's medicine was stronger than the combined medicine of several medicine men.

Crying Wolf's story had given Mitch an eerie feeling. Turning to Rhea, he changed the subject. "How is Marliee Steiner?"

"She's all right. After you were at the clinic the last time, I sat down with her and let her talk through her grief. She can't talk to her boyfriend. Evidently he was jealous of her friendship with Hatch. I insisted that she take the next day off. Since then she's been quiet, subdued, maybe even depressed, but she's doing her job and I haven't found her crying again."

"Good," Mitch said. "When I talked to her, she was unhappy enough that I wondered—well, I was afraid she might turn to drugs to help her through it."

Rhea nodded. "I talked to her about it. She swore she was finished with that, and I haven't seen any sign of drug use."

Crying Wolf said, "I will go and rest for a while now, Rhea."

She went to him and kissed his cheek. "Be right back," she said to Mitch. She took her grandfather's arm and walked with him down the hall.

When she returned to the kitchen, she said, "We're going to a stomp dance later. They don't usually have them during the winter months, but when it turned warm, they decided to call a special dance. People miss seeing each other."

Mitch knew that stomp dances were held monthly from March through October at three or four ceremonial grounds in the area, but he'd never been to one.

He couldn't delay his departure any longer. "I'd better be going home."

She nodded. "Your daughter will be wondering where you are."

"Actually, she's spending the night with a friend."

"Emily, isn't it?"

"You know Emily?"

"Not really. I saw her at a couple of high-school football games last fall. She's a lovely girl."

Mitch smiled. "You'll get no argument from me on that." He got to his feet and reached for his jacket.

"Grandfather likes you," she said.

"How can you tell?"

"He doesn't tell that Fire Carrier story to just anybody. And, besides, when I went back to the bedroom with him, he told me to ask you if you'd like to go to the stomp dance with us."

Mitch was surprised and inordinately pleased. "I've never been to one," he said hesitantly. "I don't want to make a fool of myself."

She laughed. "You won't. It's very laid back. I'd better warn you, though, it'll probably last all night, unless it turns really cold."

He grinned. "I'd like to go with you."

"Okay. Be back here at eleven-thirty."

"That late?"

"Oh, they don't really get started until midnight, and people keep coming all night long. Grandfather is the medicine chief, so he has to be there to get things going."

She followed him to the door. Mitch was excited, but still a little hesitant. "What do the men wear?"

"What you have on will be fine. Maybe a warmer jacket. Oh, and thanks for letting me know I'm off the suspect list."

He paused, his hand on the doorknob. "You weren't really worried about that, were you?"

She laughed. "On the contrary. I'd have wondered myself, if I wasn't sure I never hit Hatch at the base of the skull."

"Well, I sure didn't want it to be you."

She held his gaze for a long moment. "Thank you."

They joined a line of vehicles, mostly pickup trucks, turning off Highway 10 on a rough country road eight or nine miles from Buckskin. Mitch had offered to drive his Landcruiser, and Rhea had taken him up on it. Now he could see why. The road was full of ruts and gullies that would have been hard on an ordinary car. Mitch followed the truck in front of him through a wide gate with a hand-lettered sign tacked to the gatepost. The sign said: No Drugs or Alcohol Allowed.

He followed the truck as it wound through cedars and bare-limbed blackjack oaks and hackberries to a narrow clearing hidden in the trees. A few pickups were already parked there and several others followed the Toyota into the clearing. Rhea had brought a couple of blankets, a camp stove, and several containers of food. Even though they'd had dinner, Rhea said they'd be hungry again after they'd danced a while. Besides, eating was part of the fun. Mitch helped her carry the food to a grassy spot near the edge of the ceremonial ground, a big circle of bare earth. In the center of the circle, long logs were arranged in the shape of a tepee, which was about fifteen feet across at the base. Beneath the log tepee a fire already burned.

Mitch looked closely at the log construction and the fire as they walked nearby. The fire burned on a mound of earth two or three feet high. At the edges of the fire were four long logs, pointing in each of the four directions. "This fire is as old as the *Di-jal-agi*," Crying Wolf said. Seeing Mitch's confused expression, he translated, "As old as the Cherokee people."

Rhea, who was walking on Mitch's left, added, "At the end of tonight's ceremony, somebody will carry off some embers and keep them alive until the next dance."

Crying Wolf nodded solemnly. "Someone carried this fire over the Trail Where They Cried from the old Cherokee country." Mitch had heard other Cherokees use the same phrase to refer to the Trail of Tears.

Several women had already started their cook fires. Some were using camp stoves, others cooked over open wood fires. The smell of hot grease hung in the air. The women called to them in Cherokee. "*O-si-yo!*" Rhea and Crying Wolf returned the greeting in Cherokee, while the women eyed Mitch curiously.

As Rhea got her fire going and took the covers off big bowls of fry-bread batter and chicken ready to be fried, more people arrived and gathered in clumps to talk or settled, facing the ceremonial fire, on log benches that encircled the dance ground.

Mitch followed Crying Wolf from one group of people to another. He already knew many of them, at least by sight. Most of the men, he noticed, wore cowboy hats. They were friendly, and though they conversed mostly in Cherokee, after Crying Wolf explained that Mitch did not speak his father's language, somebody usually took the time to translate the gist of the conversation for him. Several people seemed curious about his relationship to Rhea and Crying Wolf, whom everybody clearly held in high regard, but they were too polite to ask the direct question. "Tonight he will see his first stomp dance," Crying Wolf said each time they joined a different group of people.

About twenty minutes after the evening shift ended at midnight, Virgil and Trudy Rabbit showed up at the ceremonial ground. Trudy waved at Mitch and started cooking, and Mitch wandered away from Crying Wolf to talk to Virgil's brother, Ernie Pigeon, who was a mechanic at the Ford garage in Buckskin. Virgil came over to slap Mitch's back. "Hey, man, what are you doing out here?"

"I was invited," Mitch said.

Virgil had invited him several times in the past, but Mitch had always declined. "By who?" Virgil asked.

"Rhea Vann."

Virgil and Ernie exchanged a glance, causing Mitch to decide that further explanation was called for. "Her grandfather thinks I need to be educated in the way of the Cherokee."

"I've been telling you that for years," Virgil said.

Ernie grinned. "But you ain't a pretty woman, Virg."

The crowd had grown steadily since Mitch's arrival. Although Virgil and Trudy had left their kids at home in the care of their high school–age son, many couples brought their children with them. Mitch saw quite a number of teenagers, both boys and girls in jeans and warm jackets and athletic shoes. They gathered at the edge of the woods, laughing and joking with each other in English, but Mitch noticed that they addressed the older people in Cherokee. On the drive over, Rhea had said that Jessie Hatch usually attended the stomp dances. Mitch looked for her and for Jason and Harry, but he didn't see them. Probably it was too soon after Hatch's death.

Ernie and Virgil were talking now about somebody Mitch didn't know. Virgil stopped abruptly in the middle of a sentence, looked toward the ceremonial ground, then said, "Crying Wolf's getting ready to start. It's time to go smoke the pipe, Mitch."

What pipe? Mitch wondered. "Me too?"

"No, you're a visitor tonight. Where are you sitting?"

Mitch looked around at the log benches which people were leaving now as they walked to the circle of bare earth where Crying Wolf stood. He had taken a long-stemmed pipe from the leather pouch tied at his waist and was filling it with tobacco from the pouch. Everybody had been so friendly since his arrival, Mitch had relaxed, but now he felt unsure again. "Does it matter where I sit?" he asked Virgil.

Ernie laughed, and Virgil said, "I don't guess you know which clan you are."

Mitch knew that the ancient Cherokees had been separated into clans, but it was a surprise to learn that the ones who attended the stomp dances still knew which clan they belonged to. "I don't know anything about clans," he admitted.

Ernie left, shaking his head. Virgil said patiently, "There are seven clans, Mitch. Deer, Wolf, Wild Potato, Paint, Blue, Long Hair, and Bird. The Rabbits are Long Hair. Trudy's Wolf. Crying Wolf is Wild Potato and Rhea's Bird. We sit with our clans."

"Oh." Mitch noticed for the first time that the log benches did indeed seem to be arranged in seven groups. "Where should I sit, then?"

Virgil looked past Mitch and smiled. "Here comes Rhea. You can sit with her on the Bird clan benches."

Rhea was carrying a big mug. "It's getting nippy," she said, handing the mug to Mitch. "I thought you might like some coffee." Virgil left them, and she said, "I have to go smoke the pipe, Mitch. Then I'll come and sit with you."

Mitch still thought he might seem too forward if he sat on one of the benches without being specifically directed to do so. "Where?"

She pointed to the Bird clan benches and then walked toward the line of people forming in front of Crying Wolf. Carrying his coffee, Mitch made his way to the group of benches she'd indicated and sat down to watch. He felt conspicuous, sitting there alone.

Rhea took her place at the end of the line, which circled around the ceremonial ground. Mitch spotted Virgil and Trudy about halfway back in the line. Even the children were in line.

Crying Wolf raised his hands and spoke loudly in Cherokee. Mitch guessed it was some sort of blessing. Then the old man walked to the center of the bare circle, took a pinch of tobacco from his pouch, and threw it into the fire, still chanting in Cherokee. An offering to the fire, Mitch guessed. Then Crying Wolf lit the pipe, moved back to the head of the line, and raised the pipe to his mouth. After drawing on the pipe, he used both hands to rotate it in a circle and handed it to the first man in line. Then he moved to the edge of the clearing. As each person, including the children, smoked the pipe, rotated it, and handed it to the next person, he or she went to stand at the edge of the clearing with Crying Wolf.

When everybody had smoked the pipe, they left the circle. Rhea got herself a mug of coffee and came to sit beside Mitch. She wore a heavy car-coat and carried a blanket, which she spread over their knees. "Are you bored?" she asked.

"Bored?" He shook his head. "I'm fascinated. Virgil has tried to get me to come out here with him and I always thought I'd feel out of place. But people couldn't be more friendly."

"We'll have to figure out what your clan is," Rhea said. "Was your mother Cherokee?"

"No, just my father."

"Then you'll have to go back to *his* mother. Clan descent comes from the woman's side. What was your grandmother's maiden name?"

"Roach."

"Maybe grandfather can find out what clan she was. He mentioned that he used to know some of your grandparents' people." Mitch never knew his paternal grandparents. They had both died before he was born. He barely remembered his father, who had died when he was eight years old, but the few memories he had retained were pleasant ones. His sense of his father was of a tall, quiet man who had made him feel loved. Suddenly, he had a memory of the dim living room of the house in Oklahoma City where he'd grown up. After his father's death, his mother had kept most of the lights off because she couldn't stop weeping, thinking that eight-year-old Mitch wouldn't notice. But he had. All at once he was seized by the confused grief he'd felt then and the feeling that everything was lost. Years later, his mother had told him that she had never remarried because God made only one James Bushyhead, and after him anybody else was bound to have been a disappointment.

"People eat whenever they're hungry," Rhea was saying. "There's fry bread, fried chicken, potato salad, and peach cobbler on the table by the camp stove. Dancing makes you ravenous. Help yourself whenever you feel like it."

Crying Wolf walked up to the fire in the center of the clearing and began to speak in Cherokee. Several small children gathered around him. "What's he saying?" Mitch asked.

"It's a sort of homily. A sermon, you might say. He's telling the people to live at peace with their neighbors, be honest, help each other, that kind of thing."

"I've never been around people who spoke much Cherokee," Mitch said. "I like the sound of it. It's sort of hypnotic."

"There have always been Cherokees in Oklahoma for

whom it's a first language, even though for years the government tried to stamp out the native languages. The kids were sent to boarding schools where they were punished if they spoke the only language they had known since birth." She glanced over at Mitch. "The government position was that the Indian dialects were barbarous and a detriment to the speakers."

That was almost too stupid to be believed. "You're not joking, are you?"

"Absolutely not. It's in the history books. Boarding-school teachers were ordered to teach only in English. The Commissioner of Indian Affairs said that the language that was good enough for a white man or a black man ought to be good enough for a red man."

"That's the most arrogant thing I ever heard," Mitch said.

"It's pretty typical of the government's attitude toward Indians until well into this century."

"The children must have hated those boarding schools."

"I'm sure they did. But, after a while, most of them were brainwashed into believing they should give up their language and all the old traditions. Fortunately, there were a few who kept them alive in the face of a dominant culture whose attitude was formed by official government policy toward the Indians. That attitude didn't start to change radically until the sixties, and I suppose some people still think of Indians as an inferior species. I'm sure you must have experienced that prejudice, growing up."

"I can't really say that I did. I was just eight when my dad died, but I don't recall his ever mentioning Cherokee tradition."

"That just backs up what I said. The boarding schools and the general public—even popular books and movies—had convinced us it wasn't cool to be Indian."

Mitch wondered if she wasn't just a tad bit defensive. "I have to say," Mitch repeated, "I don't remember experiencing any bias because I was Indian. I guess I wasn't really affected by it."

She looked at him disbelievingly. "Tell me, when you were a kid did you ever play cowboys and Indians?"

"Sure. What boy didn't? We'd go to the Saturday afternoon shoot-em-ups, then go home and pretend our back yards were the Old West."

"And which role did you play?"

The question brought Mitch up short. He'd never really thought to ask the question of himself. "I wanted to be a cowboy," he admitted a bit sheepishly. "We all did."

She grinned. "I rest my case."

Crying Wolf had stopped talking, and the children crowded closer around him, shouting at him in Cherokee. Rhea leaned toward Mitch. "They want him to tell a story before the dancing starts."

Crying Wolf, who at some point had gotten the other blanket and had it wrapped around him, laughed and raised his hand to quiet the children. Then he said loudly, *"Gil' Li'ut-sun' Stanun'yi!"* and the children clapped.

"He's going to tell the one about how the Milky Way was created," Rhea said. "Do you know it?"

"No." Mitch had finished his coffee. He set the mug on the bench beside him and shoved his hands under the edge of the blanket. "Tell me."

She set her mug aside long enough to put on the gloves she pulled from her coat pocket. Then she took the mug and leaned forward, cradling it in both gloved hands. "This is the way my grandfather tells the story. A long time ago, back in the old Cherokee country, the people discovered that something had been stealing their cornmeal at night. They found giant dog prints around the place where the meal was stored. They held a meeting to decide what to do about the thief. An old man suggested that everyone bring noisemakers that night, and they would hide and wait for the dog. So that night, a huge dog appeared from the west. His fur shone like silver in the moonlight. He was so big that the old man was afraid at first to give the signal. Then the dog began to eat great bites of meal. Finally, the old man gave the signal and everyone beat drums, shook their rattles, and shouted loudly. The dog was so scared that he ran around in a circle and then gave a giant leap straight up, and the meal pouring out of his mouth made a white trail across the sky. That is what we call the Milky Way and what the old Cherokees call to this day *Gil' Li'utsun' Stanun'yi*, which means, Where the dog ran."

Mitch had been watching her as she talked, her voice soft and melodious, as smooth as rippling water. He was entranced, transported almost, as though he had known these words and the rhythm of them in another lifetime. For the first time in his memory, he felt a strong connection to his father and to his father's ancestors.

When she looked around to find him studying her intently, she gave a self-conscious little laugh and said, "They're about to start dancing. Want to try it?"

"Who, me?" Mitch chuckled. "I don't think so."

"Well, I'm going." Her eyes were dancing with excitement.

"Go ahead. I'll watch."

Some of the teenage girls and younger women had tied terrapin shells filled with stones to their legs. They began to move with quick, sliding steps, stomping their heels on the ground to make the stones rattle in the shells. Stomp-slide, stomp-slide.

A group of men in the center of the clearing sang in Cherokee, and others pounded out the rhythm on small skin drums. People came into the circle behind the singers and drummers and the women wearing the shell rattles. They joined hands and moved in the same quick, stomp-slide steps as the women. The hiss of the turtle shells and the singing went on and on, the drums beating in the background, until it began to seem that the rhythm was coming from deep in the ground and entering Mitch's body. It was as though he could feel the earth's heartbeat.

Except for the area lighted by the fire, the night was dark, the woods beyond the ceremonial ground black and mysterious. In the brief intervals of silence, Mitch could hear the rustle of bare tree limbs as they moved in the wind, as though

Cherokee ghosts had gathered to whisper an accompaniment to the dancing.

Every once in a while, Crying Wolf held up his hands and everybody stopped dancing and shouted at the sky, like a single thunderous voice, whooping.

After a while, Mitch's butt felt numb from sitting and he was stiff with cold. He got up and walked around for a while. Then he found the food Rhea had prepared and put a couple of chicken legs and fry bread on a paper plate. The apple pie a la mode he'd eaten earlier hadn't stayed with him. He refilled his mug with coffee from the pot that simmered on the camp stove and took the food back to his bench. Shortly Rhea joined him, smiling and breathless and combing her hair back from her face with both hands. She looked about sixteen years old.

"Doesn't it look like fun?"

Mitch gnawed the last bit of meat from a chicken leg before he said, "Yes, it does. I don't know what I expected. Fancy headdresses and costumes like I've seen at powwows, I guess."

She laughed. "Powwows are as much for the tourists as they are for us. This is just for us."

"As soon as I'm through here, I might try it."

"Oh, good." She waited patiently while he finished eating. Then she grabbed his hand and pulled him into the circle where a boy about ten years old grinned at him and took his other hand. Mitch watched Rhea and imitated the steps she took. It was easy. Before long, he didn't notice the cold. Soon he was actually enjoying the dancing and feeling himself a part of the circling Cherokees. His people. When Rhea said she was going to get something to eat, he stayed with the dancers.

Later, after Rhea introduced him to everybody he hadn't yet met, they sat side by side on a Bird clan bench, eating peach cobbler from paper bowls. In the clearing, the dancing continued.

"What are they singing?" Mitch asked.

She lifted her head and listened for a moment. "This one is a love song. A young man is casting a spell on the woman he's attracted to. He's saying that she will soon be gazing at him all the time, she'll be unable to look away from him."

Mitch couldn't believe it was close to 5:00 A.M. when people began gathering their things and leaving. They had been there for five hours, and it seemed like about an hour to him.

The spell of the evening clung to him even after he had dropped Rhea and Crying Wolf off at her house and gone home. His house was cold and unwelcoming without Emily. The creak of the stairs as he climbed them in the darkness was like the protesting of old bones.

He realized that his calves were sore as he crawled into bed. They'd be even sorer tomorrow. A small price to pay for the most fun he'd had in a while.

Just before he fell asleep, it occurred to him that he hadn't thought of Lisa all evening. He'd been too involved in the present moment as he became a part of ancient ceremonies and tribal oneness. It was much bigger than any one person.

Keeping busy, he thought sleepily, was the antidote to unhappiness.

12

He was measuring coffee grounds into the Mr. Coffee the next morning when Emily ran into the house. "Forgot my history book," she said and disappeared.

"Hey," he called after her. "Who won the ball game?"

"We did," she called back. "By one point in overtime." She ran upstairs and, a few minutes later, ran back down.

"Forgot to tell you," she said at the kitchen doorway. "Lisa called yesterday afternoon. The phone was ringing when I got home from school."

Mitch turned on the coffee maker. "Oh?"

"We had a good talk, about her new job and what was happening here. She wanted you to call her. I'm sorry I forgot to leave you her message."

"I wouldn't have had time, anyway. I was busy last night."

Emily frowned. "Was there a car wreck or something?"

"No. I spent the night at a stomp dance."

"Really?" Her smile was delighted. "Did you actually *dance?*"

"Yep."

"That is *so* cool, Daddy. I wish I could have gone with you. Would you take me to one sometime?"

Cool? Emily never failed to surprise him. "Why, sure. When the weather warms up, they'll have them regularly."

"Great. I *am* a quarter Cherokee, you know. I'd kind of like to know more about it."

Another surprise. She'd never mentioned that before. "Okay."

"Cool," she said again. "Oh, and don't forget about Lisa."

He murmured noncommitally and reached for the *Tulsa World*, which he had earlier retrieved from the front walk. He sat down at the table and opened it.

Emily hesitated in the doorway. "You will call her, won't you?"

"I don't know."

He could feel her staring at him. "Why are you acting so strange?"

He lowered the paper, stuck out his tongue, and crossed his eyes. "I've always been strange. You just now noticing?"

"Dad-dy," Emily groaned. "What's going on with you and Lisa?"

"Nothing." He lifted the newspaper. "She's in California. I'm here. What could be going on?"

There was a silence during which he didn't look out from behind his paper. Finally Emily sighed and said, "I have to go to school. See you later."

When he heard the front door close behind her, Mitch laid the newspaper on the table. What did Lisa want from him, anyway? Permission to see somebody else? Someone to talk to about her budding romance with the college administrator? *Was she sleeping with him?* Stop that, he told himself. Maybe Lisa just wanted to know he wasn't angry with her anymore.

But as he recalled their last conversation, he couldn't think what else they had to say to each other. It occurred to him that he might be sulking, but he didn't care. He wasn't going to call her. What was the point?

A little later that morning, Mitch drove by the Kirkwoods' house and left the china plate with Polly at the door. She wanted him to come in for a cup of coffee, but he pleaded urgent police business. Stopping by the Chevrolet dealership en route to the station, he found Elwin Marshall, the owner, in his office wearing a bright-plaid flannel shirt, his feet, in tasseled loafers, on his desk, and a big mug of coffee, with a big-busted woman painted on it, in one hand.

When Mitch walked in, Marshall set his mug down and threw up his hands. "Don't shoot, Chief. I'm innocent." Then he laughed uproariously at his own humor. Marshall's laugh was high and shrill, like a teenage girl's, an immature teenage girl. Come to think of it, his jokes were pretty adolescent too.

Mitch dropped into a chair. "That's what they all say, Elwin."

"You mean I ain't original?"

He was an original, all right. "Not hardly."

"Shucks." Marshall took his feet off the desk. He was a ro-bust man with a ruddy complexion, getting a good-sized belly on him. From sitting behind the desk with his feet up too much of the time, Mitch thought. Marshall scooted forward in his chair so he could prop his elbows where his heels had rested. There was what looked like a toast crumb, left from his breakfast, clinging to his chin. "You want some coffee, Chief?"

"No, thanks."

"Hey, you heard the one about the traveling salesman and the widow woman?" He proceeded to tell the joke without waiting for Mitch's response. In fact, Mitch had heard it be-fore, several times. The joke was so old it had cataracts. He tried not to stare at the toast crumb, which bobbed up and down as Marshall talked. When Marshall finished, he laughed loudly, even though he'd probably told it at least a hundred times before. The toast crumb wobbled precariously but didn't fall off Marshall's chin.

When he stopped laughing, Mitch asked, "You rented many trucks lately, Elwin?"

Marshall looked a little glum as he picked up his mug and slurped some coffee. "Not so's you'd notice. We're lucky to rent out a truck every month or two. Two rentals a month is a boom. Tell you the truth, I been thinking about getting out of the rental business. Can't make any money with those dang trucks sitting on the lot, taking up space, and depreciating every day."

"When was the last time you rented one?"

"Let me think, now." He wheeled his chair back to lift his loafered feet up on the desk. "Must've been three, four weeks ago. Guy was moving over the weekend. Took out a big truck with a dolly on Friday, brought it back Sunday night."

"What time Sunday night?"

Marshall took another sip of coffee. "Don't know. He left the truck in the lot with the keys under the driver's seat. It was here when I opened up Monday morning."

"Did he use a credit card?"

His brow creased with thought. "Can't remember. I can find out in a minute, though." He set his mug down, wheeled around to face a metal file cabinet, pulled out the middle drawer, and leafed through some folders. "Here we go." He extracted a folder and opened it. "No credit card. He paid cash in advance for the whole weekend."

"You got his name there?"

"Sure." He scanned the sheet again. "Bill Smith."

"You saw his driver's license?"

"Yep." He glanced up at Mitch. "What're you looking for, Chief?"

"Just following up an idea I had. Several of the horse ranchers around here have been burglarized lately. Ten burglaries in the last six weeks, always on a weekend. I thought maybe the thieves were renting a van to haul the goods."

"If they are, they ain't getting it here. Like I said, this fellow is the only rental customer I've had in the last couple of months."

"This Bill Smith, do you know him?"

"Nope. Never saw him before or since."

"Can you describe him?"

He shook his head. "Not really. He was young, about your height, I guess. Six foot, six-one." He frowned. "That's about all I can recall. I had a buyer waiting, money burning a hole in his pocket, and I was anxious to get back to him. Bought a new Camaro loaded with all the bells and whistles. That's where my profit is, you know, in selling new cars."

Mitch felt discouraged. But, then, he guessed it would have been too easy if he'd discovered where the thieves were getting the truck on the first try. They could be going to a different place every time they needed one, of course, so as not to arouse suspicion. The only Bill Smith he knew of in Buckskin was about sixty-five years old. But if the young guy who rented Marshall's truck was one of the thieves, he'd have given a false name and have had a fake license to match.

When Mitch reached the station, he called Shelly and Duck into his office and sent them to find out where Alice Browne and Earlene Downing were the previous Monday night, preferably from somebody besides Browne and Downing.

They reported back within the hour. Alice Browne's roommate said that she and Alice had gone to their room together Monday evening, and neither of them had left again until they went to breakfast the next morning. Earlene Downing's husband, whom Duck had tracked down at the local high school where he taught social studies, said she was at home with him from about five-thirty Monday evening until Tuesday morning.

That virtually eliminated Browne and Downing as suspects. Since Jason and Jessie Hatch had been eliminated too—more or less—Mitch was left wondering what to do next. He remembered Henderson Sixkiller and, more out of desperation than anything else, told Duck to go to the Hatch house—in Duck's car, not a patrol car—make himself unobtrusive and keep an eye out for Henderson Sixkiller for the rest of the day. If Jessie left the house, he was to follow her.

Then Mitch got a call from the chairman of the city council, wanting to know what progress had been made in the investigation of Tyler Hatch's murder. After all, Hatch had been a respected citizen of the town, and the council members were getting concerned calls from other respected citizens. The chairman went on and on about what a loss Hatch's death was to the town. He evidently didn't know Hatch had been a wife beater. And he would be skeptical of it, now that Hatch was dead, so Mitch didn't bother telling him. Instead, he assured the chairman that he had some promising leads, but it was going to take some time to follow up on all of them. That seemed to satisfy the man for the time being.

Mitch hung up, grumbling to himself about the irritations involved in being a city employee in a small town. Then he put the city council out of his mind and pulled the Hatch file to bring his notes up to date. There was little enough real information to add. He made a note of his conversation with Rhea Vann the previous evening, stating that the doctor had reiterated her certainty about not hitting Hatch at the base of the skull, adding his opinion that she was telling the truth.

He dropped his pen and leaned back in his chair. It squeaked loudly, reminding him that he needed to bring the WD-40 from home and give the chair's swivel mechanism a few squirts. Idly, he picked up the Hatch file and leafed through it, in case something jumped out at him that he'd missed before. Nothing did.

He closed the file and tossed it on the desk. If Duck located Henderson Sixkiller, and they could prove he'd been in town Monday night, they might finally have a suspect they could build a case against. If Sixkiller didn't turn up, however . . .

Which was a real possibility, Mitch admitted to himself. Maybe he should go back out to the Job Corps Center and talk to some more people. Maybe he'd learn of other women Hatch had been involved with. Might even turn up a jealous husband or two. Or a jealous boyfriend.

Wait a minute. Rhea Vann had said something about a jealous boyfriend, hadn't she? He went through last evening's conversation at her house, trying to remember, until finally he had it. Marilee Steiner had talked to Rhea about Tyler Hatch because she couldn't talk to her boyfriend, who was jealous of the friendship. Hmmm. Maybe the boyfriend thought it was more than friendship.

Marilee had mentioned her boyfriend's name. Hammer, Hasher, something like that . . . Handler, that was it. Charlie

Handler. Mitch grabbed the phone book and turned to the *H*'s. Only one Handler was listed, Roy Handler, east of the city. He reached for the phone.

When a woman answered, he said, "Is Charlie there?"

"No. He's at work. Who's this?"

"I'm a friend of Charlie's. When do you expect him home?"

"He doesn't live here. He stays in town."

"Do you have his phone number?"

"He rents a sleeping room. He has his own phone, though." She gave Mitch the number.

"What about his work number?"

"I don't have it handy, but it's that shopping-cart factory out at the industrial park. They're in the book."

Mitch hung up and dialed Charlie Handler's home phone. No answer. He looked at his watch. If he hurried, he might catch Charlie Handler before he took his lunch break.

"I don't follow you. What is this all about?"

Charlie Handler did look puzzled. He was about twenty-five, Mitch guessed, medium height and build, with dark-blond hair cut long enough to cover his ears and sweep in a wave across his forehead. He was very ordinary-looking, except for his eyes, which were an arresting bright blue. Mitch bet those eyes drove the ladies crazy.

Mitch had stopped en route to issue a traffic ticket and therefore hadn't arrived until after noon. But he'd tracked Handler down in the employee lunchroom. The man sitting with Handler excused himself when Mitch asked if he could speak to Handler. Unlike the other people in the lunchroom, who were dressed in gray work shirts and trousers, Handler wore a dress shirt and tie. He explained that he worked in the office. He was the sales manager, a job that required him to be on the road, calling on customers, about a third of the time. As he talked, the few remaining employees vacated the lunchroom, leaving Handler alone with Mitch.

"I'm investigating a murder," Mitch said.

He looked startled. "Whose murder?"

"Tyler Hatch. Know him?"

"No. I've heard the name." He pulled off a piece of cheese-and-ham sandwich and stuck it in his mouth.

"From Marilee Steiner?"

He frowned. "Yeah, probably. Hatch worked at the Job Corps Center and Marilee was a student there. What's Marilee got to do with this?"

"What did she tell you about Hatch?"

He put his sandwich down. "I don't remember her telling me anything about him. To tell you the truth, I'm not even sure she ever mentioned him to me."

"You just said you'd heard his name from Marilee."

"I meant I *might* have, because she was at the center. But I don't really remember." He took a drink of Coke from a can. "I wish you'd tell me what this is all about."

"According to Miss Steiner, you had dinner with her last Monday night and then the two of you went to your place to watch a video."

The brilliant blue eyes clouded over with irritation. "What about it?"

"She said you were running late, so you asked her to meet you at the restaurant. Why were you running late, Mr. Handler?"

He stared at Mitch. "Hey, hold on here," he said with a snap of his fingers. "Monday night. That's when Hatch was killed."

"You seem to know quite a bit about it."

He shrugged. "Just what was in yesterday's paper."

Mitch had forgotten. The local weekly, which came out on Thursdays, had carried the story on the front page. "Please answer my question, Mr. Handler. Where were you Monday evening before you met Marilee for dinner?"

"Look, I didn't even know this Hatch guy. Why are you asking me these questions?"

"Because you didn't like Tyler Hatch. You were jealous of his relationship with Miss Steiner."

"Jealous!"

Mitch could sense his rage, though he was struggling to contain it. And his eyes had gone past cloudy to downright stormy.

"What the hell are you talking about?" He paused. "What relationship?"

"Miss Steiner has already admitted to me that she and Hatch were close."

"Close?" He shot to his feet, tipping his chair on its back. "You better not be saying what I think you're saying, mister!"

Mitch rose slowly from his chair. He had three or four inches on Handler and, besides that, he was wearing a gun. "What is it you think I'm suggesting here, Mr. Handler?"

"That Marilee was screwing Hatch, dammit!"

"That's not what I said," Mitch said calmly. "I said they were close."

"Exactly what do you mean by *close?*" he demanded.

"Miss Steiner says Hatch was largely responsible for her getting off drugs and staying off. I can't believe she hasn't told you this."

He glared at Mitch. "She may have mentioned it a time or two."

"And every time she did, you acted jealous, so she didn't talk about Hatch to you again."

He was breathing audibly through his nose. He studied Mitch, his eyes narrowed. "That's a load of crap."

"Not according to an unimpeachable source."

"Source? Oh, yeah, that's what you cops say when you're really making something up."

Mitch didn't rise to the bait, merely stared at him.

"I had no reason to be jealous of Hatch," Handler went on. "Marilee left the Job Corps Center not long after we started dating, and neither of us has dated anyone else since." Mitch wondered how sure of Marilee's faithfulness he really was. She was a fine-looking young woman. Furthermore, Handler was out of town a lot, and his reactions to Mitch's questions seemed a bit too strong for someone who had complete faith in his girlfriend.

Handler bent over and jerked his fallen chair upright. "If you'll excuse me, I have to get back to work."

Mitch came around the table. "Not until you've answered my question. I want a rundown of your activities last Monday evening and night."

He stood there with his hands clenched at his sides, his jaw working, until he got control of himself. "I was at my folks' house, east of town, near the lake, from about four o'clock until after six-thirty. I called Marilee from there and we made plans for dinner later. I hadn't been out to my parents' place for several weeks. I'd been out of town, calling on customers, and when I'm here I spend most of my off-work time with Marilee. Anyway, my folks and I got to talking and the time slipped away from me. When I realized it was too late to go to town and pick up Marilee and make it back in time for our dinner reservation, I phoned and asked her to meet me at the lodge."

"Eagle's Nest Lodge?"

He nodded. "That's where we had dinner."

For some reason, Mitch had assumed they'd met at a restaurant in town. But he knew better than to assume anything in an investigation. He should have asked. "Go on," he said.

"Marilee wasn't happy about having to meet me. But she did, and we had dinner and went to my apartment. Well, it's just a sleeping room, really. It's in Buckskin on Sixth Street. My landlady has a rule that guests have to leave by midnight, but we stretched it a little. Marilee left about fifteen minutes after twelve. When I called her from my folks' house, she was real upset about Hatch breaking into the clinic that afternoon, and she was still pretty tense at dinner. That nut case crashing through the window really shook her. But by the time she went home, she'd calmed down."

So Marilee had told him about Hatch breaking into the clinic, and Handler had lied when he said he couldn't remember her mentioning Hatch to him. Why had he lied?

"When she left—" Charlie hesitated.

"What?"

"Nothing really. It's just that she seemed kind of down. Said maybe we shouldn't see each other till she was feeling better." He shrugged. "Marilee is moody. I've seen her depressed before. She always comes out of it in a few days. I told her to call me as soon as she got home, so I'd know she was okay. She called in about ten minutes. Then I went to bed."

Mitch could check with Handler's landlady to see if he was lying about going straight to bed. She would probably know if he'd left the house after Marilee went home. But if Handler had killed Hatch, he could have done it *before* he met Marilee at the lodge for dinner. That could be the real reason he hadn't had time to go to town and pick up Marilee. Driving to the lodge, he would have been in the right place to run into Hatch on the road. He could even have phoned Hatch from his parents' house and asked him to meet him there.

But if that's what happened, what was his motive? Why did he choose that particular time, when he had a dinner date at the lodge? Had Marilee's talking about Hatch coming to the clinic sent him into a jealous rage? Clearly, Handler had a temper. Maybe it wasn't jealousy at all. Maybe he'd exploded because he thought Hatch was out to harm Marilee. Or maybe she'd told him something else that set him off.

"Why did you lie to me, Mr. Handler?"

"What lie?"

"You said you couldn't remember Marilee mentioning Hatch to you. Now you're saying she talked about him Monday evening. Why?"

He shrugged. "I didn't want to get involved."

Duck checked in at the station that afternoon before going off duty. He'd spent the whole day, except for a quick lunch break, watching Jessie Hatch's house. The woman hadn't set foot outside, not once.

13

Henderson Sixkiller sat in the dark eating chicken-noodle soup, the last can of soup in the cabin. All that was left now was a can of pork 'n beans and another of tomato sauce.

But he'd been thinking all day about leaving. Sitting in the cabin with nothing to do was getting to him. Hatch was out of the way and Jessie would probably be okay. She was in a financial bind, but he couldn't help her there, and he figured she could get welfare benefits if she couldn't find a job. He hadn't seen her since he'd tapped on her kitchen window and she'd let him in the house.

When was that? Tuesday night? Wednesday? He thought today was Friday, but he wasn't sure. He was losing track of time. His throat was sore and he thought he was feverish again too. His skin felt hot and dry to the touch.

In addition to being sick, he was downright depressed. When he showed up at Jessie's house, she sure hadn't thrown him a welcome-home party. She'd acted kind of weird and panicky. But he'd figured she was still in a state of shock over Hatch's murder. Now he wasn't so sure. He wondered if she'd just wanted to get him out of the house before the boys realized he was there. He'd left, feeling indignant and hurt. After all, he broke out of jail to save her, and she didn't seem to appreciate it at all. She'd said it was stupid. She'd said she had enough trouble without him showing up and what on earth was she supposed to do now? Like he was the cause of all her problems. She didn't want him hanging around her and the boys, that was for sure. Like his old cellmate always said: The people you try to help are the first ones to turn on you.

If he left, where would he go? The Buckskin Police were probably looking for him, and the longer he hung around, the better chance they had of catching him. He'd reached the point the last few hours, he'd even been thinking that getting caught might not be so bad. At least, in jail he could get a decent shower, clean clothes, and hot meals. He'd rinsed out his shirt—yesterday, he thought it was—and had taken another spit bath and walked around with the blanket over his shoulders while the shirt dried. But he could already smell himself again.

When he realized how low his food supply was, the thought had flashed through his mind that he might just throw in the towel, walk to town, and turn himself in. He wasn't the kind of guy who could go to another part of the country, find a job, and live the rest of his life as somebody else. He wasn't lucky enough or clever enough. The fact that he was Indian would make him stand out in a place where there weren't as many as there were in Cherokee County. He'd be apprehended sooner or later.

If he turned himself in, maybe they'd give him less prison time for the jailbreak than if he waited until they caught up with him. He vacillated between the two alternatives, unable to make up his mind. The last day or two, he didn't seem to be thinking too clearly. He probably wasn't getting enough to eat, besides which, he was so blue that it had been an effort to get on his feet and open the can of soup.

He finished the soup and sat, staring toward where he knew a window was. It was too dark to see it, and he didn't have enough energy to go in search of the flashlight. He wondered if it was late enough to go to bed. It got dark early, and the trees were too thick to let in the moonlight, so it could be anytime from six or seven to midnight. He wished he could think straight, figure out what to do.

If he went outside and walked around a while, maybe the activity and the cold air would clear the fog out of his brain. He felt a little frisson of unease at the thought of going out in the dark. But he hadn't seen that light since the first night he'd spent in the cabin, and he'd almost convinced himself he'd dreamed it. He sat there a while longer, until he lost consciousness. He woke up with a jerk of his head, his neck stiff.

How long had he slept? He made himself stand up. Needles pricked his feet. Damn, they'd gone to sleep. He yelped and stomped them a few times. Then he felt around in the dark for his coat. It was several moments before he realized he was wearing it. He found the blanket, wrapped it around his shoulders, and let himself out of the cabin.

He forced his feet to keep moving and walked away from the cabin. He didn't consciously choose a direction. It was so dark in the woods that one direction was as good as another. Eventually he'd end up at the lake or on a road or in somebody's field. He could figure out then where he was and where he wanted to go from there.

For about the tenth time, Amos Flycatcher walked through his house, checking the locks on windows and doors. Then he stood in the dark in his kitchen and peered out at the woods through a couple of slats in the horizontal blinds.

After four days at his son's house, he'd had to come home. That morning, Mark had hinted strongly that he'd overstayed his welcome. Mark thought the story about the Fire Carrier was just an excuse for Amos not to stay at his own house, now that Mark's mother had left.

Still, Amos thought it was really Mark's wife who wanted him out, but she'd made Mark tell him. That uppity Choctaw woman had never liked Amos. Well, he wasn't crazy about her, either, and he could take a hint. He'd tinkered with his old car until he got it started, about ten that morning. After picking up a six-pack of beer and a bottle of scotch, he'd returned to the house he'd shared with his wife, who still wouldn't take his phone calls. She'd talked to Mark, though, and had told him she was going to see a lawyer about a divorce. Amos was resigned to it now.

He'd been home for hours and he hadn't opened the scotch, which ought to prove that he didn't have a drinking problem. He had nursed the last can of beer while he ate a bologna sandwich for supper, but Amos didn't believe beer was strong enough to make you an alcoholic, even if that woman doctor at the clinic had as much as called him one. Tried to get him to go to an AA meeting. What he didn't need was to sit around listening to a bunch of alkies on the wagon, telling how pathetic they used to be when they drank, "sharing," they called it, trying to outgross each other.

No denying, the house was lonely with his wife gone. But he'd been feeling fine until it got dark. Then he'd started to realize how loud the ticking of the kitchen clock was. It had never bothered him before, but after an hour of trying to ignore it, he'd finally grabbed it off the wall, wrapped it in a blanket, and stuck it in a bedroom closet where he couldn't hear it.

By then his nerves were frazzled, and he started to think about that bottle of scotch in the cabinet. But he was determined to prove he didn't need it, so whenever he started feeling like he was going to jump out of his skin, he'd check the windows and doors again, even though he could remember clearly the last time he'd checked them and knew they were locked. Then he'd go stand at the kitchen window for a while. He figured if he stood there long enough, he'd get so tired, from sheer boredom if nothing else, he could sleep. Part of the time, he knew that wasn't actually why he was standing there in the dark, but he was trying not to think about the real reason.

He wondered what time it was. Ten o'clock, at least. Until recently, he'd always watched the ten o'clock news, but now he didn't want to turn on the TV. He wanted it quiet, so he could hear if somebody tried to get into the house.

Thinking about an intruder reminded him of the bottle of scotch again. In truth, everything reminded him of that scotch. He was halfway across the kitchen, going to check the windows, when he stopped himself. This was crazy stuff. He *knew* the windows were locked. Was he losing his mind?

He turned around and went back to the window, just in time

to see a light flickering through the woods. He froze. The light floated slowly from east to west, disappearing when it moved behind several trees growing close together, but reappearing again on the other side.

The Fire Carrier was back!

Amos's heart slammed against his ribs, pounding in his ears louder than the noise the kitchen clock had made before he'd put it in the closet. He tried to calm himself, reminded himself that the house was locked up tight. But since when did locks keep out the Fire Carrier? He'd heard tales about him going through solid brick walls like they weren't even there.

He jumped back from the window and stumbled through the dark kitchen to the cabinet. He didn't have to prove anything, did he? To hell with that. He took down the scotch, opened it, and drank straight from the bottle. The liquor burned warmly in his chest for a moment, then the warmth spread throughout his body, and shortly he began to feel a little calmer.

He went back to the window, stood there for several minutes, but the light didn't reappear. At first, he was greatly relieved, but then it occurred to him that only when he could see the light did he know where the Fire Carrier was. Now, he could be any-where—moving toward the house, right outside the front door.

Oh, Lord. He took another slug of scotch.

He should never have come back to the house. It was too iso-lated. He was a sitting duck out here. He couldn't stay. He had to get out, go back to town. He thought he had enough cash on him for a cheap motel room, but he'd sleep in the car if he had to. He got his coat from the living-room couch where he'd thrown it when he came in, put it on, and felt for his car keys in the coat pocket.

Before he left the house, he walked through it once more, looking out every window. He didn't see the light. He tucked the bottle in a coat pocket and quietly unlocked the door leading from the kitchen into the attached garage. He opened the door a crack and listened, but heard nothing. He raised the garage door, which seemed to make enough noise to wake every corpse in the nearest graveyard.

Pursued by the demons in his mind, he ran to his car and got in. After assuring himself that all the doors were locked, he stuck the key into the ignition and turned it. Nothing happened. His hand shaking, he tried again. And again and again. He tried a dozen times. Each time he heard a click, but the engine wouldn't turn over. The battery was dead. The damned car wouldn't start! Cursing, he jerked the key out of the ignition and flung it to the floorboard.

Panic threatened to overcome him. He swigged scotch and tried to think what to do next. The only thing that was perfectly clear to him was that he had to get out of there. He had to get to town where there were other people. The last time he saw the light, it had been moving away from the highway. He would go the other direction. If he could reach the highway, he could hitch a ride to town.

He opened the glove compartment and got his flashlight. He'd need it if he was going to walk through the woods. He got out of the car and crept from the garage. He heard nothing but the far-off howl of a coyote, and he saw no light. Leaving the garage door open, because closing it would make too much noise and signal to the Fire Carrier his intent to leave the house, he walked as fast as he dared, into the inky blackness of the woods.

Mitch switched off the TV and turned out the downstairs lights. He went upstairs and tapped on Emily's bedroom door.

"Just a sec. Come on in, Daddy."

She was lying on her bed in a pink flannel nightgown, with her hand between her mouth and the telephone receiver.

It was almost midnight. "Who're you talking to?" Mitch asked.

"Jimmy."

She'd left the house with Jimmy Doolittle at seven-thirty and he'd brought her home half an hour ago. They'd taken in a movie, then gone for a Coke, Emily had told him. While he was waiting for her to come home, Mitch had pictured them in Jimmy's old Pontiac, parked in the local lovers' lane, a country road between Buckskin and the lake. Over the years, he'd rousted a number of teenage couples parked out there. So he'd been tempted to ask if Emily and Jimmy had gone there after the movie. He was pretty sure she wouldn't tell him if they had, so he'd kept the question to himself. Why force her to lie to him?

Now she was on the phone with Jimmy Doolittle. What in heck could they have to say to each other after spending four hours in each other's company?

Emily was looking at him expectantly, waiting for him to explain what he wanted. "Just wanted to say good night, sweetheart," he said. "You better get to sleep soon too." He bent to kiss her forehead.

"Okay. 'Night, Daddy." By the time Mitch closed the door behind him, she was saying, "It was just my dad. What were we talking about? Oh, yes . . . I can't *believe* he actually said that, Jimmy! That is *so* majorly cheesy."

Just my dad. It kind of put Mitch in his place.

He went into his bedroom and undressed in the dark, wishing Emily felt a need to talk to *him* when they'd been apart for a short time. An unrealistic wish, he knew. He was just feeling sorry for himself. Virgil, speaking from his own experience with his kids, had told him that all teenagers pulled away from their parents, wanting to establish their independence. He was just feeling at loose ends, had all evening. He had been so restless at one point that he'd almost phoned Lisa. But then he thought she probably wouldn't be at home, she'd be in class or out with the college administrator.

It was over with Lisa, and the best thing to do was to let it go. Lisa had as much as said it.

This long-distance relationship isn't working.

Well, she was right about that. He wondered for a moment if that remark had been a subtle ultimatum. Before she left town, she'd suggested he come out to California and look for a job, which was the last thing he was interested in doing. Even if staying behind meant losing her.

She'd probably called yesterday only because she was feeling sorry for him. He didn't want her pity.

14

Henderson Sixkiller heard the crackling sound of limbs moving in the tree beneath which he'd stopped to rest. His heart leaped in his chest, but he was too exhausted to move, even to save himself.

He wondered if it was the *Uk'ten'*, the huge serpent with seven spots that Ma used to talk about. He wondered if the monster had crawled out on a limb to sleep, and if his stumbling up to its tree had awakened it. Perhaps if he didn't move, the monster would go back to sleep.

He imagined the serpent dropping off its branch right on top of him, its huge coils enveloping him and squeezing . . .

He shuddered and shook the image away. If he kept this up, he'd be a raving lunatic when he was found.

If he was found.

Sixkiller had finally admitted that he was well and truly lost. He'd walked for what seemed hours, but he hadn't found either the lake or the highway. He must have been walking in circles.

Sometime after he left the cabin, he'd had a chill that rattled his teeth and made his body shake as though with palsy. Now he was so hot, he threw the blanket off him with a grunt.

The branch overhead creaked again. He tried to gather enough strength to get to his feet, but halfway up he fell back against the tree. He told himself it couldn't be the *Uk'ten'* up there in the tree because the creature had been destroyed.

Ma's stories had always ended with a Cherokee warrior killing the monster with an arrow, smack in the middle of the monster's seventh spot.

He hadn't seen the Fire Carrier since he left the cabin, either. He just had monsters on the brain tonight.

If only he could find a house or the highway. His granddad had been lost once and, according to Ma, the Little People had found him and led the old man home. Sixkiller wished they'd find him.

"*Anigunehiyat,*" he said aloud, as if uttering their Cherokee name would make them appear. There was a loud *Whooo* and the sound of flapping wings overhead. He nearly jumped out of his skin until it registered that his voice had disturbed an owl perched in the tree.

Only an owl, not a monster.

An owl could be a harbinger of death, but you had to hear it three nights running in the same place. If he was still here the third night, he'd *want* to die.

He wasn't ready to call it quits yet. But he was losing touch with reality, and if he didn't get up, he would die where he lay. He clutched the blanket with one hand and braced the other hand against the rough tree trunk. Slowly, he got to his feet. He stood, leaning against the tree for a moment, breathing deeply. He couldn't guess how cold it was because of his fever. It wasn't nearly as cold as it had been the nights he'd trekked from the Delaware County Jail to Buckskin, but he knew it was too cold to let himself fall asleep on the ground.

A warm, dry jail cell was beginning to be more and more appealing.

He had to keep walking. If dawn found him still lost in the woods, daylight should enable him to find his way out. This night seemed endless, but surely it was almost past. Nothing lasted forever. He couldn't give up now. He'd heard tales of lost people who'd given up and died on the very edge of civilization, people lost in a snowstorm who'd died a few feet from a dwelling.

He draped the blanket around his shoulders again and trudged on through the trees.

Amos Flycatcher was hiding behind a bush whose bare limbs were covered with needle-sharp thorns. He'd discovered the bush had thorns too late, when he'd seen the flickering light again and dived for the bare suggestion of a form that might provide cover. Thorns had scraped the flesh of both hands as he hit the ground. He'd gritted his teeth against the pain and licked the blood that oozed from the scratches.

Only then did it occur to him that it was too dark for him to be seen, anyway. He didn't need to seek cover. Except maybe he did. For all he knew, the Fire Carrier could see in the dark. For all Amos knew, the Fire Carrier could see through solid objects, and, if so, he could certainly see Amos sprawled behind a pitiful little thorn bush.

The batteries in his flashlight had gone dead a while ago. He couldn't see the light from where he lay and he thought he ought to get up. But he couldn't seem to muster the energy. He lay on his belly on the cold ground and his eyes filled with hot, self-pitying tears. His fear had reduced him to a blubbering baby. No wonder his wife had left him. He was a sorry excuse for a man.

If he didn't get up and keep moving, his muscles would lock up on him and he wouldn't be able to go on. The last of the scotch would settle his nerves and give him the confidence he needed to press ahead. He reached into his pocket for the bottle and felt nothing. The other pocket was empty too. He must have lost it when he dived for the bush. He raised up on his knees and felt the ground all around. The bottle wasn't there. He'd lost it somewhere back behind him, before he saw the light.

Aw, what was the use?

He was going to die out here. Then his wife would be sorry she left him. Serve her right. He imagined himself dressed up in a suit in a satin-lined casket, and his eyes filled with tears again. Angrily, he wiped them away with the heel of his hand. *Get hold of yourself, Amos.*

He rose to his knees and peered over the bush. The light was gone. Struggling upright, he made himself walk on, ignoring the pain in his feet, holding both hands out in front of him to detect obstructions in his path before he rammed his face into them.

He was still headed in what he thought was the direction of the highway, though he couldn't be sure. But Amos had always had a good sense of direction, and now wasn't the time to stop trusting his instincts.

Henderson Sixkiller couldn't walk another step. He was shaking again, the chill penetrating to his very bones. He'd come out of the thickest part of the woods and could see the glittering pinpoints of stars between bare tree branches. But he still didn't know where he was, and at that moment he really didn't care very much. He pulled the blanket up over his chin and gripped it more tightly around him. Slowly, he sank to the ground and leaned against the rough bark of a tree trunk.

Dawn couldn't be far away. He'd just close his eyes for a few minutes and wait for daylight to show him the way out of the woods.

He didn't know how long he slept, but when he jerked awake it was still dark. And he was stiff with cold. His throat was as raw as if he'd swallowed ground glass. He struggled to his feet, hugged the blanket under his chin, and leaned against the tree, breathing heavily.

Damn, he was sick of being sick, sick of smelling himself, sick to death of this unending night. He thought about how, when he was in jail, he used to dream of camping out in the woods, living off the land, free, self-sufficient, like a damned pioneer. Well, now that he had the chance, he'd give anything to see the lights of town. In his fantasies, it had always been summer, and the woods had been full of wild game, plump and ripe for the taking. He hadn't seen any wild game since he'd killed that rabbit almost a week ago, unless you counted the owl he'd scared out of its tree.

He'd never eaten owl, but right now he was hungry enough to try, if by some unlikely stroke of luck one happened to fall into his arms. He never thought he'd miss the starchy jail food, but he did. He hadn't had a square meal since he broke out.

He didn't think he could take much more. If he ever got out of here, he was giving himself up.

Groaning, he pushed away from the tree. Did he imagine it or was the night a little less black than before? Was dawn approaching, or was his feverish brain making him imagine things?

Maybe it was only that he'd found his way into what seemed to be a clearing in the woods. He looked up. Stars winked at him. The moon was a thin wedge of silver melon. There were no tall tangles of brush here, which made walking much easier. He was trudging along what seemed to be a trail or a narrow road.

For the first time in the last twenty-four hours, Sixkiller felt his depression lift. Dawn was coming, and he was going to make it out of there. He felt a little surge of energy and picked up his pace.

That's when he saw the light ahead of him. If he kept on his present course, he would run right into it. The light wasn't moving. Maybe it was attached to a house or a barn. He halted, torn between fear of running into the Fire Carrier and the possibility that help was straight ahead.

He stood there for long moments, agonizing over what to do—run forward or back into the woods. Still, the light did not move. He crept forward a few steps and stopped. Nothing happened. He took several more steps, stopped, listened. The light remained still. It *must* be a yard light near a farm house. Encouraged, Sixkiller walked on, slowly and quietly.

What was that?

He froze in his tracks, paralyzed by fear. He thought he heard people talking, but he wasn't close enough to hear what they were saying. He took several deep breaths and waited for his heart to stop flinging itself against the cage of his ribs.

In all the stories he'd heard of the Fire Carrier, there was never a mention of the evil creature speaking, or making any sound at all. He took a step, and then another. He stopped and held his breath to listen intently. Yes, it did sound like voices. Voices meant people and rescue.

As if he'd been restrained by a leash that was abruptly released, he ran toward the light. He could see now that it was attached to something. Not a house, though. A big truck of some sort. As he drew nearer, the voices became more distinct. The voices were male.

"Hey!" he shouted. They didn't seem to hear him, for the voices continued without a break. Then he realized that he hadn't shouted at all, he'd merely moaned.

The two men were only a few hundred yards ahead now. He could almost make them out—almost.

He swallowed painfully and opened his mouth. "I'm lost!" he shouted. "Help me. Please!"

The voices stopped. The almost-forms turned to watch him stagger toward them. Even when he was nearly upon them, he still could not make out their faces. But it didn't matter. They would save him.

"Oh, thank God," he panted. "I've found you."

No reply. That was odd, but maybe he had frightened them, running at them from the woods like an apparition. He must look scary, dragging his blanket, twigs sticking out of his hair. He came to a halt, swaying a few feet from them. Let them see that he meant them no harm. "I need help," he croaked.

One of the figures reached toward the truck, or into it—Sixkiller could not see well enough to know. Then the figure moved toward him slowly, paused, and raised its right arm which, Sixkiller now saw, held something—some kind of tool?

A flicker of panic raced through him. Why hadn't they spoken to him? Maybe he should introduce himself. "I'm—"

But that was as far as he got. The form moved in closer, and

Sixkiller stepped back. "I mean you no harm," he croaked, and caught his heel on something, and fell in a heap at the feet of what he could now plainly see was a menacing figure.

It bent over him, its right arm swooped down. The last thing Sixkiller saw was that thing in its hand, coming down directly over him, and one end of the crescent moon, like a tiny silver ornament attached to his attacker's head.

Dawn bruised the horizon when Amos Flycatcher came out of the woods. He had no idea where he was. In front of him was a narrow clearing with more woods on the other side of it. But the clearing extended left and right as far as he could see.

Just getting out of the woods made him feel hopeful, but he tamped down the feeling. Many times during the past few hours, he'd wanted to go back home, but he didn't know which direction home was. His once-dependable sense of direction had deserted him. He'd lost all hope of orienting himself. Now, with the lightening horizon visible to his left, he realized that left was east. But he'd wandered around all night. He didn't know what direction would take him out of there. He had begun to doubt, in fact, that he'd *ever* get out of there.

What he did know was that he didn't want to go back into the woods, if he could help it. He chose a direction arbitrarily and started walking west, putting one sore foot in front of the other like an automaton.

He must have trudged the length of a football field before he took any notice of the ground on which he walked. It was light enough to see that he was walking between two parallel paths of bare dirt that ran through the grassy clearing. The paths were four or five feet apart and about a foot wide. Odd, and he'd think about what it meant when he could, but right now the pain in his feet held his attention. He'd started on this night journey in the stiff, black dress shoes he'd put on that morning. Stupid. The shoes had rubbed blisters on both heels and the heels of both socks were wet. With blood, he feared, but he hadn't looked. Really, he didn't want to know. The soles of his feet hurt, too, and the little toe on his right foot felt as if it had a knife stuck in it.

He tried to ignore the pain in his feet. He had to keep walking. He peered at the ground. Instead of his feet, he'd think about those strange parallel paths. What could have made them so perfectly straight like that?

His brain finally clicked in and gave him the answer. Cars. This was a road of sorts. The paths had been made by tires. He stopped and bent closer to the ground and made out what looked like the tread of a tire. The road was in use, had been used recently.

A road had to begin somewhere and lead somewhere. All he had to do was follow it and he'd reach civilization. He let out a strangled whoop and began walking again. He was shaking, but not because he needed a drink, he told himself. He was trembling with exhaustion. He didn't want to think about a drink. He'd think about that when he got out of here. But the very first thing he'd do was soak his feet in hot salt water. The mere thought made him shiver with anticipation.

The next thing he'd do was take a little nip, just one, to get him back on an even keel. He wished he could walk faster, but his heels—he heard himself moaning softly now as each foot hit the ground. And he was crying, he realized in amazement, as he touched his cheek. It was wet.

Any minute now, he'd run into someone or a house or a road with cars traveling over it. He'd be rescued and this horrible nightmare would be over. He'd probably be crippled for life, though. He hoped his daughter-in-law and his wife would be satisfied.

Something lay on the path ahead. It looked like a big bundle of trash. And trash meant there were people not far away. He hurried toward the bundle, and stopped a few feet away.

It wasn't trash. It was a man with a blanket thrown over him, as though he'd bedded down right there on the ground and gone to sleep.

"Hello," Amos said loudly.

There was no reply.

He moved cautiously forward until he stood next to the man. "Hello," he said again and reached down to shake what looked like the shape of a shoulder beneath the blanket. The man groaned but didn't speak or try to get up.

Amos bent closer, and that was when he saw the bloody mat of hair on the side of the man's head. He was hurt! He'd run into something—or somebody had hit him. Amos whirled around and peered into the woods on both sides, but he heard nothing, saw nothing but trees.

He touched the blanket again, but the man didn't moan this time. Amos was afraid to turn him over. As weak as he was, he sure couldn't carry him, even if he wanted to. But he'd always heard that injured people should not be moved.

Had the injured man met up with the Fire Carrier? "Hold on, mister," Amos croaked. "As soon as I get out of here, I'll send help."

He started hobbling as fast as he could. His heels screamed with pain, but he kept on, shaking, his heart pounding, glancing over his shoulder every few steps to see if something was after him.

He had known the tire tracks had to lead to a road eventually, but when he actually reached a two-lane highway, he thought for a moment that it was a mirage, that he was imagining it.

Then he heard a car coming around a curve to his left. He stumbled into the center of the highway, and when the car appeared he began waving his arms frantically. "Help! Help!"

Brakes squealed and the car swerved off the road and came to a screeching halt on the shoulder. The driver's door flew open and an elderly, white-haired man crawled out. "Gawd Almighty, man! What is wrong with you? I almost hit you."

"I'm hurt," Amos gasped. "And there's a man in the woods hurt worse than me." He pointed toward the trail that angled off from the highway. "Back there, on that old road."

The old man hesitated, then left Amos standing there and got back in his car. "No!" Amos cried, thinking that the man meant to drive off and leave him. But he didn't close the driver's door. Instead, he picked up something and began to punch buttons. A car phone, Amos realized, and a wave of gratitude swept through him. It was so strong it made him sob.

The old man put the phone down. "I called for an ambulance and the police. My daughter made me put in the phone, said the time might come I'd be glad to have it. I guess that's now." He squinted at Amos. "The man in the woods, is he dead?"

"No," Amos said, his teeth chattering, he was shaking so hard, "but he's unconscious. I was afraid to try to move him."

"What happened to him?"

"Don't know. I found him—just a while ago. I felt bad, leaving him there, but . . ." Amos shrugged helplessly.

The old man nodded. "We'll have to let the police and the medics take care of him. You look like you could use some medical attention too. Get in."

15

Mitch caught sight of Amos Flycatcher as soon as he walked through the hospital emergency-room doors. Amos sat on the end of an examining table, in one of the cubbyholes with the curtain pushed back. He was clutching a short-tailed hospital gown over his privates. Both hands were bandaged with gauze and young Dr. Payner, a trauma-medicine resident from Tulsa, one of several who covered the emergency room on the weekends, was bent over him, examining his feet.

Mitch walked to the cubbyhole. Amos was jerking and trembling, and looked traumatized. "Hey, Amos. How're you doing?"

"Not so good, Chief." Amos groaned as the doctor dabbed at his poor, battered heels with Mercurochrome. "I'm hurt, and I'm sick enough to puke up my guts."

Payner looked up, startled. "You need a basin?"

Amos swallowed and shook his head.

Mitch wondered if Amos was suffering from DT's, and his suspicion seemed confirmed when Payner glanced at Mitch and lifted both his eyebrows. "He had quite a walk last night," Payner said.

"My car wouldn't start," Amos said defensively.

"His feet took a beating," Payner went on.

"Ruined a good pair of shoes too," Amos grumbled.

"We'll treat these feet," Payner said, looking at Mitch,

"keep 'em from getting infected and keep Mr. Flycatcher overnight."

"I kind of got lost," Amos whined to Mitch, then addressed Payner—"and I ain't staying here 'less I get something for pain."

"I've already ordered an injection for you," Payner said. "We'll put you to sleep so you can get a good rest. The nurse will be here any minute. I've got another patient to see." Payner disappeared behind a curtain two cubbyholes down from Amos's.

"You want me to call your son?" Mitch asked.

Amos was looking around for his injection. It wouldn't be alcohol, but any port in a storm, Mitch supposed. He hoped they'd put Amos in detox. Maybe they could talk him into entering rehab when he left the hospital.

"Hell, no," Amos said in answer to Mitch's question. "Wouldn't let me stay at his place. Sent me back out there . . ." He seemed to shake off some terrible image. "What about that guy in the woods, Chief?" he asked, his eyes still darting around in search of the nurse.

"The ambulance got there about the time I did," Mitch said. "He was semiconscious when they loaded him in the ambulance. Don't think he'd been out long. They're bringing him in now. Good thing you happened by, Amos."

Sixkiller, whom Mitch had recognized immediately, might not be too grateful, though. He perhaps would rather have taken his chances out in the woods with a head injury than get medical help and be returned to a cell.

"Thought he was a bag of trash at first," Amos mumbled. Suddenly, his expression changed from peevish to fearful. "I seen the Fire Carrier again last night, Chief. When I seen it was a man in the road, I thought *he* mighta been there."

Mitch wondered if Amos had been drunk at the time. "It was a human being that hit him, Amos."

Mitch heard the ambulance siren as a nurse bustled in. "Here's your injection, Mr. Flycatcher. We'll just pull the curtain, and you turn over on your side."

"Check you later, Amos," Mitch said and went to meet the ambulance attendants. He needed to ask Sixkiller a few questions, as soon as the man was coherent. He'd hang around until they moved Sixkiller to a room, then try to talk to him.

"It's coming back to me a little now, Chief," Sixkiller said, his voice still dulled by sleep. "The guy attacked me. Out of the blue. Never said a word, just grabbed something from his truck and hit me."

Sixkiller had spent four hours in the emergency room. Examinations had been made, X rays had been taken, the radiologist had arrived and given his report. In spite of all the blood, Sixkiller had merely suffered a concussion, not a skull fracture. Twenty-four hours of bed rest was prescribed, after which, if no other medical problems presented themselves, Sixkiller could be taken into custody.

Mitch had been left alone with Sixkiller for long periods of time in the emergency room, and had tried to question him there. But Sixkiller had been woozy and couldn't remember much of what had happened to him. Dr. Payner had told Mitch that the amnesia would be temporary, but he couldn't say exactly how long it would last.

So Mitch had spent most of the day in Sixkiller's room, dozing on and off in a chair, while Sixkiller slept. At noon, he'd gone to the cafeteria for lunch and had called to check on Emily, who planned to spend the afternoon with Temple and two other girlfriends. Something about meeting with the youth minister at the Methodist church to plan a teen retreat.

"I'm sorry I had to leave before you got up this morning," he'd said. He hadn't wanted to wake her so early on a Saturday, so he'd left a note on her bedside table.

"It's okay, Daddy."

"I haven't seen a lot of you lately. When you're home, I'm working or alseep. When I'm home, you're out running around. I'm not criticizing you, sweetheart," he added hastily. "Just trying to tell you I miss you. How about a date with your old man for Sunday lunch? Maybe a movie afterward."

"That sounds great," she'd said, and she seemed to mean it. "I guess we haven't seen each other much the last couple of weeks. The film changes today at Cinema One. It'll be a Danny DeVito movie, I think." The theater's name made it sound like a fancy place, but it was just a small building housing one screen and about a hundred and fifty seats.

When Mitch had returned to Sixkiller's room, the patient was sitting up in bed, eating lunch. Mitch had watched him eat meat loaf, potatoes, English peas, bread, pudding, milk, and coffee as if he were starving. Probably hadn't been eating too regularly since his jailbreak, Mitch thought.

Then he'd asked Sixkiller if he could remember what happened last night, and Sixkiller said that it was coming back—unless he was snowing Mitch. But Mitch couldn't think of any reason he'd want to do that.

"You didn't exchange any words with your attacker at all?" Mitch asked.

Sixkiller frowned. "I think I said something. I'd been in the woods all night, lost, probably going in circles. I was trying to get to town and turn myself in." He glanced at Mitch earnestly to see if Mitch believed him. Mitch was reserving judgment. "Let me think, now," Sixkiller continued. "Yeah, I saw a light. I thought it was—" He trailed off, dropping his gaze from Mitch's.

"You thought it was the Fire Carrier, right?"

Sixkiller looked up, hesitated. "Yeah," he said finally. "I'd seen it earlier, before I set off for town, but it was moving then. This light was standing still. I was leery about going closer, but then I heard voices, so I figured it couldn't be the Fire Carrier."

"Voices?"

"Two men were talking, the one who hit me and another guy. The light was on the truck. A lantern, maybe."

"So you saw them, and you spoke to them."

"I hollered that I needed help, so I wouldn't scare them, you know. Then I went closer."

"That's when one of them got something out of the truck and hit you, no questions asked?"

"That's right. I know it makes no sense, and I didn't know what was going on till it was too late."

"Did you do anything threatening? Pull a knife or something?"

"No, man. I didn't have a weapon on me, not even a knife."

"Did you recognize either of the men?"

"Couldn't see 'em well enough." He shook his head. "Ouch!" He grabbed his head. "Every time I move my head, feels like a sledgehammer pounding behind my eyes." He dropped his hand and slowly leaned back against a pillow. "You sure nothing's broke in there?"

"Doc says not," Mitch assured him.

He was silent for a moment. Then, "It wasn't light enough for me to see their faces. I don't think I knew them—I didn't recognize their voices." He closed his eyes.

"Did you hear what they were saying?"

He sighed and opened his eyes reluctantly. "I don't think so, no."

"So you have no idea what they were doing out there at night?"

"No. I wasn't thinking about that. I was just mighty glad to see them—till one of 'em knocked the crap out of me." His voice slowed and his eyes drifted closed again.

"I have another question or two, Sixkiller. Bear with me, please."

Sixkiller dragged his eyes open.

"You broke out of jail on a Friday night, a week ago last night. When did you get to Buckskin?"

Sixkiller didn't answer immediately. He was thinking. "Musta been Sunday night. Monday morning, really. It was getting light when I found that—I mean, when I found a place to camp."

Mitch didn't believe Sixkiller had been living outdoors all that time. He'd either been at his sister's or he'd used one of the many unoccupied cabins around the lake. That wasn't Mitch's main concern at the moment, so he let it pass. "Are you aware that Tyler Hatch was murdered last Monday night?"

Sixkiller was fading, but he managed to focus on Mitch's face. Alarm flickered in his eyes. "I heard, but I didn't have nothing to do with that. By the time I got here, I was too sick to do anything. I meant to talk to Jessie as soon as I got here, but I was running a fever, and I didn't make it to her house till Monday afternoon, and she wasn't even there."

"What time Monday?" Mitch asked.

"About four, I guess." He lifted his head from the pillow, struggled to sit straighter. "I hid in the toolshed," he said. "Saw my nephews come home from school and leave a little while later. Saw Tyler come home, go through the house, turning on lights. Then I heard the phone ring and I guess he answered it. Right after that, he left again in a big rush. Seemed real pissed off about something. That's all I know. I never spoke to him, and he never saw me. I didn't know he was dead till I talked to Jessie later—Tuesday or Wednesday, I forget which." He fell back against the pillow, exhausted, then grimaced from the pain in his head. He drew in a gulp of air. "That's the God's truth, and I'll take a lie-detector test if you want me to."

Realizing he'd get no more out of Sixkiller at the moment, Mitch left the room and found the nurse in charge of Sixkiller's unit. He'd already satisfied himself that Sixkiller couldn't leave by the window in his room. They'd put him in the detox unit with Amos Flycatcher. The glass was reinforced with wire, and extra thick. The nurse said the only way to exit the unit was to pass the nurse's station, which was manned—or womaned, to be more exact—at all times. But if Mitch wanted an officer stationed outside Sixkiller's door, she'd clear it with the hospital administrator.

Mitch said he'd think about it and let her know. Sixkiller claimed he'd already decided to turn himself in before he ran into his attacker on that road, but Mitch wasn't sure he believed him. Still, he didn't think Sixkiller would try to go anywhere for a few hours. He'd station Duck or Shelly at the hospital tonight.

Since Emily wasn't going to be home, he drove to the station and phoned the Delaware County Sheriff's office to report that Sixkiller had been apprehended. The deputy on duty said they'd contact the hospital and pick up Sixkiller as soon as the doctor released him. Which should be tomorrow morning, Mitch thought as he hung up.

He leaned back in his swivel chair and tried to make some sense out of what Sixkiller had told him. Why would a man attack somebody who stumbled out of the woods, in need of help? Could be the attacker didn't believe Sixkiller, thought Sixkiller meant to rob him. But there were two men with the truck, according to Sixkiller, and Sixkiller swore he hadn't brandished a weapon, hadn't even had a weapon. If he was lying about that, the two men had taken the weapon with them—there'd been none on Sixkiller when he was found.

Mitch tried to envision the scene as Sixkiller had described it. He'd walked toward the two men, who were standing beside a truck with a lantern on it, talking. Sixkiller had shouted to alert them of his presence, had asked for their help. The men stopped talking, had remained silent while one of them reached into the truck and grabbed something—a wrench? a piece of pipe?—and brained Sixkiller with it.

Obviously, Sixkiller's appearance on the scene was totally unexpected and unwelcome. He was perceived as a threat and knocked unconscious, left lying on the ground, as the men drove away. But it was two against one, and the one was exhausted from wandering in the woods all night. Sixkiller had no weapon—Mitch was inclined to believe him on that score—and he hadn't threatened them physically. So what were they afraid of? Of being recognized? Of being seen on that little-used road? They hadn't been out for a leisurely drive, that was for sure, not there and not at that particular time.

If the moving light that Sixkiller had seen earlier was the same light that was on the truck when he approached the men, they'd been out there for several hours. What were they doing?

Mitch didn't have a clue.

But Sixkiller was his more immediate concern. He'd been

in the vicinity Monday night when Tyler Hatch was killed. Claimed he didn't do it, but then what else would he say? He'd even offered to take a lie-detector test, which was something a guilty man usually didn't do. It was enough to make Mitch think he might be telling the truth when he said he didn't murder Hatch.

Well, Sixkiller wasn't going anywhere but back to jail. If he decided to ask Sixkiller to take the lie-detector test, he knew right where he could find him. He filled out an incident report on Sixkiller's apprehension and filed it. Then he phoned Shelly at home and asked if she was free to baby-sit Sixkiller at the hospital that night. She was, and agreed to be at the hospital at seven and stay until Sixkiller was released Sunday morning and the Delaware County Deputies arrived to take custody of him.

"Thanks, Shelly," Mitch said. "I'll put in for overtime for you, but I can't promise you'll get it. The budget's pretty tight."

"Don't worry about it, Chief. Got a new book I've been wanting to read for a month. This will give me the chance to do it."

Mitch cleared off his desk and was putting on his jacket to leave, when the pager clipped to his shirt pocket went off. Since he was on call this weekend, phone calls were automatically transferred to his home phone. When nobody answered there, the answering service dialed his pager. The staticky voice from the pager said, "Chief Bushyhead, call 555–6999, please. Chief Bushyhead, call 555–6999."

The number was unfamiliar to Mitch. When he dialed it, a harried voice said, "Marshall Chevrolet. Elwin speaking."

"Elwin, it's Mitch Bushyhead."

"Can you get down here right away, Chief?" Marshall was breathless with agitation.

"What's the problem, Elwin?"

"Some dang peckerwood stole one of my trucks!"

"When?"

"Last night, I guess. The trucks are parked out back, so I didn't notice one was gone until a little while ago. Dadgummed thieves."

"I'll be there in five minutes, Elwin."

16

"It was just luck I even came in today," Marshall said as soon as he'd led Mitch into his office. "I usually let my assistant run the place on Saturday."

"Why'd you decide to come back today?"

"Had some paperwork I wanted to get done before Monday."

"And you didn't notice the truck was gone right away?"

Marshall ran a hand through his short-clipped hair. He was too indignant to sit down, so he stood in front of his desk, hands jammed into his trouser pockets, loafered foot tapping impatiently. "Like I said, it was behind the building. I don't go back there every day. I think I already told you my rental business ain't real brisk."

"This was a rental truck?"

"Yeah, didn't I say that? It was the biggest one I got, the van with the dolly. No-account hoodlum must've hot-wired it."

"Unless he had a key made when he rented it to move," Mitch mused.

Marshall stared at him. "You talking about Bill Smith?"

"If that's his name."

"Well, o' course it's— Wait a minute. You saying Bill Smith wasn't his real name?"

"Just a theory," Mitch said.

"But I saw his license."

"Could've been fake."

"You saying he rented the van just so he could have a key made and steal it later?"

"I wouldn't know about that. He may really have needed the van the weekend he rented it. He may even have used it to move, but I got a feeling that was another lie. And knowing he might need it again, he could have had a key made." Mitch shrugged. "Or he could've hot-wired it, like you said."

"I don't get it," Marshall said. "He rented it the first time. Why not just rent it again, instead of stealing it?"

"Don't know." Mitch frowned. "Maybe he didn't have the money this time."

"Well, I hope you can find the skunk. I can't afford to lose that van."

"Isn't it insured?"

Marshall sighed. "Yeah, but I kind of skimped on the insurance. I won't get full replacement value, that's for sure."

"That's too bad, Elwin."

"Tell me about it." He leaned back against the desk and raked his hand across his head again. "Wish I'd never got in the rental business. It's been nothing but a drain on me since day one. Car sales have fallen off the last couple of years too. People are buying imports. There ain't hardly any patriotic Americans left, Chief." He sighed heavily. "If I could find a buyer for this place, I'd take early retirement."

Mitch pulled a small spiral tablet from his shirt pocket. "I'll need a description and the license tag number, Elwin. Then we'll get out an APB."

Saturday night, Emily had another date with Jimmy Doolittle. They'd just left the house, and Mitch was idly flipping through television channels to see if there was anything worth watching, when the telephone rang. It was probably too soon for the thieves who stole Elwin Marshall's van to have been apprehended, but Mitch grabbed the phone, hoping, anyway.

"Hello."

"Mitch?" It was Lisa.

"Oh, hi."

"Did Emily give you my message?"

"Yeah."

"You didn't call me back."

"I've been busy."

There was a silence. He heard her sigh. "That's not the real reason you didn't call, is it?"

"Well—" He stopped. There was an injured edge to his voice that he didn't want her to hear. He tried again. "I didn't know what to say to you, Lisa."

"I know. I mean, I understand. I don't know what to say, either. I guess I just wanted to hear your voice."

The words should have been encouraging, but there was a reserve in her tone that kept his heart from leaping hopefully in his chest. "Are you still seeing the college administrator?"

"Yes," she murmured. "I get so lonely, Mitch."

"Then, we're wasting our time, talking."

"Oh, Mitch . . ." Her voice caught. "I really do care for you. I miss you so much and I don't want to lose you."

She had a strange way of showing it, he thought but didn't say. Her words melted some of the hardness around his heart, but he ruthlessly ignored that. Words were cheap. "If that's true, then why did you leave Buckskin?"

"I—at the moment, I'm not sure. I'm confused. I—" He kept silent, letting her sort herself out. Finally, she said, "No, that's not true. I've always planned to get my doctorate and teach at the college level. To do it I had to leave Buckskin. It hurts, but I would do it again."

"I see."

"Can't you understand that, Mitch?"

"Sure I can. I don't have to like it, though."

There was another awkward silence. "Let me ask you something," she said finally. "Year after next, when Emily goes to college, would you give serious consideration to moving out here?"

He'd thought about the possibility when she first told him she was moving to California. He'd thought about it again Friday morning when Emily told him Lisa had called. Now he thought about the gangs, the polluted air, the congested free-ways. He would hate getting up every morning and going to work. He'd been raised in Oklahoma City, but he'd always been a small-town boy at heart. Small towns had their unique problems, but he felt better able to cope with them than with those spawned by a city.

It was never going to work out with Lisa. He had to accept it now and go on—somehow. And, because of what they'd once had together, he owed her honesty. "I don't think so, Lisa. Emily will go to college somewhere in the state and I don't want to be that far away from her. Besides, I like it here—most of the time."

"I guess Emily will always come first," she said sorrow-fully.

"It can't be any other way. Not for several years, anyway, until she's married and settled."

"I know. If you didn't feel that way, you wouldn't be you." He could tell by her voice that she was crying. "Oh, Mitch." She drew a long, tremulous breath.

"I guess this is good-bye then, isn't it?"

"I guess it is. I just wish it didn't feel like it was killing me."

He had a sudden impulse to say, Wait! I've changed my mind. We'll work out something. But he knew it was only an impulse, that it wouldn't, couldn't last, even if right now he felt as though he too were dying. He would get over it. They would both get over it. People survived. "I want the best for you, Lisa. I hope you know that."

"I do. Good-bye, Mitch."

The dial tone had never sounded so final.

Mitch and Emily had Sunday lunch at a new steak house outside of town on the road to the lake. Surrounded by cattle brands etched into dark-paneled walls, they ate filets and baked potatoes smothered in butter and sour cream. After lunch, they'd taken in the Danny DeVito movie, and Mitch had even managed to follow the storyline and chuckle a few times, in spite of repeated intrusions of the memory of his last phone conversation with Lisa.

As they came out of the theater, Emily pulled up the collar of her down jacket against the cold. True January weather was back. The temperature hovered near freezing at three o'clock in the afternoon.

Mitch put his arm around her and they hurried to his Toyota. "Let's take a little ride before we go home."

"Where to?"

They got in the car and he started the engine. "I want to check out that country road where we found Henderson Sixkiller." He'd already told her about Sixkiller and Amos Flycatcher and what had happened Saturday.

"Sure. What're you looking for?"

He left the steak house parking lot and turned away from town. "I want to see where that road goes. I didn't have time to follow it yesterday. I had to get to the hospital and keep an eye on Sixkiller."

The heater was starting to warm the Toyota's interior. Emily, who'd been scrunched up on the seat, unscrunched. "Do you think he killed Mr. Hatch, Daddy?"

"I don't know. He says he didn't, even offered to take a lie-detector test."

"Then he must not have done it. I mean, would he let you hook him up to a lie detector if he was the murderer?"

"Maybe," Mitch said. "And maybe he's bluffing. If I decided to take him up on it, he could change his mind. The first thing you learn in the police business is not to believe anything a convicted criminal tells you."

She made a face and sighed. "Mega bummer."

"Yeah," Mitch agreed.

They drove for several minutes in silence, until he found the turnoff. He would have missed the narrow road if he hadn't been looking for it. As they bumped along, Emily gazed out the side window. "Wonder what Henderson Sixkiller was doing out here at night."

"He claims he was trying to get to town to give himself up."

"But maybe he's lying?"

"Right. He probably was trying to get to town—can't imagine what else he'd have been doing—but as for giving himself up, who knows?"

The road wound back and forth, around clumps of trees, and finally ended at a wire-and-post gate in a barbed-wire fence. "That's funny. It doesn't seem to go anywhere but to that field over there," Emily said.

"Let's check it out," Mitch said. They got out of the car and Mitch opened the gate, refastening it when they were on the other side.

Emily took his arm. "They probably drive in here to load cattle."

"They'd need a corral or at least a chute. Maybe they bring one of those portable chutes, but the only people who'd load cattle at night are rustlers, and I can't remember the last time we had any cattle rustling reported in the county. Looks like a path over there. We'll see where it goes."

The path wasn't wide enough to accommodate a vehicle. A motorcycle could make it, but it would be a rough ride. Whoever used it evidently traveled on foot. Mitch noticed a couple of limbs alongside the path had been broken off, perhaps to provide more room for whoever walked here, as if the person had been carrying something wider than himself.

"I don't think this goes anywhere, either," Emily said. Walking through the woods on a cold January afternoon clearly wasn't her idea of a fun thing to do. But she probably preferred it to waiting in the Toyota for Mitch to return.

"Another five minutes," Mitch said, "and then we'll turn back if we don't find anything."

But they did find something, and in less than five minutes. At the end of the path was an old barn which, judging from a few flakes of paint beside the door, had once been red. Now it was a weathered gray-white. But it wasn't listing to one

side, and only a few of the roof shingles were missing. It was
still a good, dry place for storing hay or equipment.

Mitch undid the homemade door latch, a piece of wood that
slid into a leather loop attached to the barn wall. He pulled
open the heavy door and stepped inside. The interior was dim
and smelled not unpleasantly of long-decomposed manure.
There had been no livestock in there for a long time. The barn
was empty except for a pile of old tarpaulins in one corner.

This must be where the two guys in the truck had gone—either before or after they disposed of Sixkiller. There was
nowhere else for them to go on that narrow road. But why? Illegal cockfights? They weren't unheard of in Cherokee County,
but Mitch could see no dried blood or feathers anywhere. Nor
could he see or smell any excrement.

Not dog fights, either, for the same reason—there was no
sign that dogs had been in the barn in the recent past.

Emily had gone to the corner where the tarps were piled
and lifted one. A mouse ran across her foot. She shrieked and
jumped back. The mouse disappeared through a small hole in
the barn wall.

Mitch grinned. "You okay?"

She took a deep breath, her hand pressed to her heart.
"Yeah. It was a mouse. I hate mice." Ellen had hated mice too.
The problem with mice was that you never knew they were
there until they streaked past you—or over your foot.

"We might as well go back to the car," he said.

"Wait a minute." She bent over to peer at the ground. "I
thought something fell out when I dropped that tarp." She
took a cautious step closer, reached down, and picked up a
small object.

"What did you find?"

"It looks like one of those big buckles cowboys wear." She
carried it back to the door where there was more light. "That's
what it is. It looks kind of expensive too." She turned it over.
"There's some writing on the back." She held it up to catch the
light. "It's too worn down to read. All I can make out is a *B.*"

17

Lex Burnside was waiting for Mitch at the station Monday morning. Mitch had called him Sunday night and asked him to come by sometime. To Lex, *sometime* evidently meant the first possible moment.

Burnside's face was still red from being out in the cold. He was waiting just inside the door when Mitch stepped inside. He stretched his neck to lean closer to Mitch, like a bird dog on point. "You find my stuff, Chief?"

"No, Lex, but I might have a lead." Noticing that Helen had already made the first pot of coffee of the day, Mitch poured a cup. "Coffee, Lex?"

Burnside shook his head. "Not for me. I already had three cups. Been up for hours, wondering why you wanted to see me."

"Sorry. Didn't mean to get your hopes up." He glanced at Helen, who was studying the *Tulsa World*'s crossword puzzle. "Any calls yet, Helen?"

She tucked her pencil behind her ear. "Yes. Doctor Pohl, for one. Nothing urgent, he said. Call him when you have time. Also, Earlene Downing called. Said she'd be in a meeting till ten, but could you stop by the Job Corps Center after that."

"Okay."

"Oh, and Shelly called. Said to ask you if she should stay at the hos—" She glanced at Burnside—"on stakeout."

"She's still there?"

Helen nodded. "She went home for a while yesterday, then went back last night. They're supposed to pick up that—er, package this morning."

"Call her and tell her to stay till Delaware County sends somebody to take over," Mitch said. "Then she should go home and get some rest. If we need her today, we'll call her."

Duckworth arrived with a gust of cold wind. "Whew, it's winter out there."

Mitch said hello, then added, "Come on in my office, Lex."

Mitch shut the office door, hung his coat on the rack, and took the belt buckle Emily had found in the barn from his shirt pocket. "Is this yours?" He handed it to Burnside, whose eyes lit up like two candles.

"Sure is. It was stolen with my other buckles. Where'd you get it, Chief?"

Mitch told him. Burnside looked bewildered. "That sounds like the barn on old lady Tellon's place."

"Edna Tellon?" Edna was a widow in her eighties. Burnside nodded, and Mitch said, "I thought she'd moved into the retirement center."

"She did, but she still owns the family farm. Probably can't stand the idea of selling. Rather let the kids do it when she's gone."

Mitch pulled out his swivel chair and sat down. "Wonder if anybody's using it," he mused.

Burnside shrugged. "Don't know. And I doubt you'd get much from Edna. Last I heard, she was pretty senile." He looked down at the buckle again. "How do you reckon this got in Edna Tellon's barn?"

"The thieves evidently know the barn isn't being used. They could be storing the stolen goods there until they can dispose of them. Two men in a big van were seen near there Friday night. They must have dropped that buckle when they were loading the van."

Burnside looked agitated. He snatched his cowboy hat off his head and crushed it in his hand. "Well, where in tarnation did they take my stuff?"

"My best guess is they took it out of state, to an auction somewhere."

Burnside groaned and dropped into a chair, hanging his hat on his knee. "You missed recovering my saddles and buckles by less than two days. Damnation, Chief. My luck ain't nothing but bad ever since I let my wife talk me into going to Vegas."

"Don't despair just yet, Lex. A van was stolen off the Chevrolet lot Friday night. I got a feeling the thieves took it. There's an all-points bulletin out on the truck. With any luck, they'll be in it when it's found."

Burnside gnawed his bottom lip for a moment, then crammed his hat back on his head. He stood. "I ain't gonna count on it. They'll probably sell the stuff and get rid of the van quick—if they got any brains at all." He sighed. "Well, keep me posted, Chief." He clomped out.

Burnside was gone before Mitch could think of anything encouraging to say. But nothing was going to lift Burnside's spirits but the return of his saddles and buckles.

Mitch reached for the phone and dialed Dr. Pohl's office in Tahlequah. It was early enough that he caught Pohl in. "You wanted me to call, Doc?"

"Is this Chief Bushyhead to whom I'm speaking?" Pohl barked testily.

"I guess I didn't identify myself, did I? Thought you'd know my voice."

"You're as bad as Molly Bearpaw," Pohl grumbled. "No time for chitchat. Get right down to brass tacks."

Molly Bearpaw was an investigator for the Cherokee Nation in Tahlequah. Mitch had never met her, but he'd heard good things about her work. "Sorry, Doc. You sound like you had a bad weekend."

"My wife dragged me to Tulsa," Pohl said. "Made me buy a whole houseful of new furniture. Southwestern style, it's called. Looks like it's upholstered with saddle blankets." Mitch was tempted to say there were worse things. Ellen had labored lovingly over every detail of the old Victorian they'd remodeled several years ago. She'd been so proud of that house. He'd worried about the expense, but now he'd give anything to have her around, coaxing him to buy new furniture. Mitch had done nothing to the house since her death; it was exactly as she'd left it. Not because of a sentimental desire to freeze it in time, but because Mitch never gave much thought to what the house looked like.

"Well," he said, "you know women and their houses."

"Don't I." Mitch heard the sound of shuffling paper. "What I called about, Chief—I got some test results back on Hatch. Something interesting turned up. Can't see what it has to do with his murder, but I figured you'd want to know." He paused.

Mitch had already been barked at once for hurrying the doctor. He wasn't about to make the same mistake twice, not today. He waited silently while Pohl cleared his throat and rattled papers.

"You still there, Mitch?"

"Yep."

"This is confidential, mind you. I'm not sure what the law says about a dead person, and I suppose the wife has to be told, but leave me out of it, okay?"

"Sure, Doc."

"Here it is, then. Hatch was HIV-positive."

For a moment, Mitch was too surprised to respond. Pohl was right, the fact that Hatch was HIV-positive didn't seem connected to his murder, but it was indeed interesting. "I didn't know you tested for AIDS when you autopsied," he said finally.

"I don't, usually. We protect ourselves as though every corpse is HIV-positive. But in Hatch's case, I saw a little spot that looked like a lesion. It was next to his hairline in front. His hair was kind of long there, so it probably covered it. Anyway, it made me curious, so I ordered the test."

"A lesion?" Mitch recalled Jessie Hatch saying that her husband had had the flu recently, or something that acted like the flu, but she hadn't mentioned a lesion. "Does that mean he actually had the disease?"

"That's right. One of them, anyway. AIDS is a whole range of diseases, Chief. Hatch was in the early stages of Kaposi's sarcoma. He was fixing to be real sick when he died. You didn't hear it from me, now. All this right-of-privacy business surrounding AIDS is a bunch of craziness. We make people get tested for syphilis before they can get married. Not AIDS, though. Go figure."

"He must've had the virus a long time."

"Not necessarily. People are different. Some can have the virus for ten years without developing AIDS. Others start manifesting AIDS-related disease within months."

"Okay, Doc. And thanks."

Mitch hung up, spun the swivel chair toward the window, leaned back, and locked his hands behind his head. The few people walking along Sequoyah Street, Buckskin's main drag, had their heads down against the wind, hurrying to get where they were going. Mitch gazed at them without really seeing them. His mind was still working through what Pohl had told him.

Had Hatch known he had AIDS? Had anyone else known? Hatch's wife, for example? If she found out he'd exposed her to the virus, she'd have wanted to kill him. Sure sounded like a top-notch motive for murder to Mitch. But if she hadn't known . . .

Oh, Lord, Pohl was right—somebody would have to tell her. But he saw no reason to rush over to the Hatch house. He decided to put off giving Jessie Hatch the bad news.

At ten o'clock, Mitch went to the Job Corps Center. He met Earlene Downing in the hallway, carrying a stack of manila folders. "Just got out of a meeting," she said. He followed her to her office. She moved a folded newspaper from a chair so that he could sit down, then stacked all the folders on her desk and sat down behind it.

She had on a deep-purple blouse with long, billowing

sleeves. She rested her elbows on the desk and looked at him over interlocked hands. "I wasn't sure I should even call you. I mean, I'm not sure this is police business. They're both over eighteen, you see."

"Who?"

"Tim and Martin Kramer."

The fact that the brothers were adults under the law was hardly a hot news flash. "So?"

"Let me start at the beginning."

Sounds like a good place to me, Mitch thought.

"Tim and Martin told me Friday that they were going to visit their mother over the weekend." She picked up a pen and rolled it between her thumb and index finger. "But when they weren't back here this morning, I asked around to see if anybody had heard from them. That's when I learned they'd moved out. One of the other students saw them putting all their clothes and other belongings in a car late Friday night. Their old Ford wouldn't start, and it turns out the car they were using belonged to another student. Martin had asked him to take them to the bus station. He left them there with their luggage. They always took the bus to Dallas to visit their mother." She made some random marks on a memo pad with the pen. When she looked up, she seemed almost embarrassed. "At least, that's where we thought they went. I realize now we should have checked up on them sooner—considering their past record . . ."

Mitch sat forward in his chair. "You're saying they *didn't* visit their mother last weekend?"

She nodded. "I phoned Mrs. Kramer this morning. She told me she didn't see them last weekend. Not only that, they weren't with her the other weekends when they told us they were going home. They took Tyler Hatch's money for their bus tickets and heaven knows what they did with it. Drugs or alcohol, I suppose. Neither is permitted at the center, of course."

Puzzle pieces were falling into place. Mitch didn't think the Kramer brothers had spent the money on drugs or alcohol. It was looking more and more as though they'd used it to rent large trucks. All the tack burglaries had occurred on weekends, and that barn on Edna Tellon's farm had served as a temporary storage place, until the past weekend when it had been cleaned out. Even the intense conversation he'd interrupted when he'd visited the Job Corps Center earlier now made sense. Tim's "it's over" had evidently referred to the burglaries. After Hatch's death, there was no more money to rent vans. But Martin had said it wasn't over yet. So they stole Elwin Marshall's van and took off with the goods. Did Hatch find out what they were doing with his money? He wished he knew the answer.

"I'm not sure what you can do," Earlene Downing was saying. "As I told you, they're adults. They can drop out of their program here if they want to. It was my understanding, though, that finishing their course was a condition of their parole. That's why I finally decided to call you. Thought you might want to be the one to notify the probation office in Tulsa."

"I'll take care of it," Mitch said. He hesitated. Then, "I wonder if I might have a word with Alice Browne before I go."

She frowned. "She's in class."

"This is important."

She was clearly curious about why he wanted to talk to Alice again, but she didn't ask. "All right." She picked up the phone and told the receptionist to send Alice to her office. When she hung up, she said, "I'll work in the conference room while you speak to Alice." She took the top two manila folders from the stack on her desk and left, leaving her office door open.

Two minutes later, Alice Browne halted in the doorway. Clearly, she had expected to see Earlene Downing.

"Come on in, Alice," Mitch said.

"You're the one who sent for me?"

"Yes. We need to talk." When she cleared the doorway, he got up and closed the door. "Sit down, Alice."

She took the chair he had vacated. Mitch remained standing. He was too uncomfortable to sit. "Alice, uh—well, I've learned something and, uh—I, well, I need you to be real honest with me."

Her brow furrowed. "You found out who killed Tyler?"

"No, it's not that." Mitch clasped his hands behind his back and tried to think how best to approach the subject. "It's, uh—" Good Lord, he was stammering like an idiot. "Alice, I know you told me you never slept with Tyler Hatch, but—"

"You think I lied?"

"Look, Alice, it's none of my business whether you did or you didn't. But in case you did, I really need to know. I swear it will go no further than this office."

She stared at him. "But I didn't." She drew in a deep breath and looked at her hands, which lay, palms up, in her lap. "I'll admit that's what Tyler wanted." She looked up quickly. "I know I said we were just friends, and we were. But Tyler wanted to be more than friends. I found out later he'd had affairs with other students here in the past." She shrugged. "But I knew he was married, so I kept saying no." She blinked hard a few times. "He was so good to me. If I'd known he'd be dead in a few days, I might have given in."

Thank your lucky stars you didn't, Mitch thought. He wondered if Hatch had known he had AIDS and had tried to get Alice in bed, anyway. If so, how *long* had he known? More good questions. If only he knew where to look for answers.

At least he didn't have to tell Alice that Hatch had had the virus. "Okay, Alice. You can go back to your class now."

She looked startled. "That's all you wanted to talk about?"

"That's it."

She left the office, frowning, plainly wondering why her sex life, or lack of it, was important enough for the police chief to come to the center and question her again. Mitch hoped she never learned what a close call she'd had. Ignorance could be a blessing. Would it be kinder to leave Jessie Hatch in ignorance too?

Thinking of Jessie, he returned to the station. He knew it

was cowardice more than kindness that was making him procrastinate, but he couldn't bring himself to give Jessie the news just yet. Instead, he went back to thinking about Hatch and wondering if he'd known what was making him sick. The aches and pains he could have easily put down to another cause. But surely the lesion had worried him. He might even have seen a doctor about it. Wait . . . he *had* seen a doctor.

According to Jessie, Hatch had visited a doctor a few days before he died, and the doctor had given him pills for his flu-like symptoms. Now Mitch knew why they hadn't made him feel better.

As soon as he got back to his office, he phoned Jessie and asked the name of the doctor Hatch had seen before he died.

She thought it over. "I don't think he said, but it was probably Dr. Rapicorn in Muskogee. Tyler saw him a few times last year for minor things. He could have seen Dr. Vann at the clinic for free, but he didn't like her."

Because she knew his dirty little secret, Mitch thought. Hatch had been ashamed to see Rhea, or he hadn't wanted to be confronted by her about the battering.

Mitch thanked Jessie and dialed Information for Dr. Rapicorn's number. The doctor was with a patient. Mitch left word for Rapicorn to return his call. The receptionist warned that it might be several hours; the doctor had a very full schedule.

18

Monday night, Mitch had difficulty getting to sleep. He lay staring into the dark, thinking about all that had happened since Friday, and trying to make the new data fit into a logical pattern. He was confident he'd solved the tack burglaries, even if he didn't have the thieves in custody yet. What he didn't know was how, or if, the burglaries were connected to Hatch's murder.

Actually, he had a theory, but no evidence to back it up. He worked out the details as he lay sleepless. Hatch had been giving the Kramer brothers money for bus fare to visit their mother. They then disappeared for a weekend, used Hatch's money to rent a truck, and committed the burglaries, hiding what they'd stolen in Edna Tellon's old barn.

Henderson Sixkiller, who, as of that morning, resided once more in the Delaware County Jail, had seen a light on the truck, probably a lantern. The Kramers had had to carry the stolen items, traveling the path on foot at night, from the gate leading to Edna Tellon's field to the barn. They would have carried a lantern to light their way. The recent sightings of a light, which had given rise to fear among some Cherokees that the Fire Carrier had returned, could well have been the Kramers' lantern. Another mystery solved, though this one wasn't in Mitch's jurisdiction. Crying Wolf and the other medicine men, however, would be pleased to know that the Fire Carrier hadn't overcome their medicine and returned.

How the Kramers, who weren't from the area, had known about Edna Tellon's barn in the first place, and how they had targeted certain horsemen to be burgled, were questions Mitch couldn't answer. He put them aside for the moment and thought about Hatch's murder. According to his theory, which he'd run past Virgil Rabbit that afternoon, Hatch found out what the Kramers were up to, threatened to expose them, and they killed him. Virgil had been unable to punch any holes in it.

A tidy solution to both crimes, except for the one detail that kept floating around in his head, bugging him, the fact that Hatch had AIDS. Chances are it had nothing to do with anything else, but it kept nagging at Mitch. He wanted to know if Hatch had known he had AIDS. If so, how long had he known? And did anyone else know? Hatch's physician, Dr. Rapicorn, would have been the first to know, but Rapicorn hadn't gotten back to Mitch yet.

It was close to midnight and he still wasn't asleep when the telephone rang. It was Virgil Rabbit, the officer on call that night.

"Sorry to wake you, Mitch, but I thought you'd want to know this."

"I wasn't asleep."

"Oh. Well, I just talked to a sheriff near Phoenix. One of his deputies spotted Marshall's stolen truck parked at a truck stop out there. Martin and Tim Kramer were in the restaurant, trying to find somebody to work on it. Seems it conked out on 'em."

"What about the stolen goods?"

"Still in the truck."

"Lex Burnside will be ecstatic."

"Yeah. Anyway, one of the Kramers told a long-hauler that they'd been hired by several horsemen to take the stuff to an auction somewhere in California."

"So where are the Kramers now?"

"On the way back here. The real reason I didn't wait to tell you until tomorrow was that I wanted you to know I might've crawled out on a limb. I told 'em we'd pay expenses if a couple of their deputies could bring the Kramers back."

"Good work, Virg." Mitch would get the city council to pay for the trip somehow.

"I knew you were hot to talk to them about Hatch's murder."

"You better believe it."

"The deputies are gonna spell each other driving, so they should get here sometime tomorrow evening."

Mitch waited until he reached the station Tuesday morning to phone Earlene Downing and tell her the circumstances under which the Kramer brothers had been found. "I guess they won't be back to class, then," she said. "Too bad. It was their last chance to get their act together and stay out of jail. Why are some people so attracted to crime?"

"I wish I knew," Mitch said. "Maybe it's the risk of getting caught that thrills them. Living on the edge, you know?"

She sighed. "There's enough of that in everyday life for me. Well, thanks for calling, Chief."

"You bet."

Next, Mitch phoned Lex Burnside and gave him the good news. Burnside was so moved he got all choked up. After snuffling and coughing and clearing his throat a few times, he finally managed to say, "I hope they didn't damage anything. When can I have my stuff?"

"It may be a while before we can get it back here. The thieves stole a van to haul it in, and the van broke down. It's in the possession of the sheriff's department out there. Don't worry. It's safe. As soon as I have more information, I'll let you know, Lex."

"Thanks, Chief," Burnside said brokenly.

Elwin Marshall wasn't so grateful. "You mean the deputies ain't bringing my truck back?" he demanded when Mitch told him the truck had been found.

"I think it broke down."

"Hell's bells, they probably tore it up. Probably cost a fortune to fix it. The insurance company's gonna raise my rates again." He sighed. "Where is it now?"

Mitch gave him the phone number for the Arizona Sheriff's

Department. "You may have to send somebody after it, Elwin. You need to make arrangements with the sheriff out there."

Marshall hung up, still grumbling.

Helen brought in a bag of gourmet coffee—cherry chocolate—and they all tried it. The unanimous decision was that they preferred plain old Folgers.

Duck and Shelly got in an argument about a remark Duck made that Shelly took as sexist. Duck accused her of setting him up so he'd say something she could yell at him about.

To which Shelly replied, "That's right, Duckie. I live to torment you. You're my life."

Mitch sent them on patrol so he wouldn't have to listen to them.

In other words, it was an ordinary day. Except that this one seemed to take forever to pass while Mitch waited for the Arizona deputies to arrive with the Kramer brothers.

A little after three that afternoon, Dr. Rapicorn, the Muskogee physician, returned Mitch's call.

"I understand the late Tyler Hatch was a patient of yours," Mitch said.

"Yes," Rapicorn said slowly. "I've been so busy I haven't even had time to read the newspaper, so I learned about Hatch's death only yesterday. It was quite a shock."

The doctor seemed to be weighing his words with care. So Mitch decided on a small deception. "According to his wife, you saw him a few days before he died."

There was a pause. "I'd have to check my records to be sure."

"You tested him for the HIV virus, didn't you?"

An even longer pause. "Where did you get *that* information, from his wife?"

Mitch cut in. "No. Look, Dr. Rapicorn, I know Hatch had AIDS. I also know how sticky the situation can be with living people who are HIV-positive, their right to privacy and all that—but Hatch is dead. He was murdered. And your information could be important to the investigation." To be honest,

Mitch thought he was overstating the case. He doubted that Rapicorn had any vital information.

"Chief Bushyhead, these days physicians are a beleaguered lot. We can get sued over the slightest misunderstanding. You wouldn't believe what I pay for malpractice insurance."

It's rough all over, Mitch thought. "I just want the answers to a few questions. Nobody will know you talked to me, I assure you."

He hesitated. "I won't know if I can answer your questions until you ask them."

"Okay. Did you see Hatch a few days before he died?"

"Yes."

"Did you test him for the HIV virus?"

"Yes."

"Was he aware of what was wrong with him when he came to you?"

"He had no idea. He said he had the flu and couldn't seem to shake it."

"And the lesion?"

"Oh, you know about that, do you?" He sounded depressed. "Mr. Hatch thought it was ordinary skin cancer. Of course, when I saw it . . . well, I ordered the test, told him it was necessary as part of a complete workup."

"Did you tell him you thought he had AIDS?"

"Not until I got the test results."

"And when was that?"

"The following Monday. I got the lab to rush it. I called Hatch at home . . . oh, I guess it was shortly after five. When I told him the test was positive, he was shocked, said it wasn't possible, and so on. I suggested he have another test. A false-positive result isn't all that uncommon. But I had to tell him that the biopsy on the lesion showed Kaposi's sarcoma and, therefore, it was highly unlikely the HIV test result was wrong." He paused to clear his throat. "I started to tell him about recent advances in AIDS treatment, but he hung up on me. I thought I'd give him a couple of weeks to come to terms with the news and talk to him again." He cleared his throat once more. "At least, he won't have to go through the last stages of AIDS now. Perhaps he would have preferred it this way."

"Maybe," Mitch said, "but now his wife has to be told."

"I've been thinking about that. I'll phone her in a few days and ask her to come to my office."

Mitch felt a weight slide off his shoulders. Thank God, he wouldn't have to be the one to tell Jessie Hatch that her husband may have infected her.

"Thanks for your candor, Doctor," Mitch said.

"I'm counting on your discretion," Rapicorn cautioned as he ended the conversation.

Mitch was still at the station at 5:25 when the Arizona deputies arrived with the Kramer brothers. Virgil and Roo's shift had started at four, but Roo had gone to a local bar in response to the owner's call for help in thwarting a fight that seemed to be brewing between two customers.

The Arizona deputies turned over their charges and left to find a place to eat and a motel room for the night. Mitch and Virgil took the Kramers into the interrogation room, a small cubicle tucked into one corner of the station. It had been converted from a storage room. So far, Martin and Tim hadn't opened their mouths. One of the deputies had told Mitch that they'd stopped talking somewhere around Amarillo.

The brothers slumped in two chairs and stared sullenly at the floor. They looked like twenty miles of bad road—dirty, disheveled, and much the worse for wear. Virgil sat on a corner of the small table next to a tape recorder and waited for Mitch to take the lead. Mitch, standing with his back to the door, nodded, and Virgil turned on the recorder. Mitch pulled a card from his back pocket and read them their rights, then asked if they wanted to contact a lawyer.

"We don't need a lawyer," Martin snapped. "They ain't never done a thing for us."

"Well, then," Mitch said, "we got you on possession of a stolen vehicle and a truckload of stolen goods and transporting them across state lines." He'd obtained warrants on those charges while waiting for them to get there. But he needed more evidence to get a warrant for the attack on Henderson Sixkiller and for Hatch's murder. He hoped to have it when he left the interrogation room. "There's also the little matter of violating the terms of your probation. What've you got to say for yourselves?"

Tim glanced at Martin, who snorted contemptuously. "Just lock us up and be done with it. We ain't slept worth shit since last Friday night."

"The night you transferred the stolen goods from Edna Tellon's barn to the stolen van," Virgil observed.

Tim looked confused. "Edna who?"

Martin glared at him. "Shut your trap."

"It's kind of late to play innocent, Tim," Mitch said. "How'd you find out about Edna's barn, anyway?"

Martin tipped his chair on its back legs, laced his fingers behind his head, and looked as if he could sit there all night. Tim shuffled his feet and heaved a loud sigh.

"And how'd you know when those horse ranchers would be away from home so you could burgle them?"

"We got ESP," Martin snarled.

"Okay, Martin, if that's the way you want to play it." Mitch looked at Virgil. "Lock 'em up, Virg." He turned to the door, put his hand on the knob, and paused. He turned around. "By the way, there're a couple more charges pending against you I failed to mention. The attempted murder of Henderson Sixkiller, for one."

"Who?" Tim asked in confusion.

"The man who caught you out there at the Tellon place. You clubbed him and left him for dead."

The brothers exchanged a long look. Martin gave a slight shake of his head, but Tim said, "You mean that guy who ran out of the woods and came after us?"

Mitch couldn't believe these stupid clods. "He'd been wandering in the woods all night. He was ready to drop. I doubt seriously that he came after you."

"If we'd wanted to kill him, he'd be dead," Tim insisted and winced at Martin's glare. "He's not dead, is he?"

Mitch shook his head.

Tim took a deep breath. "We just gave him a little tap, just enough to put him out of commission while we got down the road."

"Jeez, Tim, who pulled your chain?" Martin snarled. "Whyn't you just confess to all the unsolved crimes in Cherokee County while you're at it."

Mitch looked at Martin for a long moment. Then Tim said tentatively, "You said a couple of pending charges. What's the other one?"

"Murder one," Mitch said.

The front legs of Martin's chair hit the concrete floor with a crack. "Murder! Who're we supposed to've murdered? You're bluffing, copper."

Mitch continued to look at him steadily. "Tyler Hatch found out you'd been using the bus money he gave you for other purposes, like renting trucks and stealing from ranchers. He threatened to expose you, and you killed him. That's the case we think we can make. It'll be up to a jury to decide who's bluffing."

"We didn't murder nobody!" Tim's voice rose in a frightened squeak.

"I tol' you to shut up!" Martin barked.

Tim glared at his brother and shook his head. "I ain't taking the rap for no murder."

Martin got red in the face. He was obviously used to telling his brother what to do and being obeyed. "Dammit, Tim—!"

Mitch stepped up to the table, planted his hands in the middle of it, and leaned toward Martin. "*You* shut up. If you won't cooperate, at least let Tim talk. Either that, or you can haul ass to your cell." He looked at Tim. "And believe me, it'll go on record who cooperated and who didn't."

"The judge will take that into consideration when he imposes sentence," Virgil murmured while examining his fingernails.

Mitch straightened up and inclined his head in Tim's direction. "Cooperate or not. Up to you."

"You want to know how we knew about the barn, how we knew where to go to steal stuff?" Tim asked defiantly. "Hatch told us."

Mitch tried not to show his surprise as he watched Tim. "You're gonna blame it all on Hatch, huh? A dead man can't defend himself."

"We didn't want him dead!" Tim wailed. "We never wanted nobody dead."

Martin glared at him and mumbled, "You're wasting your breath, bro. They ain't gonna believe a thing you say."

Mitch shot him a warning look. "We're still here and we're still listening."

"Yeah, right," Martin muttered.

"Maybe you want us to call a lawyer now," Mitch said.

"No, thanks," Martin said. "Last one we had screwed us over good."

To Mitch, it seemed the lawyer had done a great job for them. He'd kept them out of jail, got them probation. "Okay, it's your call," he said. "But, keep in mind, you've made a lot of bad decisions in the past. The latest being to go back to your old thieving ways."

Martin laughed contemptuously. "We didn't have all that much choice in the matter."

"Somebody hold a gun to your head and make you steal?" Virgil inquired in a sarcastic tone.

"He didn't have no gun," Martin shot back. Since he couldn't shut Tim up, he'd evidently decided to put in his two cents' worth too. "He just threatened to see we got in trouble at the center and report it to our parole officer."

"Hatch again?" Mitch asked and looked bored.

"Yeah, Mr. Big Upstanding Citizen Tyler Hatch." Martin snorted. "Crooked as a coiled snake."

Mitch pulled out a chair and sat down. "Okay, tell it from the beginning."

Martin looked at his brother, then back at Mitch. "Why bother? You already made up your mind we killed Hatch."

"Convince me I'm wrong."

The brothers exchanged another glance. Tim said, "It was all his idea. Hatch's, I mean."

"Stealing from the horse ranchers?" Virgil asked.

Tim nodded. "Yeah. He knew about that old barn where we could store the stuff until we got a big enough load to haul to California. They have some big farm and ranch auctions out there, and Hatch said the stuff would bring more money in California. But he couldn't do it by himself."

"He came to us not long after we enrolled at the center," Martin put in, eager to set the record straight now that he'd started. "Said he had a deal for us, a way we could have some money saved when we finished our training course."

"We said no, at first," Tim said. "We wanted to graduate from the center and find jobs."

"We figured we'd give up our evil ways," Martin added in a self-deprecating tone. "Only problem was, Hatch wasn't having any."

Mitch searched their faces for evidence that they were lying. Or that they were telling the truth. The only thing he saw was self-pity. "So Hatch threatened to see you washed out at the center?"

Tim sighed. "Yeah. That might not have been so bad, but he said he'd report us to our parole officer and we'd go to jail. So we agreed to help him."

"Did you ever think of coming to the police?" Mitch asked.

The only answer was Martin's contemptuous snort. Then he said, "Hatch would tell us when some horse rancher was going to be out of town on a weekend and give us money to rent a truck. Everybody else at the center thought we went to visit our mom. We'd steal the stuff, and Hatch would meet us out at that old barn and help us unload it. Usually it was dawn by the time we finished. Hatch said the old lady who owned it was in a nursing home. The last haul we made was a bunch of fancy saddles and stuff. Hatch said they'd bring big bucks in California and we had a vanload, so he wanted us to take it out there. He was supposed to get half and we'd split the other half. We were gonna tell the people at the center that our mom was sick and we had to go home for a week."

"Then he went and got himself killed," Tim added.

"We didn't do it," Martin put in, emphasizing each word separately. "No matter what you think. We didn't like being forced into partnership with him, but why would we want to kill him? He was running the whole shebang. Financing it too. He might have needed us, but we needed him more."

Virgil scratched his head. "If you didn't do it, who did?"

"We asked ourselves that a hundred times," Tim said and shook his head. "But we can't figure it out. After he died, you know, I thought, well, at least the burglaries are finished. But Mar—" He caught himself. "I mean, we decided we might as well sell the stuff. It was just sitting out there in that old barn. I wish we'd just left it there and stayed at the center."

Martin scowled at him. "Nobody twisted your arm, Tim."

Tim slid down in his chair and did not reply. It was clear that Martin was the leader, and that Tim had gone along with Martin's decision to take the stolen goods to California. Now he was going to be charged with burglary and vehicle theft along with his brother. Maybe the attempted murder of Henderson Sixkiller. And possibly the murder of Hatch. Mitch had hoped they'd admit to killing Hatch, claim self-defense, maybe. But it wasn't going to be that easy.

Mitch took them back through their story a couple more times, but it remained basically the same. Finally, he told Virgil to put them in a cell. When Virgil came back, Mitch was in his office, putting on his coat.

"Well, what do you think of their story, Virg?" Mitch asked.

"They're lying through their teeth. About Hatch, I mean. They're trying to cover their backsides."

"Yeah," Mitch said. "Well, maybe they'll confess after they've been in that cell for a while. Right now, we don't have enough to take it to the D.A."

19

Next day the D.A. petitioned the judge for a hearing on the burglary and stolen-vehicle charges. The hearing was set for the coming Friday. The Kramer brothers received the news impassively. Mitch talked to them about the murder that morning and again in the afternoon, hinted he thought it could have been self-defense, said if that were the case he'd do what he could to get the charge reduced to manslaughter. But it was clear he was wasting his time. They continued to insist they didn't kill Hatch and didn't know who did.

At four-thirty, Mitch went home and dished up the beef stew that had been simmering in the crock pot all day. They ate at five because, as usual, Emily had plans for the evening. After dinner, she changed to her cheerleading outfit for a basketball game at the high school. "Don't forget, Daddy," she said as she was leaving the house. "There's a dance afterward, so I won't be home until late."

"Eleven o'clock," Mitch called to her. "Not a minute later. It's a school night."

"But Jimmy might not even get there until ten."

"Eleven o'clock," Mitch repeated.

He heard the front door close and the receding sound of her footsteps on the porch and front steps. Then she was gone. He cleaned up the kitchen, got a beer from the refrigerator, and took it to the living room. Sprawled on the couch, he switched on the TV and watched the early news on one of the Tulsa stations.

The report of two robberies of elderly people in north Tulsa led the newscast. Two teenagers had been arrested and charged in both incidents. Texaco was laying off forty more people in Tulsa, and Whirlpool was hiring thirty-five new workers. OSU and TU had won their latest basketball games; OU had lost to Kansas.

Mitch followed the newscast with only half his attention. The other half was going over his interrogation of the Kramer brothers, searching for holes in their story. The more he thought about it, the easier it was to believe that Hatch had been the brains behind the burglaries. How else would the Kramers have known about Edna Tellon's old barn and when the targeted horse ranchers would be away from home? And it had already been established that Hatch had a dark side that not many people saw. So that part of the Kramers' story hung together.

And they had dug in their heels on the murder. They'd deny it with their last breath. Mitch kept coming back to the same question: If the Kramers didn't murder Hatch, who did? Jessie, because he'd exposed her to AIDS? No, that wouldn't work because, according to Dr. Rapicorn, Hatch had found out he had AIDS on Monday evening, after Jessie had accepted Rhea Vann's invitation to hide out at her house. Unless Jessie was lying, she didn't see her husband alive again after Rapicorn gave Hatch the bad news. Mitch tended to believe her because there was only about a half hour of her time Monday evening unaccounted for.

As Mitch put it together, Hatch left the house for the clinic immediately after Rapicorn's phone call. Henderson Sixkiller had been hiding in Hatch's shed at the time, and he said Hatch left the house in a rush. Probably in a daze too, considering what he'd just learned. But he'd gone straight to the clinic in search of his wife. Knowing what he now knew, Mitch thought that seemed odd. How could a man who'd just learned he had AIDS be thinking about anything but that?

Was it possible Hatch thought Jessie had infected *him?* Was that why he was in such a rage by the time he reached the clinic?

Mitch found that well-nigh impossible to believe. Jessie

was too frightened of her husband ever to have looked at another man. It was Hatch who had played around, apparently throughout the marriage. When he died, he had been working on getting Alice Browne in bed. Just as he'd seduced other students at the center.

Mitch scratched his head, closed his eyes, and concentrated. Okay. Hatch had learned he had AIDS. He'd gone immediately to the clinic in a rage, looking for his wife. Mitch heaved a sigh. The events didn't seem connected. Mitch sensed he'd missed a link somewhere.

He started playing around with possibilities. He had Rapicorn's testimony that Hatch had learned he had AIDS just before he left the house. And he didn't question that Hatch had gone straight to the clinic; he hadn't had time to go anywhere else. And he had Rhea's and Marilee's testimony that Hatch had demanded to see his wife, had threatened to kill her. He had even threatened to kill Marilee because she was calling the police. *I'm gonna kill you, bitch!* had been his exact words, according to Rhea and Marilee. It didn't track. Mitch finished his beer and lay back on the couch, still trying to figure out what he'd missed.

As the minutes passed and his frustration increased, he toyed with ever more outlandish possibilities.

Among them: Hatch was so devastated by what Rapicorn had told him, he had to kill *somebody,* and Jessie was the most likely candidate. Why should she live when he was going to die? But that didn't explain his fury. Surely he didn't think Jessie gave him the virus. Mitch's thoughts stalled for an instant and then a thought came to him from out of left field.

Maybe Hatch hadn't been looking for Jessie at all when he went to the clinic. And if not Jessie, then who *was* he looking for?

Mitch got up restlessly and went to the kitchen, where he rummaged in the cabinet for a handful of cheese crackers. He looked up Rhea Vann's home phone and called. He let the phone ring four times and was about to hang up when she answered.

Mitch identified himself, then said, "You sound out of breath."

"Had to run to catch the phone. We worked late this evening," she said. "Marilee's still there, catching up on some paperwork. What can I do for you?"

"I'd like you to go over everything Tyler Hatch said and did when he broke into the clinic."

"Why? I've already told it two or three times."

"I just had a wild hair," Mitch said. "Humor me, okay?"

She sighed. "Okay. Let me get out of my coat first." She put down the phone, came back after a few moments. "Now."

"Start with when Marilee came back to your office and told you Hatch wanted in."

She did, recounting the incident almost exactly as she had before.

"You said Hatch threatened to kill his wife. Did he actually ever use her name?"

She thought about it. "I don't think that he did. No, he referred to her as a whore who had ruined his life. I can't see what difference it makes."

"It doesn't, unless he wasn't talking about Jessie."

He heard her indrawn breath. "But of course he was talking about Jessie. Who else could he have been talking about?"

Mitch told her about his last conversation with the medical examiner and then he told her about his new theory. "I can't believe that," she said.

"Like I said, it's a wild hair. But I think I'll have another talk with Marilee."

"Maybe I should be there too." She sounded worried.

"I'd rather you stayed put."

"Then will you call or come by here after you've talked to Marilee?"

He promised that he would. He hung up, strapped on his gun, grabbed a jacket, and left the house. Driving to the clinic, he was assailed by doubts. It was a crazy idea. But he kept coming back to the fact that seeing Marilee on the telephone had infuriated Hatch. Why? He should have expected them to call for help. So, according to his theory, Hatch's fury had had nothing to do with the phone call. It was simply seeing Marilee that set him off. Even as he thought it, he shook his head. Hatch and Marilee had been friends. According to Marilee. But maybe they'd been more than friends, in spite of what Marilee said.

Filthy whore's gonna pay for ruining my life.

I'm gonna kill you, bitch!

Marilee had been a drug addict. Hard-core, Rhea had said, and that meant needles.

When he reached the clinic, the lights were on in the reception room but the door was locked. Marilee's car wasn't in front, but it could be parked behind the clinic. Mitch jammed the bell with his thumb and left it there. After several moments, Marilee Steiner's face appeared at the window. He let up on the bell and gestured for her to open the door.

Mitch stepped inside and looked around. "Working late, Marilee?"

She looked as if she hadn't slept in a while. There were dark smudges under her eyes, and her cheeks seemed more hollow than Mitch remembered, as if she'd lost weight. "Trying to get caught up on some reports," she said woodenly, but there were no papers on the counter or on the desk behind it. She glanced toward the hallway.

"Are you alone here?"

She hesitated so briefly before she nodded that he hardly noticed. "We have to talk, Marilee."

She nodded again, moved to one of the vinyl chairs, and sat down abruptly. Something wasn't right about her. Her eyes looked glazed—or maybe it was only a trick of the light.

Mitch remained standing, his back to the dim hallway, which was lined on both sides with closed doors. "Something new has come up in the murder investigation."

She looked up at him without speaking.

"When you left town that night to meet your boyfriend at the lodge, Hatch followed you, didn't he?"

"Don't—" She turned her head quickly to peer down the

hallway. Looking for a way out? Mitch wondered. After a moment, she turned and gazed at him, as if from a distance, and finally she covered her face with her hands and began to weep silently.

"Did he try to run you off the road?"

She shook her head. For a long moment, she cried without making any noise, tears streaming down her cheeks from behind her hands. Finally she dropped her hands and wiped her eyes with the back of her hand. "I didn't know he was following me," she said, so low that Mitch could barely hear her.

"You did have an affair with him when you were at the center, didn't you?"

She nodded dully. "I'd been there a couple of months when it started, and when I'd try to break it off, he'd always get around me somehow. I felt so indebted to him—" She took a deep breath. "So, it went on like that until a month or two before I left the center."

Mitch had to step closer to hear her. "So, when you drove out to the lake to meet Handler, Hatch followed you."

She clenched her hands together and nodded. "I guess he waited for me to come out of the duplex, but I never saw him. Then, on the lake road, I had a flat and got out to change it. All at once, he was just there." She gestured helplessly. "His car came around a curve and he jumped out almost before I knew what was happening. He was yelling at me"—she shuddered involuntarily—"horrible things. I didn't know what was going on."

"What happened then?"

She said dully, "I—I thought he'd flipped out. I didn't have time to do anything but react. He grabbed me, tried to choke me. I struggled free and picked up the tire iron to protect myself. He—he just kept coming. I got away again and he tripped. But he got up and came after me again, and I—I hit him. It didn't slow him down much, so I hit him again. He fell and just lay there without moving. I couldn't believe he was dead." She seemed to be gazing at something far away. "But he was. I dragged him into the woods and drove his car in too.

I don't remember much of what happened afterward. I must have finished changing the tire and then I drove to the lodge."

"He accused you of infecting him with the HIV virus, didn't he?" Mitch asked gently.

For the first time, she looked truly desperate. After a moment, she looked down at her hands. "It didn't really hit me until the next day," she whispered. "I didn't believe him, but I went and had the test, just to be sure." Her voice broke and, when she looked up, her eyes swam with tears.

For several moments, neither of them spoke. Finally, Mitch said, "The test was positive," the sound of his voice too loud in the silent clinic.

Marilee looked past him and her eyes widened. At the same moment that she gasped and jumped to her feet, Mitch heard a sound behind him.

"I told you to keep the lounge door closed and wait for me!" Marilee cried.

Mitch started to turn and caught Charlie Handler's white, stunned face in the corner of his eye. Handler made a strangled sound and grabbed Mitch's gun from its holster.

"Get back!" Handler yelled. His face was like the face of a corpse, and the gun in his hand shook uncontrollably. The guy had flipped out. He turned the gun on Marilee. "How could you do this to me?" he choked out. "How could you not have told me?"

"That's why I asked you to meet me here." She was crying, and the words wobbled out with great effort. "I was going to tell you, but Chief Bushyhead came before I had a chance. I only got the test results today."

He stared at her as if he'd never seen her before. "I'm dead!" he said, his voice shattered. And then the gun went off. A hole appeared in the wall next to Marilee. She clapped both hands over her ears and staggered back. "I didn't know, Charlie," she wailed. "You have to believe me."

Mitch chose that moment to go for the gun. It went off again, and another bullet lodged in the wall. Handler jumped back and stared at the gun, as if he had no idea how it had gotten in his hand, more surprised than anybody that the gun kept firing. He waved it wildly. "I wish Hatch had killed you!" A sob shook his body.

"Give me the gun, Handler," Mitch said quietly. "You don't want to shoot anybody."

"I loved you," he said to Marilee, his voice anguished.

"Give me the gun, Handler," Mitch repeated.

Handler shook his head, sobbing. "I'm gonna kill her. I swear I am!" He lifted the gun and tried to aim, but his hand was shaking too badly. Marilee just stood there, weeping. She didn't try to get away, didn't even move. She didn't seem to care whether he killed her or not.

"I'm so sorry, Charlie."

Mitch took a step toward Handler, but Handler caught the movement and turned the wobbling gun toward Mitch. "Don't make me shoot you too!"

"Give me the gun," Mitch said. "You're only making your situation worse."

"Worse?" A desperately harsh sound erupted from Handler. "How could it be worse?" Tears glistened on his cheeks and he stared at Mitch with tortured eyes and gripped the gun with both hands. "Get over there against the wall. I don't want to hurt you, Bushyhead."

"No," Mitch said. "You'll have to shoot me."

Handler stared at him, unequipped to deal with Mitch's refusal to obey the order of a man with a gun. "I said—get over there!" But Mitch had seen his hesitation.

"No," Mitch said.

"Oh, God," Handler cried. He looked around, wide-eyed, like a cornered rabbit. Then he raised the gun to his own head.

Mitch tackled him. The gun flew from Handler's hand and slid across the floor. Mitch scrabbled for it, got it in his grip, and rose to his feet. Marilee hadn't moved. Handler lay on the floor, sobbing.

"Maybe," Marilee said, "you should have let him kill me."

20

Charlie Handler was still a basket case when they got to the police station. Mitch called Charlie's parents and sent him home with them. He'd decide later whether to charge Handler with anything.

As for Marilee, she barely seemed aware of her surroundings. She didn't even ask for an attorney, but Mitch didn't have the heart to question her any more then, anyway.

He phoned Rhea Vann from the station and filled her in on what had happened at the clinic. Then he went home.

Two weeks later, Mitch ran into Rhea at the Three Squares Café. It was the first time he'd seen her since Marilee's arrest. She was having lunch and invited him to share her booth.

She had on a red sweater that looked good with her black hair and tawny skin. She filled it out just fine, too.

After he'd ordered, Mitch said, "I hear you got Marilee some hot shot defense lawyer from Tulsa?"

She nodded. She'd finished her burger and now pushed the plate aside. "He says it's as clear a case of self-defense as he's ever had. He thinks he can get her off without any prison time at all."

"I hope so," Mitch said. Marilee needed help she probably wouldn't get in prison, medical as well as psychological. "She's lucky to have a friend like you. The night-duty officers tell me you visit her four or five evenings a week."

She shrugged off the compliment. "They've been good about letting me see Marilee, even though it's not regular visiting hours."

"What's your take on her mental state?"

She frowned slightly. "It seems to be improving. At first she would hardly speak to me. I was terribly worried about her, but the last few times I've been to see her, she's been better. I keep telling her that she could live AIDS-free for a long time if she'll take good care of herself." She paused, her dark eyes full of sadness and a flicker of hope. "The researchers come up with new treatments all the time. By the time Marilee develops symptoms, we can only hope for a cure." She reached for her coffee cup, and Mitch wondered which one of them she was trying to convince. "Anyway, she seems to be coming out of her depression. She's talking to me now." She sipped her coffee and set the cup down. "Have you heard anything about Charlie Handler?"

"I've talked to his mother a couple times." Mitch had called to tell her there would be no charges filed against Charlie. That had been one load off her mind, but the bigger load remained. "Charlie's test was positive. His doctor's got him on a diet-and-vitamins regimen and he's joined a support group. A group might help Marilee too, when she gets out."

"I've been checking into that."

"What about Jessie? Wasn't she supposed to see a doctor this week?"

She brightened. "Oh, you haven't heard? Jessie tested negative. The doctor at the Indian hospital wants her to have another test in three months, but I think she's safe. She told me that she and Tyler hadn't had sex for more than a year before he died." Her mouth twisted. "He said she was old and ugly and she disgusted him."

"He had other fish to fry," Mitch said wryly. And younger women to lay, he added to himself.

"Poor Jessie. She kept trying to make herself more attractive for him, but it didn't work."

"Lucky for her."

"How true," she said earnestly.

The waiter brought Mitch's barbecued beef and milk.

She watched him thoughtfully as he took a bite of the sandwich. Then she said, "I have to get back to the clinic." She slid across the seat. "Oh, I almost forgot. Grandfather checked on your grandmother's people. You're a member of the Wolf clan."

He took a drink of milk to wash down the barbecue. "Really?" He grinned, thinking of Emily's reaction when he told her. No doubt she'd say it was cool.

"Hey, that's Trudy Pigeon's clan. Does that mean Trudy and I are related?"

"Sort of." There was a teasing twinkle in her eyes. "For one thing, you couldn't marry her. Marriage within the same clan is taboo."

"I don't think Virgil would let me, anyway."

She smiled and started to rise.

"Do people still keep those old laws?" Mitch asked.

"Some do."

"Would you—"

She laughed. "You mean would an educated person like myself worry about some old Indian taboo?"

He felt embarrassed but curiosity won out. "Well, would you—marry somebody in your clan, I mean?"

She gave it a few moments of thought. "I don't think so. It would upset Grandfather." She rose to her feet.

"As I recall," he said hastily, "you're not Wolf clan."

"That's right." She studied him, her eyes crinkled at the corners. "Not thinking of asking for my hand in marriage, are you?"

"No, but I am thinking of asking you to dinner." He saw her hesitation and amended quickly, "Sometime."

She tilted her head to one side, her expression quizzical and faintly bemused. "Call me," she said, and then she was gone.

Mitch finished his sandwich, paid for the meal, and walked out to his car. He headed back to the station. Call her, she said. Well, he surely meant to do that.

Welcome to the Island of Morada—getting there is easy,
leaving . . . is murder.

Embark on the ultimate, on-line, fantasy vacation with
MODUS OPERANDI.

Join fellow mystery lovers in the murderously fun MODUS OPERANDI, a
unique on-line, multi-player, multi-service, interactive, mystery game
launched by The Mysterious Press, Time Warner Electronic Publishing and
Simutronics Corporation.

Featuring never-ending foul play by your favorite Mysterious Press authors
and editors, MODUS OPERANDI is set on the fictional Caribbean island of
Morada. Forget packing, passports and planes, entry to Morada is
easy—all you need is a vivid imagination.

Simutronics GameMasters are available in MODUS OPERANDI around the
clock, adding new mysteries and puzzles, offering helpful hints, and taking you virtually by the hand through the killer gaming environment as
you come in contact with players from on-line services the world over.
Mysterious Press writers and editors will also be there to participate in
real-time on-line special events or just to throw a few back with you at
the pub.

MODUS OPERANDI is available on-line now.

Join the mystery and mayhem on:
- America Online® at keyword MODUS
- Genie® at keyword MODUS
- PRODIGY® at jumpword MODUS

Or call toll-free for sign-up information:
- America Online® 1 (800) 768-5577
- Genie® 1 (800) 638-9636, use offer code DAF524
- PRODIGY® 1 (800) PRODIGY, use offer code MODO

Or take a tour on the Internet at
http://www. pathfinder.com/twep/games/modop.

MODUS OPERANDI—It's to die for.